ON YOUR LEFT

ON YOUR LEFT

Duane A. Eide

iUniverse, Inc.
Bloomington

On Your Left

This is a work of fiction. All of the characters, names, incidents, organizations, and dialogue in this novel are either the products of the author's imagination or are used fictitiously.

iUniverse books may be ordered through booksellers or by contacting:

iUniverse
1663 Liberty Drive
Bloomington, IN 47403
www.iuniverse.com
1-800-Authors (1-800-288-4677)

Because of the dynamic nature of the Internet, any web addresses or links contained in this book may have changed since publication and may no longer be valid. The views expressed in this work are solely those of the author and do not necessarily reflect the views of the publisher, and the publisher hereby disclaims any responsibility for them.

Any people depicted in stock imagery provided by Thinkstock are models, and such images are being used for illustrative purposes only.
Certain stock imagery © Thinkstock.

ISBN: 978-1-4759-2962-1 (sc)
ISBN: 978-1-4759-2963-8 (ebk)

Printed in the United States of America

iUniverse rev. date: 06/12/2012

Acknowledgements

Thank you to my wife, Patricia, for her patience during the months of my writing and for her help in editing *On Your Left*. Thank you, also, to Wallace Wierson, friend and former teaching colleague, for his suggestions and helpful editing.

CHAPTER 1

The early morning sun blinked through the trees lining the bike path. Clay Pennell rode carefully, watching the path both in front of him and with a slight twist of the head behind him. For the first time since the accident, he had returned to one of his favorite forms of exercise, biking.

For Clay, biking gave him the chance to organize his thoughts, to contemplate the day ahead of him, to assess the day gone by, or simply to be alone. This morning, an image out of the past that eluded him for years suddenly strayed into his mind. His imagination grabbed the image as well as his attention.

In that image, two people walked hand in hand in the darkness of a narrow path lighted only by a distant street light.

"Do you often walk out here at night?" Clay lowered his eyes to view in the shadows of the tree lined walkway the petite, attractive, young woman who walked beside him.

"No, definitely not alone." Robin Foster spoke firmly, punctuating her response with a soft bump on Clay's shoulder.

A brief silence hung over the two as they walked slowly toward Friendship Park, the pride of Packwood, a small town in south eastern Iowa.

"So, you feel safe with me?" Clay asked with a smile concealed by the darkness.

"I don't know. I guess I do. Honestly, I haven't done anything like this before."

"What do you mean? You have never walked with a man at night before?" Clay knew what she meant. He just felt playful. After all he met Robin only a few hours ago. Now they walked together in the darkness toward a park he had not even seen in the daylight.

"Not much chance for walking with an almost stranger in this town." Robin momentarily removed her hand from his. She slowly turned to face him, moonlight sparkled in her clear blue eyes. "Maybe we should turn back. It is getting late."

Clay reached for her arm, held it gently, and stopped to face her. "You're probably right. I have an early morning date with my bike. Tomorrow is the last leg of the tour. Then it's packing up the bike and heading back to Minneapolis."

As they stood facing each other, a force over which they had no control moved them closer together. In the darkness Robin smiled, her eyes emitting a tiny sparkle. Clay reached for her shoulders. She did not resist.

Suddenly, Clay's arms encircled her, drawing her body close to his. He looked down upon this small face clearly visible even in the darkness. Robin met his eyes. She smiled, reaching up to accept his kiss. Passion bolted through their bodies. Clay's hands moved frantically over her shoulders, down her back, coming to rest on her well formed bottom. He pulled her body against his. She willingly succumbed to his lead. In seconds they parted, breathing heavily, staring at each other without a word.

No words could convey the intensity of the moment. They stepped off the path to settle on the grass that marked the beginning of the park. Carefully, Clay knelt down. On his knees he placed his hands on Robin's hips, encouraging her to follow him down on the grass. She submitted to his silent commands.

As they lay together, the passion increased until clothes were shed, and he was positioned on top of her. Her movements signaled the urgency with which she awaited his entrance. Gently their bodies engaged. Rhythmic movement intensified, as did breathing. At the height of sensual pleasure, their small world exploded in climatic delight.

Breathless, they lay side by side, looking into the night sky. Neither moved for several minutes. Sitting up, Clay reached for Robin's hand. With a tender pull, he helped her to her feet. They reached for clothes thrown recklessly on the grass. Dressed, they moved back to the path which brought them to the park.

"Do you work in the morning?" Clay was the first to speak.

"Yes, at seven o'clock." Robin answered tersely.

Again silence fell over them. For several steps, they said nothing, both thinking about what to say.

Clay urged her to stop. He faced her, looking first at the dark sky and then at the ground, obviously searching for the right words. "Robin, I'm really sorry if I pushed myself onto you. I don't want you to get the idea that I think you're some kind of easy girl. Honestly, what we just did was wonderful."

Robin looked away, too, confronting her turn to say something, anything. "I'm sure that in a few days you won't remember much about our little episode together. I really don't know what happened tonight. I'm not used to having sex with strange men. Some kind of spark ignited between us, I guess."

"Believe me. I'm not used to having sex with a strange woman either. But it was good."

"Yes, it was."

They continued the short walk back to the church from which they had departed following a dinner served there for dozens of across-Iowa bikers. Standing before the church, Robin and Clay embraced. They exchanged a brief kiss. She turned to enter the church; he turned toward the large campground where he would spend the night in a tent. In the morning, he would begin the last day of the famous ride across Iowa.

The tinkle of a bell from behind brought Clay out of his reflection. He turned to see several bikers approach. "On your left," the first rider called out. Clay thanked the riders for the courtesy to signal their presence. Under different circumstances, very few riders would pass Clay. Under different circumstances, he would not have ridden on a bike path. The accident several months ago changed all that. Now frequent pain from a broken leg reminded him of that accident and the months of agonizing recovery and therapy.

CHAPTER 2

In the garage, Clay parked his bike in its usual place of honor. Spending over two thousand dollars on a bike demanded he exercise sound judgement about where he parked it. He removed his water bottle, took a long swallow before limping outside to empty the water that remained on thirsty flowers decorating the side walk leading to the front door. As he emptied the water bottle, he paused to look across his front yard at nothing in particular. His thoughts returned to the morning ride when suddenly he relived that moment, now, almost ten years ago when a complementary dinner at a small church in rural Iowa ended with a walk in the park and more with a woman who served him his dinner.

During the many intervening years, he rarely, if ever, thought about Robin. He had to search his memory to remember her name, even though it was, to him, a very common name. Clay smiled as he recalled that night and the next day with its frantic preparations for the final leg of the bike tour across Iowa. The events of the night before remained vivid in his mind. He recalled his misgivings about the encounter. Also he remembered worrying about what Robin would think about the night before when she arose the next morning. However, the long ride on that last leg, the preparations for transporting his bike back home, and his securing his own transportation soon started the gradual process of that night's experience slipping into a remote corner of his mind.

He turned to walk back into the garage. His right leg throbbed with a dull, grinding pain. Clay braced himself against the wall of the garage, relieving pressure on his right leg. Vicky told him before he took off on the bike that maybe he was pushing his return to riding. The leg had not responded to treatment, had not healed properly. He ignored her caution. He would wait no longer to return to his bike.

Removing the small cycle computer fastened to the handlebar, he checked his mileage for the morning. His ride, seventeen miles, a meager total considering he used to average over three thousand miles a season. Still, that he rode at all gave him confidence that sometime in the future he would regain the strength and stamina that previously enabled him to ride, at times, a hundred miles in one day. At this moment, though, pain burned through his leg.

Completing the ride, failed to give Clay the satisfaction that he anticipated. Concern for his right leg, now throbbing with a dull pain, obscured any chance at satisfaction. His shoulder, also severely damaged in the accident, healed relatively quickly. According to his doctor, watching his diet carefully and following a regular schedule of physical exercise influenced greatly the speed of his recovery. However, neither diet nor exercise could combat the infection that settled in his right leg. Only antibiotics could do that. So far they were losing the battle. After several weeks, the incision required to repair shattered bone in Clay's leg failed to heal. Several times a week drainage from the incision required Clay to change the bandage that encircled his leg.

"How was your ride?" Vicky, Clay's wife of nearly ten years, stepped into the garage dressed in her typical business attire, charcoal grey pant suit, white blouse, and conservative heels. A vivacious, charming woman, she retained the physical appeal that attracted Clay so many years ago. At thirty-two years old, she easily attracted attention. Flowing black hair resting on her shoulders framed and accentuated the tan glow of her prominent cheeks which gave definition to full lips and gleaming white teeth. A gracious smile shared those teeth with the rest of her world.

"Not very good. I think I should have listened to you." Lately, Clay and Vicky listened to each other very little. Far too often their conversations degenerated into bitter arguments over petty topics.

"What happened?"

"Nothing happened. It's this damned leg. The pain's back." Clay slumped against the wall.

"How far did you ride?" Vicky moved toward her car, a late model BMW, speaking over her shoulder which carried her large briefcase.

"Seventeen miles."

"Well, that probably wasn't such a good idea. Is the pain worse than before?" Vicky's voice reflected her concern.

"Yes, it's that dull ache that travels up my leg." Clay approached his wife's car, leaning on the front fender.

Talking over the top of the car, Vicky advised, "Maybe you shouldn't go to work today."

Clay ran his hands through his thick, dark hair. "I don't know. I can't keep taking time off work. Ross needs me at the shop. He has other things to do." He looked over the top of Vicky's car directly into her eyes. "Will you be home for dinner?"

That question, recently, ignited several of their arguments. As a buyer for an electronics firm, Vicky assumed considerable responsibility, often working late hours. Lately, Clay began to question just what transpired during some of those late hours. The critical time Clay spent in the hospital, the many hours in rehabilitation, both guided by a therapist and self-directed, and the days and weeks that Clay required assistance in performing simple acts like taking a shower or drying his hair, or getting to work had imposed on Vicky's freedom to do her job. The many hours Clay sat at home, alone, while the infection delayed healing also promoted suspicion about the demands of Vicky's job. As vice president for purchasing, her job required her attention more than just forty hours a week.

Until recently, Clay attributed the tarnish on their relationship to the accident and all that resulted from it. However, recent events, such as more than usual late nights for Vicky at the office, generated doubts which only further weakened their marital relationship. Though he probably should have addressed the issue with Vicky, he had not, believing that his frustration with his leg and his inability to resume life as he had known it created the suspicions. Bringing up his suspicions, he concluded, would only irritate the already tenuous relationship.

A frown crossed Vicky's face. "Of course, I will." Her voice betrayed a tension that too often accompanied the subject of her professional day. She resented Clay's questioning her hours. They both knew that her salary, which exceeded his, helped sustain their life style, not extravagant but still beyond what he alone could afford. "I do have a meeting late this afternoon, but I should be home around six. I'll call if there's a delay."

She quickly placed her brief case in the back seat of the BMW then slid behind the wheel. Clay moved away from the car. Backing out of the garage, she gave her husband a quick wave before driving off to work.

Clay entered their modest three bedroom, two story home located only blocks from historic Lake Minnetonka. Living close to the lake satisfied them both. Besides living on the lake entailed property taxes neither Clay nor Vicky wished to pay or what their budget would allow. Nonetheless, their double income assured them many of life's comforts.

For nearly five years they lived in their current home secured after an exhaustive search for one that satisfied both of them. Clay harbored no illusions about his status in the community. Image made little difference to him. Vicky did not share his indifference. After all, she did hold an important position at Wagner Electronics. Following their marriage, they rented a small two bedroom apartment just minutes from Vicky's office in suburban Minneapolis. That their apartment required Clay to bike nearly three miles to his office at the bike shop made little difference to him. Eventually, they agreed they deserved a more permanent home in a respectable neighborhood. They found that home in a quiet neighborhood not far from a large shopping center or from the freeway, a quick access to Clay's bike shop office in suburban Long Lake.

CHAPTER 3

Vicky parked in her spot, one of the important symbols of her status in the company. For nearly ten years, since shortly after graduation from the University of Wisconsin, Stout, she worked for Wagner Electronics, no significant competition to companies like Best Buy but still a growing, dynamic company that commanded a sizable share of the burgeoning electronics market. A degree in marketing prepared her well for her position as Wagner Electronics' vice president for purchasing.

Over the years she advanced from part-time buyer and part-time sales assistant to her current position. Those who knew Vicky only assumed that eventually she would rise to a position of importance in whatever she chose to do. As early as junior high school, she displayed a dedication to winning that attracted the attention of both coaches and teachers.

At five feet nine inches and one hundred twenty-five pounds, Vicky lacked the appearance of a dominating athletic threat. Still, as a ninth grader, she started on both her high school softball and basketball teams. She proudly remembered her senior year when she scored thirty-three points, leading her team to the Wisconsin State High School basketball championship. The same drive that made her an athletic talent also equipped her to excel in the classroom. She simply refused to permit anyone else to surpass her academic performance.

Combined with her talent, Vicky enjoyed a physical appeal which she had yet to exploit but was certainly not lost on the boys who shared her life in a small Wisconsin high school. Her slim figure with curves in all the right places, her sparkling smile accentuated by dancing blue eyes, and black hair made her the envy of other girls. A charming confidence added to her appeal.

For all her talent and all her physical appeal, Vicky paid a price. She rarely felt the soothing touch of happiness. At school or in public, she played the role of this vibrant, captivating teen. At home in the privacy of her small room, she would lie on her bed, distraught and depressed over some, in her perception, failure or an only marginal success. Whether a test on which she scored a mere 95% rather than 100% or a softball game when she struck out twice, Vicky possessed no tolerance for what she considered failure.

Rarely did she confide in her parents, who relished what they considered the boundless potential of their daughter. To them, she truly was the vibrant girl she portrayed to the rest of the world. Not including her parents in her private life only exacerbated the struggle that she faced much too often. Her escape to the privacy of her room, her parents interpreted as simply her need for rest from the demands of her full academic and athletic schedules.

During her junior and senior years in high school, she longed to share her troubles with somebody, especially with her parents. Ironically, in this most important aspect of her life, she lacked the courage to admit to anyone her limitations. Besides, why tarnish the polished image she portrayed to her parents and to the rest of her small Wisconsin world.

Only rarely did Vicky now suffer from the misgivings that plagued her teen years. Maturation as well as persistent success combined to limit moments of anxiety she suffered growing up in Wisconsin. Nonetheless, a compelling drive not just to succeed but to surpass others produced an aggressive competitiveness that so far aided her in her climb to importance in the corporate world.

Indeed, Clay's accident did influence Vicky's life both at home and at work. She loved her husband. They both found great satisfaction in biking. It's how they met. The accident imposed a strain on their relationship which troubled both of them. Until recently, Clay tolerated the inconvenience of his infected leg and, earlier, the crushed shoulder. Now, she too often heard him grumble about that "damned leg." Vicky willingly helped him with routine tasks he could no longer perform including driving him to work and in most cases home again. The extra demands on her time disrupted the smooth flow of her day. She needed consistency. Over time these demands chipped away at their relationship. She deplored the strain imposed upon their marriage and upon their daily personal interaction.

Vicky secured her BMW, another symbol of her success in a male dominated, corporate world.

"Good morning, Mrs. Pennell. How are you this morning?" The sweet, customer service voice of receptionist Abby Firth typically was the first voice Vicky heard upon arriving at the office.

"I'm fine. And you?" Vicky responded a bit too perfunctorily.

"Oh, I'm fine. How is Clay getting along?"

For months, Vicky responded to that question. Recently that response assumed a tone of indifference. She had heard it so often, and each time it only reminded her of the agony Clay faced and the personal problems for both of them that followed his accident. To this point, she believed she fulfilled her part in Clay's recovery. She now wished to move on to topics less repetitious. "He's getting better."

"That's great." Abby smiled that corporate smile she was hired to share. "Is he back to work?"

Eager to get to her office, Vicky moved passed Abby's reception desk then turned to say tersely, "Yes, he is."

Assuming a much more impersonal role, Abby announced, "Mr. Wagner wants you to contact him right away this morning." Abby looked down at a list in front of her.

The comment stopped Vicky in her haste to end the conversation about Clay. "Thank you. Did he say why?"

"No. He just wanted you to contact him when you arrived."

Vicky nodded an acknowledgement then turned to continue to her office, intrigued by her boss's uncharacteristic request. To Vicky, Madison Wagner was more of a coworker than a boss. She considered him honest, fair, and a quiet but effective leader. Rarely had he asked her to contact him under such detached circumstances. If he wished to discuss something with her, he usually just appeared at her office door with an apology for interrupting her day. That he wished her to contact him upon her arrival provoked questions about his purpose.

Vicky checked her appearance in the full length mirror installed in her private restroom. She adamantly believed in the power of appearance to persuade. Unless you looked good, what existed beneath the surface made little difference. This philosophy had evolved over the years as Vicky competed in a world of male egos. And it paid dividends. As vice president for purchasing, she stood above most other employees, except, of course, the three other executives besides Madison Wagner, the CEO. Giving herself a last perusal, she pictured in her mind those three, her eyes rolling up when she thought about Brian Tarlton, president of the company, who considered himself the answer to every woman's dream. The other two, Thomas Morgan, the company comptroller, and Sid Hayes, vice president for personnel, Vicky found both professional and respectful.

Vicky's advancement in the company left her integrity unblemished. Yes, temptations presented themselves, especially early in her career. She possessed the strength, the devotion to her marriage, and the intellectual agility to resist them. Still vice president for purchasing failed to quench her thirst for more authority, more power and, of course, more money. She aspired to work more closely with major company decisions, not only decisions about purchasing, but also decisions about company policy.

For only a moment, she paused before that full length mirror reflecting not on her image but on her ambition. Indeed, she envisioned Madison Wagner as the company CEO consulting her on company policy. At quiet times allowing for reflection, she considered her qualifications for president of the company. She could find no reason why she would not make an excellent president. A smile spread across her face as she pictured herself assuming responsibility for the future of the company. Only the intrusion of current president Brain Tarlton's image erased the smile. Vicky shook her head in disgust.

She refocused on herself in the mirror. She admired what she saw. For someone for whom appearance ranked above most other qualities, attention to her own required no justification. Even at thirty-two, she retained an attractive figure, admired by anyone who appreciated femininity. She had not changed sizes in years. Her smile revealed gleaming white teeth accentuated by full lips which Clay once, playfully, said were the most kissable in the county.

Giving her hair a gentle fluff, her breasts a gentle boost and her lips a touch of color, Vicky walked confidently to the office of Madison Wagner, CEO of Wagner Electronics.

Responding instantly to the knock on his door, Madison ushered Vicky to one of the chairs positioned in front of his relatively modest executive desk. The son of the founder of the company, Madison made everyone feel comfortable in his presence. Over the years a little too much weight gathered around his middle. Still, his six foot frame gave him a commanding presence as did his full head of hair now dominated by gray and meticulous attention to his attire. Unassuming, friendly and engaging, he possessed a gift for dealing with his employees as well as his customers. Though at times tentative in his relationships with others, he willingly sought their advice in decisions related to the company. But when situations demanded action, Madison acted decisively.

Nearly ten years ago, he hired Vicky. Then, he held the position of president. His father served as the company CEO. During the interview process, Madison made Vicky feel comfortable. His candor, his eagerness to listen to a prospective employee, and his suppressing any desire to embellish his position in the company or to dominate the interview with attention to his own career impressed Vicky. After one more short interview with Madison's father, she received, what Madison termed, an invitation to join the team at Wagner Electronics.

Before assuming his place behind the desk, Madison briefly glanced at Vicky. "Thank you for coming at such short notice." He smiled then added, "As usual, you look great."

Vicky settled into her chair, crossing her legs while discreetly arranging her skirt. "Thank you," she smiled.

As he sat down across from Vicky, Madison asked, "By the way, how is Clay doing?"

For a fleeting moment, she again felt the tip of resentment over that incessant question. "He's getting better. It's taking much longer than we expected."

Madison smiled. "You wish him the best for me. I know how these injuries can linger. It's frustrating, I'm sure."

Madison leaned forward, folding his hands on top the desk. "Though obviously we all are concerned about your husband, honestly, that's not the reason I asked you to see me this morning."

Vicky tensed momentarily, wondering if she had done something wrong?

Madison continued. "You've been with us now for what, nearly ten years? During that time you have proven yourself

19

a capable, talented employee, an important member of our leadership team. This company has grown impressively over the years, thanks to people like you."

Vicky smiled, still intrigued by where this conversation was headed.

Madison sat back in his chair. "I'm sorry. This isn't intended as a history lesson on Wagner Electronics. What I want to ask is a favor. In about three weeks, an international trade show will be held in Orlando at the Orlando Convention Center. In the past I've not felt attending such an event would prove worthwhile for our small company. Now that our company isn't so small anymore, I've decided that we should attend, and I want you to be a part of our group."

Vicky uncrossed her legs, sat up straight, a smile confirming the delight with which she received the invitation. Thoughts of president of the company again skipped through her mind.

CHAPTER 4

In the master bedroom, Clay replaced his biking clothes with a light summer robe. His medication reduced the throbbing in his leg. Determined to go to work, he refused to let a poor decision to bike keep him away from his job.

Turning to leave the bedroom, he glanced at their wedding picture in its place of importance on a small end table whose only purpose was to provide a resting place for that picture. Hundreds of times Clay walked in and out of the bedroom. Hardly ever anymore did he pause to study the picture that represented a much happier time in his life.

Grasping the picture, he held it up in front of him. A mental image emerged of that day when he and Vicky got married. How proud he was. How lucky to have such a marvelous woman for a wife and partner. A petite brunette, gracious and attractive with a disarming smile, Vicky Dumont captured Clay's affection from the moment they met. And they met riding in a bike tour around the Twin Cities.

Vicky grew up on a prosperous dairy farm located in central Wisconsin. She acquired an interest in biking as exercise even before high school. In high school her biking served as an important part of her conditioning for both basketball and softball. When weather didn't permit riding outdoors, she rode on a stationary bike set up in her room. She retained this interest as she moved on to the University of Wisconsin Stout where she earned a degree in marketing. From there she traveled to the Twin Cities where she began her career as a buyer and occasional sales clerk for an electronics firm.

On a hot Saturday in August only months after she settled in the Twin Cities, Vicky set out on a bike ride that would pass through miles of beautiful Minneapolis/St. Paul scenery. An experienced rider, she kept up with the leaders even though the tour did not qualify as a race.

As she rode, enjoying the tree lined streets and marvelous views of the sky blue lakes, she happened to find herself next to young man who even under his biking helmet exuded male appeal. Riding side by side, relatively close, she could almost feel the magnetism of this lean, tall cyclist. She could feel his eyes taking furtive glances at her. A couple times they looked at each other simultaneously. Each offered a smile but exchanged no words.

Finally, after riding a few blocks side by side, Vicky broke the silence. "I like your bike." Not one to struggle in a search for words, at this moment, she didn't know what else to say. She did know what she did say likely sounded a bit trite.

However, it got Clay's attention, not that he wasn't already aware of her presence. He slowed his pedaling, looked over at Vicky, his eyes tracing her from helmet to shoes. A broad smile lighted his face, "I like your helmet."

Vicky returned the smile. "Thank you. Not a fashion statement but it serves its purpose."

"I don't know about that. It sure looks good on you." With that compliment, a slight blush spread over Vicky's face. "You from here?" Clay asked.

"I am now. I just moved here a few months ago. How about you?"

"Been around here all my life. Not much for adventure, I guess." Clay shifted his bike into a lower gear slowing his pace. "Where did you live before coming here?"

"On a farm next door in Wisconsin. Kind of your typical farm girl." Vicky's smile betrayed her sense of humor about her rural background.

Clay laughed out loud. "Typical farm girls in Wisconsin certainly aren't like typical farm girls in Minnesota." He hesitated, again searching to keep the conversation going. "No doubt you had lot of space to bike on the farm."

"Yes, I did. But only after I finished my chores." Vicky's response retained its playful tone. "How about you? Have you ridden long?"

"Nearly all my life, I guess. My dad says that I rode a bike before I walked. I don't really believe that, but I know I've been biking for a long time."

"By the way," Vicky added. "I was serious about your nice bike."

They rode several miles, exchanging more casual conversation when the route enabled them to relax their vigilance for a few moments. At the conclusion of the ride, they sat together in the grass surrounding Minnehaha Falls where the ride had started hours before and now finished. Their conversation revealed for her that he managed a bike shop. It revealed for him that she worked as a buyer for an electronics company. For both of them, it revealed phone numbers.

Only days later Clay assembled the courage to call Vicky. He had to leave a message. She failed to return the call. Not one blessed with confidence in his attraction to the opposite sex, Clay retreated. Weeks passed, yet he could not dismiss from his mind this vivacious, beautiful, Wisconsin farm girl. Reaching for his limited store of courage, he tried calling again. When Vicky answered, Clay hesitated, suddenly not knowing exactly what to say. Eventually, the conversation did lead to a date, then several dates.

On a glorious summer evening a few months after their first date, they decided to spend a Saturday night biking around some of the same lakes they rode around that day they met. During their ride, they talked briefly, when on the bike path, traffic permitted. They laughed at a few roller bladders for whom standing up produced the greatest challenge.

At the completion of their ride, Vicky invited Clay to her small apartment. The stimulation of the ride, the romanticism of a serene summer evening, and the love that had grown between them inflamed their desire. Upon entering the apartment, they rushed into each other's arms. Their tight riding clothes magnified the feel of each other's body. They stood pressing against one another. Vicky gently guided Clay's hands to her swollen breasts. They kissed deeply; lips pressed tightly. The next moment they parted, stepping back, eyes locked on each other. No language communicated their desire more articulately than that instant of eye contact. Immediately, they moved to the sofa where they vanished into a world of ultimate pleasure. One year later they were married.

Their mutual interest in biking, at least for several years, helped to ensure a compatible relationship, something they both considered essential for a lasting marriage.

Clay slowly shook his head, his hand brushing the wedding picture as if to retrieve a bit of the thrill of that day. A heavy heart followed him into the shower as he prepared for another day at the bike shop where he had worked for what seemed forever.

CHAPTER 5

Clay watched as the water swirled around the drain at the bottom of the master bath shower. He inspected his legs, noting the difference in their size. His right leg still had not regained its original size or strength since the accident. Each time he showered required rewrapping of the leg to cover the incision. He reached down to touch the tender wound. Even a touch sent tiny sensations through his calf.

Out of the shower, he dried his hair with a towel. The process reminded him again of his damaged shoulder as twinges of pain shot through the shoulder and down his back. He slumped in frustration. The countless hours he devoted to guided therapy along with the daily regimen of exercises designed to strengthen both shoulder and leg had gone on for months with only marginal improvement. His shoulder had responded much better than his leg. Still, certain routine movements caused sudden pain there too. He sat on the special stool placed in the bathroom expressly for him to rest or to re-bandage his leg.

Through the months of therapy, Clay could only dream about biking. So much of his life involved biking, for him, always a source of relaxation as well as both mental and physical exercise. Returning to a regular schedule of biking served as a major motivation in his commitment to the months of physical therapy. This morning's ride crushed any hope about returning to regular biking anytime soon. Clay deplored the thought that just maybe his body would never again enable him to engage in the physical activities, especially biking, he so enjoyed. Even at thirty-three years old, he felt, what he considered, the effects of getting old. At thirty-three, one should never have to deal with thoughts of growing old.

He moved to the sink. He leaned heavily against the vanity, bracing himself with rigid arms. Gradually, he raised his head to study himself in the mirror. Vibrant brown eyes that at one time reflected vigor and energy had grown dull with tiny red veins visible in each eye. Even his hair, at one time dark, thick and wavy, had thinned and stiffened. Stepping back from the vanity, he checked his torso. He took such pride in his appearance, watching his diet, exercising and, of course, biking. Now his shoulders slumped. He had to force himself to straighten up. His skin had paled from the hours he spent inside tending to his therapy. Even his once gleaming white teeth reflected a slight yellowish tint. He turned just enough to see the small tattoo on his right shoulder, the picture of a cyclist, the result of a wild weekend with college friends. Even that tattoo lacked its original, distinct color.

Through all the physical pain and emotional agony, Clay held firm to his determination to return to life as he once knew it. Recently, however, the prolonged recovery required more pain pills. At times even the pills failed to relieve the constant ache in the severely damaged leg. On a rare night out with college friends, the conversation drifted to Clay's accident and its repercussions. Reluctant to taint the gathering with complaints about his leg, Clay did confess his frustration with the prolonged healing.

The conversation expanded, aided by another round of beers, to descriptions of accidents experienced by his friends. Nearly all the five of Clay's friends seated around the table could remember an accident or an illness that, for them, had created pain and suffering. The conversation, then, moved on to a discussion of how each dealt with pain and suffering. Eventually, one of Clay's friends mentioned marijuana which he found effective in suppressing pain. At first, Clay rejected that as an option. However, others at the table reinforced marijuana's effectiveness to combat pain. Ultimately, Clay returned home that evening with samples, carefully wrapped joints, of something a bit different from his usual, prescribed pain killers.

Several days passed before Clay seriously considered trying the marijuana his friend had given him. Years of warnings by concerned parents implanted in his mind the dangers of substances like marijuana. However, after a particularly painful day, Clay succumb to marijuana's promise of relief.

The first time he tried it the powerful effects amazed him. As the smoke encircled his head, the persistent ache in his body subsided. At least, the marijuana masked the pain. Whatever it accomplished, Clay liked it. However, liking it and using it on a regular basis were not the same. Though given the chance as a college student, Clay, then, also refused to use substances like marijuana wishing to avoid their addictive potential as well as the penalties associated with their use. Consequently, the few joints in Clay's possession ended up in the back of his dresser drawer. Besides the problems he faced, he did not want to deal with an issue like marijuana. Those parental precautions echoed through his mind with just a thought about smoking marijuana. Instead, he would stick with the medications prescribed by his doctor.

He didn't need the complications involved in dealing with pot or whatever term described it. Sneaking the use of it to control pain was only part of the problem. Acquisition and cost were another. Yes, the few joints his friend gave him cost nothing. What would replacements cost? Clay knew about people who found themselves shackled to the euphoric escape of a few puffs of marijuana. Confining himself to traditional pain relievers made much more sense to Clay.

Of course, he said nothing to Vicky about his brief venture into the world of controlled substances. She would never have accepted their use. Besides, his decision to avoid them made discussing them needless. If Ross, the owner of the bike shop where he worked, had rules about controlled substance use, Clay did not know. He simply had no reason to inquire.

Momentarily, he reflected again on his parents. Thinking of them, he shook his head. Knowing he used anything like marijuana would devastate them. Smoking anything, to them, was not only bad for your health but also just plain stupid. Clay simply could not dismiss vivid memories of his parents admonishing him about the evils of "drugs."

More important than a concentration on pain medication, Clay was determined to return to his favorite activity, biking. He paused before getting dressed. Sitting down on the large king sized bed that he and Vicky shared, he smiled, a faint smile, as he thought about his early years of biking. In his mind he could see, vividly, that little boy eager to take off, for the first time, on a bike without training wheels.

Harold and Agnes Pennell stood side by side at the head of their driveway. The Saturday morning sun spread warmth over the Twin Cities. For days, three year old Clay begged his dad to remove the training wheels from his bike.

"Do you really think he's ready?" Agnes reached for her husband's arm, tension etched across her face. "He could easily fall and hurt himself."

"Sure he can. That's always a possibility." Harold acknowledged. "But he can fall out of the bed and hurt himself, too." He bumped his wife playfully.

"Oh, you guys are so tough." Agnes turned her head away to study her young son waiting restlessly for his father's permission to take off on his bike.

"I don't think it's that. You just can't shelter him from all those things that could hurt him. You'd have to keep him in a cage."

"Harold, I don't want to shelter him from everything. I just don't want him to fall off that bike."

"Look, sweetheart. Clay has been riding that bike for almost a year. He's ready to get rid of the training wheels. Just ask him. He's talked about it for a long time.

From an early age, Clay displayed an affinity with things on wheels. Before he walked, his favorite toy was a small scooter which he propelled around the house bumping into chairs, tables and walls. From the small scooter, he advanced to a miniature trike, his first toy he could ride in the garage and on the driveway. Zipping around the garage and driveway proved the highlight of many of his days.

Though the Pennells lived on a cul-de-sac, Clay's mother refused to let him ride on the street. She worried enough over his riding on the driveway. Harold urged her to relax, to have a little confidence in their son's ability to ride safely on a trike. However, she did not limit her protective instincts only to his riding. She watched over him regardless of his activity. Eventually, as Clay grew older, his need to escape his mother's hovering over him magnified his need to ride his bike. Doing so gave him some peace.

From a mere infant, Clay evinced an independence, a need to do it by himself. From rolling over in his crib, to sitting on the toilet, to climbing into his high chair, he insisted on doing it himself.

Determination supported that independence. Clay did not give up easily. His persistence in wishing to climb into his high chair offered a compelling example. At just two, Clay refused any assistance whenever a meal required him to use his high chair.

After just a few failed attempts, he succeeded in doing it himself. The first success found him sitting proudly in the high chair, a smile spread across his face.

At the same time that Clay exhibited independence and determination, he also possessed a need to please. At some level contradictory, these qualities gave Clay a uniqueness which appealed to all who knew him. As years passed, he never changed; except as he grew older, his desire to please guided more of his decisions.

When the desire to please did conflict with his determination or his independence, he turned to his bike. Biking gave him the chance to be alone, the chance to sort out conflicts created by his unusual combination of character attributes. He loved the solitude of a ride around Lake Minnetonka only blocks from his home. He delighted in the contact with nature, particularly early in the morning. When his mother hovered over him insisting that he clean his room, or read a book, or sweep the garage floor, his need to please collided with his independence. A quiet bike ride released the tension of those conflicts. As he advanced in age, riding his bike made easier coping with demands of home and friends.

"Go ahead, Clay. Jump on the bike. We're watching and will pick you up if you fall." Clay's dad urged playfully.

Though he had ridden his bike for months with the training wheels, this represented his solo ride unsupported by training wheels or even a guiding hand from his dad. Clay adjusted his small helmet. Even riding on the driveway required a helmet. His mom would tolerate nothing else. With his left foot planted on the left pedal, Clay swung his right leg over the seat, stretching for the right pedal. Instantly, he shot forward, pedaling to the end of the driveway and out into forbidden territory.

"Clay!" his mother yelled. "You get back here right now!"

Harold placed his arm around his wife's shoulder. "He's fine." He assured her. "He has it under control."

With legs working like pistons, Clay circled the cul-de-sac and back to his driveway. He stopped in front of his parents, a wide grin showing his satisfaction.

"Nice going, son." Clay's dad patted him on the top of his helmet.

"Yes, we're proud of you. But you need to be careful about riding on the street," his mom warned, reluctant to sanction the ride with too many compliments.

Through the subsequent years, late childhood, early teens, high school and even college, biking retained for Clay a high priority. Despite reaching the age that qualified him for a driver's license, he still found biking his escape. When other kids headed for the swimming pool or the park or the baseball diamond, Clay often headed out on his bike. He did strive to compete athletically and with some success. He ran the 880 meters in track and covered left field for the high school baseball team. But biking gave him the greatest satisfaction, and as he grew older, working with bikes became a career as well as an excellent way to stay in shape.

CHAPTER 6

Miles Hunter parked his gleaming, white pickup in the remotest corner of the lot, away from other vehicles and the chance for dents from wayward doors. He sat for a moment admiring the elaborate dashboard features of his Cadillac Escalade EST with pickup options. He simply could not satisfy his obsession for his most important possession. Even as a young boy, cars, trucks, vehicles of all descriptions intrigued Miles. While other young boys treasured a bike, a baseball glove, a professional athlete, or even reading, vehicles excited him. More than any other desire, he yearned for the day when he could acquire his driver's license and then his own vehicle. By the time he reached sixteen, that vehicle obsession demanded a pickup. Money to buy one mattered little. His father owned a prosperous law firm.

In the years since his first one, several times, Miles savored the unique smell of a new pickup. Last year when he reached the magic plateau of thirty years old, he bought, in his judgement, the supreme pickup, the Cadillac Escalade.

Miles smiled as his hand moved tenderly over the padded steering wheel. He opened the driver's side door, stepped down to the parking lot surface, pressed the lock button on the remote key, and walked slowly around to the other side of the truck, his hand softly tracing the contours of the hood.

As he approached the right front fender, he paused to stare at a faint red smudge marring the shiny surface. Miles rubbed the smudge as he did numerous times before. His attempts to remove the stain proved futile. Even an application of polish failed to do the job. The smudge served as a constant reminder of an incident he strived to forget. For his own protection he knew better than to take his pickup to a body shop.

A sneer crossed his face as he mumbled, "Damned bicycle riders." His eyes lingered on the small mark which awakened his memory to an incident last fall on a warm, sunny, Saturday morning.

Free from any responsibilities at his father's law office, he eagerly awaited the chance to give his new pickup a workout. An extensive system of blacktopped, county roads encircled the historic Lake Minnetonka area where Miles lived his entire life. These mostly country roads served as race tracks for Miles and his passion for giving his vehicles a workout.

Speeding over one of the few straight sections of County Road 19 in rural Hennepin County, Miles saw in the distance a cyclist, for Miles one of the biggest hazards on the road. He simply could not tolerate sharing the road with a wimp on a bike. To Miles, these people needed to stay on the miles of bike tails traversing the Twin Cities. Still, not just individual cyclist but whole groups of them frequently spilled out on the roadway, not content to stay on the shoulder. Miles found their arrogant behavior intolerable.

In his contempt for cyclists, Miles often envisioned brushing one of them off the road, not to hurt them, though Miles cared little about what happened to others, just to remind them the priority of the road belonged to vehicles. Over the years, he suppressed this urge not out of concern for the riders but out of his fear that one of them might inflict damage to his cherished vehicles.

Rapidly approaching the cyclist on this sparkling, autumn morning, Miles felt no compunction for maintaining his place on the road. He determined not to swerve around the rider who, as Miles neared, did ride outside the white line. He grinned, thinking of passing closely this pesky cyclist as a reminder that the road was not built for him.

Generally, he had few problems with individual riders. The groups of riders, eight-ten in a bunch, pissed him off most, not because they created the greatest hazard to motorists but because their refusal to ride single file infringed on his right to all the road. Their riding side by side or even triple invariably placed them in competition with him and his pickup.

In the seconds it took for Miles to reach the cyclist, these thoughts rushed through his mind. At times things happen for no apparent reason. For no apparent reason, this cyclist inched over the white line into the main road surface. In a near fulfillment of his vision to brush a biker off the road, Miles heard a barely audible squeak as he raced by. A brief sensation raced through his body. What had he done? Had he really brushed this guy? His contempt for bikers, so far, had translated into intimidation, not injury which could cause him serious trouble. Working in his dad's law office, he did know about such things.

He gripped the steering wheel. He glanced at the huge side mirror. He saw rider and bike careening across the shoulder of the road, through a shallow ditch, and crashing into the foliage that lined the road. Brushed by the front fender of his speeding pickup, the rider had lost control.

Instantly, Miles slowed, trying to follow the violent course of the bike. The fear of consequences, not fear of injury to the cyclist, produced indecision. What should he do? He slowed almost to a stop, stretching to see in the side mirror just where the rider ended up. He considered backing up for a better view of the scene. But what could he do about an injured biker? It was only an accident. He was not going to risk losing his pickup over some stupid biker. Besides, he thought the biker should have exercised more care riding on a busy road.

Finally, Miles did stop, more out of curiosity than compassion. When he did, he noticed the biker crawling from the foliage that ended his wild ride. With a twisted sense of satisfaction that the incident caused no serious injury, he put the pickup in gear and sped off, eager to examine damage, if any, to his prized vehicle.

"Hey! Miles. You coming to work or are you going to stand there staring at your truck?"

The voice of his father jolted Miles out of his trance. He turned in the direction of his father's voice, pushed his hands into his front pockets and uttered, "Yeah, I'm coming."

His father stood at the front entrance to his law office, arms folded across his chest, watching every step as his son sauntered across the parking lot.

"Someday, son, you might get a bit more serious about life, like arriving on time for your job." Chester Hunter, for years, entertained such thoughts and discussed them with his youngest son, to no avail. To Miles these discussions mattered little, only more nagging from his father who didn't understand what Miles faced growing up in a family of siblings who did everything right.

Miles never demonstrated any seriousness about life. He stumbled through school, some private, some public as his parents sought solutions to their complacent, indifferent youngest son. Two older brothers and an older sister established early in their lives a commitment to success in whatever they chose to do. They achieved that success. Perhaps, out of resentment or due to something genetic, Miles simply did not possess the same drive and sense of responsibility that marked the rest of his family.

A successful personal injury lawyer, Chester Hunter tried desperately to motivate his youngest son. Ultimately, he had to accept the fact that Miles would not earn a college degree as had his other children. Miles barely survived high school. However, in his law office, Chester made a place for Miles. That place involved performing menial tasks, such as document duplication and assembly, or document delivery. He also ran errands for the office staff. Even enrollment in a junior college program leading to a certification as a legal aid ended in failure. Miles did not find time to embrace academics or even to attend classes regularly.

On occasion, the memory of the incident with the cyclist intruded into Miles' daily routine. If nothing else, it strengthened his resentment of cyclists using his roads, those intended for motor vehicles. In the months since the incident, Miles heard nothing about it on the news. He rarely read the newspaper so could not know of any coverage there. Since he heard nothing and since he saw the rider crawl out of the foliage, he assumed he could forget about the whole thing. That he hadn't, only fueled his resentment.

CHAPTER 7

"How was your ride?" Ross Langer stood behind the counter studying an invoice for yesterday's late shipment of bicycle helmets.

"I should never have taken it." Clay walked by his boss and into the small office that served him as the manager of the bike shop as well as Ross, the owner.

Ross turned and with his eyes followed as Clay slouched in the chair behind the one desk. He watched Clay's shoulders slump while he sat in the chair and stared at his hands folded in his lap.

Stepping into the office, Ross leaned on the desk. "Are you all right, Clay?"

Clay looked up at his boss, the only one he'd known for nearly ten years. "Yeah, I'm okay. Just a bit tired."

"Not sleeping well?"

Clay turned in the chair, stood up with a grimace, seeking the desk for support. "It's this damned leg. I can't get comfortable at night. If I turn too quick, sharp pain shoots through the calf. If

I don't move at all, the leg gets stiff. Riding this morning didn't help."

"It's the infection, isn't it? Have you talked to the doctor about it lately?"

Clay rubbed his eyes, slumped against the desk, and breathed deeply. "I've talked to doctors too damned much. For six months I've talked to doctors, nurses," Clay slowly shook his head, "therapists and even receptionists. It's an infection around the incision. They all say it takes time. I'm taking antibiotics, strong ones, I guess. The bone, I understand, has mostly healed?"

Clay shifted his weight off the damaged right leg. A young couple entered the bike shop. Ross hurried out to greet them. Clay leaned more heavily against the desk. He reflected on the conversation with Ross. He worried about the damned infection. Why didn't the antibiotics do something? His increased dependance on pain medication had not entered the conversation. It entered the conversation only when his doctor renewed the prescription. Beyond that he only wondered about his dependance. It developed into a preoccupation with Clay that not even his wife shared.

With the departure of the young couple, Ross returned to the office. He stayed in the doorway where he observed Clay before suggesting, "Why don't you take some time off. You know, try to get some rest. Talk to a different doctor."

"Thank you, but I can't just sit around the house either. Already my wife gets impatient with me. I shouldn't have ridden. This morning was the first time in weeks that I felt some energy. But, who knows. Maybe I'm pushing it too fast."

"God, how long has it been?" Ross asked

"About six months."

Ross shook his head. "You'd think that's long enough. But I've heard these infections can be damned tough."

"I can agree with that. I just don't know what's happening or not happening with the infection." Clay sat heavily back in the chair.

With the arrival of more customers, their conversation ended. However, in his own mind, Clay revisited it several times during the day. He worried about his attachment to pain killers. That his marriage suffered because of the accident only deepened the frustration Clay experienced. At home, petty differences developed into bitter arguments. Too often he and Vicky hardly spoke to one another. When they did, it typically involved some contention. Though he tried to suppress such thoughts, his suspicion grew that her hours on the job involved more than a devotion to work. Lately, she followed her schedule, and he followed his. They rarely intersected, on too many evenings, not even for dinner.

Clay literally limped through the day. Light business only stretched the day out more than normal. Clay's managerial duties included doing whatever needed doing: waiting on customers, taking inventory, assessing repair needs for customers, or ensuring a full supply of merchandise. As the owner, Ross also assumed responsibility for a range of duties. However, he devoted more and more of his time to promoting his shop and the sport of cycling.

Clay's early affinity with biking influenced many of his decisions, even where he would attend college. His choice of St. Thomas in St. Paul ensured that for much of the academic year, he could bike to his classes, freed from a worry over parking a car. At that time in his life, he didn't own a car, but he would have if not for his bike.

Considering the cost of tuition at St. Thomas, Clay's parents questioned the need for a liberal arts degree since Clay decided he wished to stay with Ross at the bike shop after graduation. Lacking a compelling argument, Clay reminded them that a college education qualified a person for more than just a job. Working at the bike shop, for Clay, served as more than just a job. It gave him the chance to associate with people who shared his passion while allowing him to work with all aspects of the cycling world.

Six months had elapsed since the accident. Yet healing slowed in the injured leg. The longer the delay in healing the more often

Clay revisited, in his mind, that morning on County Road #19. This slow business day found him repeatedly slipping into the memory of that Saturday morning.

A gorgeous autumn morning, a bright sunshine, a gentle breeze rustling autumn leaves clinging to the trees made for perfect riding conditions. For years Clay rode the miles of black topped roads around Western Hennepin County and the Lake Minnetonka region, roads that often carried little traffic.

A careful cyclist, Clay adhered to all traffic rules for bikers, essentially the same rules as those for motorists. He made sure he followed the white line, riding to its outside whenever possible, striving to avoid intruding on motorist space. Even at that he knew that some motorists resented sharing the road with cyclists. In his years of riding, those most guilty of this resentment drove pickups.

Even six months could not erase the memory Clay had of a vehicle presence behind him. The sudden bump against his handle bars triggered events that easily could have killed him. The force of the bump propelled Clay into an out of control plunge down the shallow ditch bordering the road. The momentum carried him through the ditch over a culvert and into thick brush. The collision with a tree sent shearing pain through his shoulder, tossing him to the ground, tangled with his bike.

He had no idea how long he lay stunned, trapped in the heavy foliage with his bike on top of him. Ultimately, attempts to move sent sharp pains through his shoulder.

His right leg was twisted, at an unnatural angle, around the bike's fork. In the haze which clouded his vision and despite the pain that shot through his body, his struggle to sit up gave him a glimpse of a white pickup speeding away.

Eventually, he regained some sense of what happened and where he was. A pickup had pushed him off the road. His sense also told him he needed to do something. From the road he likely wasn't visible to passing motorists. He also sensed he needed medical attention.

For weeks Vicky urged him to take his cell phone on his rides. Recently, he gave in to her suggestion. With painful effort Clay secured his cell phone. By noon on that Saturday morning, he rested in the hospital lucky to be alive but suffering a crushed shoulder and a broken leg.

While still in the hospital, Clay reported the accident to the Hennepin County Sheriff's Department. He spoke with an Officer Stewart Cook, describing what happened and confirming the driver of the pickup slowed but sped away. Officer Cook noted all the details and assured Clay he would alert other police departments in the western suburbs. An appeal went out both in the newspaper and on TV for anyone who might have witnessed the accident.

For several days, members of the sheriff's department spoke with residents in the area of the accident. A major problem with the attempts to acquire information was the fact very few people lived around the area where the accident took place. After a few days, the department curtailed its investigation only to retire the file until something concrete gave them a justification to renew the search. Nothing emerged to warrant reopening the case.

Though Clay faced critical therapy, he never completely gave up on the officials finding the white pickup and its careless driver. In his very private moments, he resolved that someday he would discover the one responsible for dramatically altering his life.

"Clay, why don't you take off. I can handle things by myself. You look worn out." Ross placed his hand on Clay's shoulder.

"Do I really look that bad?" Clay responded with a smile.

"Well, let's say you don't look like you're ready for a century ride. It looks like every time you move it hurts."

Clay took a deep breath and shook his head. "You're probably right." He glanced at his watch. "Maybe I will take off." He trained his eyes on his right leg. "Maybe, for a while, I'll stay off my bike too."

CHAPTER 8

"You are going when?" Clay confronted Vicky rinsing dishes at the kitchen sink.

Dinner gave Vicky the chance to discuss with Clay the impending business trip to Orlando. The topic plunged them into an argument that crushed calm discussion.

"In about two weeks." She answered, her eyes focused on the dishes in the sink.

"When did this come up?" Clay struggled to control the volume of his voice.

Vicky turned to face her husband. Calmly, she explained. "Mr. Wagner talked to me this morning, the first I knew anything about it."

"Why do you have to go?"

Vicky's shoulders slumped, her head dipped. "I am part of the executive team. I'm expected to work with the others."

"Going to Orlando is work?" Clay leaned heavily against the kitchen counter.

"Honey, I'm sorry I have to do this, but I . . . ."

"You don't have to do this!" Clay interrupted.

"If I want to keep my job, I think I do." Vicky trained her eyes on her husband. "You just never have accepted the fact that I have an important job that demands my attention. Can't you see it from my perspective? I've always wanted to do the best I can. Is that so bad?"

"No, it's not so bad. You do have a husband, though."

Clay's words ignited a flame of resentment in Vicky. "God! How can you even suggest that I neglect you! For the last few months I've done about all I could do to help you through this crisis. Now, you don't want me to do my job. Just what else do you want me to do?" Vicky paused. Breathing deeply, she turned away from her husband.

"I appreciate what you've done and the sacrifice you've made." Clay's voice now much more controlled. He stepped forward to touch Vicky's shoulder. He turned her so they stood face to face. "Are you happy with our marriage?"

Vicky's head jerked up, and her mouth dropped open. "What are you saying?"

Clay folded his arms across his chest. "Lately, we've spent more time arguing than we have doing almost anything else. We don't discuss any more. We just argue. We hardly do anything together. You spend more time with those guys at work than you do with me." Clay shifted his weight off his right leg. With deliberate hesitation, he carefully considered his next words.

"Sometimes, I wonder if all the time at the office involves only work."

Shocked by his implied accusation, Vicky rushed by Clay. "I don't have to listen to this. I don't know where you get these ideas. I don't want to hear any more of this . . . this damned nonsense!" Vicky charged out of the kitchen seeking refuge in the quiet of the bedroom.

Slamming the door, she flopped down on the bed. She buried her face in her pillow, striving to hold back the tears that threatened to spill out. "How ungrateful!" She whispered into her pillow. She recalled the countless hours she devoted to her husband after the accident. He could do very little for himself. The injured left shoulder and right leg had rendered him nearly incapacitated. He needed help from getting out of bed in the morning to drying his hair to visiting the doctor. Now his suspicions extinguished much of the excitement of a business trip to Orlando.

Vicky moved over on her back, gazing into the emptiness of the bedroom ceiling. She had respected her marriage vows through the years at Wagner Electronics. Yes, the many meetings, Christmas parties, and occasional company celebrations had created temptations. She accepted the fact that she did have appeal. Men looked at her, some with desire, wherever she went, the grocery store, the shopping center, or the gas station. If she wished, she could have violated her marriage vows many times. She had not. Nonetheless, she believed in the power of appearance. She believed in exploiting her physical attributes to achieve what she wanted. Why wouldn't she? What she always wanted transcended simple success. She offered no apology for her commitment to achieving number one.

Clay knocked gently on the bedroom door. He listened carefully for any sound from within. He knocked a second time then eased the door open. Vicky lay on the bed, watching him enter.

"You all right?" he asked.

With eyes still trained on the ceiling, Vicky, in a voice hardly more than a whisper, replied, "I guess so."

Clay walked in to sit at the end of the bed. "I'm sorry. I didn't mean to offend you. I miss what we once had." He ran his fingers through his hair then rubbed his eyes. "What has happened to us?"

"I wish I knew." Vicky looked away from her husband.

Clay moved to her side of the bed. "I don't think it's just the accident. But, that's a part of it, I guess. I know it's made me moody and frustrated. You too. Maybe we have become too selfish. You have your life. I have mine."

Vicky sat up on the edge of the bed, turning her head to face Clay. "I know the accident hasn't helped our marriage. Shouldn't adults adjust better to adversity?"

"Yes, they should."

Silence settled over the bedroom. On the bed, each sat contemplating what to say next.

Vicky reached, placing her hand on her husband's arm. "Clay, what are you going to do about the infection in your leg? Something is just not right."

"For weeks, I've asked myself that question." He gazed down at the floor, slowly shaking his head. "I've asked my doctor that question."

"What did he say?"

"He has repeated that the infection is not easy to combat. He repeats that it takes time. I've asked how much? He always says, 'Everyone's different.'"

Vicky's shoulders slumped; she breathed deeply, exhaling frustration. She looked into Clay's eyes, a smile spreading her lips. "Honey, I think you should get another opinion. You probably should have gotten one a long time ago."

Clay moved toward his wife, kneeling carefully in front of her as she sat on the edge of the bed. With conviction he announced, "Tomorrow, I'm going to contact the Mayo Clinic. If any one can find some answers to my problem, they should be the ones. I'm not sure what getting an appointment there involves. I'll find out."

Vicky leaned forward placing a kiss on Clay's cheek. "I agree."

Clay smiled. "It's great to agree about something." He paused, almost reluctant to bring up the issue. "When do you leave for Orlando?"

Vicky smiled. "Are you sure it's okay for me to go?"

Clay exhaled, hanging his head. "Of course, it's all right. I'm sorry I questioned you. You shouldn't have to get my permission to do your job."

Vicky reached to touch Clay's chin, gently urging him to look at her. "We leave in a couple weeks. The whole thing lasts about five days." Vicky lifted her legs in a type of yoga position on the edge of the bed. "Are you sure about being here alone? Can you handle everything with that leg?"

"Look, my parents live near by. If I needed help, they could be here in minutes. Besides, Josh next door is always willing to give a hand. Maybe, I can get an appointment at the Mayo Clinic before you leave. That could give us more information about what to expect."

Clay reached up to pull his wife closer. He kissed her deeply. She wrapped her arms around his shoulders. They kissed again, passion building as they embraced. Standing up, Clay urged Vicky back on the bed. He crawled in beside her. Quickly, they reached for reach other, hands searching for bare skin. With awareness of his injuries, Clay removed his trousers. Vicky slid out of her shorts. With bodies pressed together, they kissed passionately.

Clay urged Vicky onto her back. She responded by pulling him with her. Almost as if their first time, they plunged into sex, exploring and ultimately exploding in mankind's most glorious moment.

CHAPTER 9

"Hey, Jamie, where was your dad yesterday?"

"Maybe, he doesn't have a Dad. Hatched from an egg."

Two boys from Jamie's class cornered him on the play ground. They delighted in their assault on him. The previous day, Dad's Day in Jamie's classroom, featured Dads and what they did. He didn't have a Dad, at least not a living Dad. He knew his dad died in an accident a long time ago. Some of his classmates ignored that fact. Making Jamie suffer offered more entertainment than accepting the truth.

At ten years old, Jamie Foster ranked as one of the smallest in his class. For that he could thank his mom, petite at only five feet two inches. He never knew the joy of having a Dad. He watched with envy and a bit of mystery as other kids came to school with their dads or whose dads dropped them off at school. The joys or the sorrows of having a Dad completely eluded him. Nothing, so far in his short life, gave him a clear idea of life with a Dad.

That evening before dinner, Jamie approached his mom. "Mom, tell me about my dad again." He looked pleadingly at his mom.

"Honey, I've told you many times already." Robin, Jamie's mom, reached for her son, holding him close.

"I know you have. I want to hear it again," his voice muffled as his mom pulled him closer.

She tilted her head to kiss the top of Jamie's curly head, a tear forming in each eye. "Let's sit down over there by the table. We can talk better that way."

Jamie rushed to grab a chair. His mom pulled a chair away from the kitchen table and slowly sat down.

"Now, what exactly do you want to know that I haven't already told you about your dad?"

Jamie pulled his legs up under his chin. Tiny inquisitive wrinkles creased his forehead. "What did he look like, really? Pictures don't count. What did he look like in real life?"

Robin smiled as she studied the serious expression on her son's face. "He was handsome. He was tall, more than six feet tall."

"Will I be six feet tall someday?" he interrupted, his light blue eyes sparkling with anticipation.

Robin laughed. "I don't know about that. Maybe, if you eat only good food."

With mild alarm, he declared, "I can't eat at MacDonald's any more?"

Robin enjoyed her son's innocent sense of humor. "Maybe not just so often. As I started to say, your dad was tall, dark, and handsome. You might have heard that description before, but it really did apply to your dad. Like you, he loved to ride his bike. Nearly every day he spent time on his bike. Because he did, he stayed in excellent shape." Discussing these details disturbed her, knowing that they represented a fabrication. "If you continue riding and eating only healthy food," she playfully nudged her son's shoulder. "You may not reach six feet tall, but you will stay in good shape." Robin leaned forward in her chair, placing a hand on her son's shoulder. "Always remember, Jamie, your dad was much more than an avid cyclist. He loved his family, especially his son."

A broad smile spread across Jamie's face. His mom patted his head as he rested it upon his knees still tucked under his chin. When she talked about his dad's love, more guilt tainted what she said. Over the years, she fabricated much of what she told her son. She fashioned a family in her mind, a family she envisioned and likely would never have. She worried about the future when Jamie grew older with a deeper curiosity about the reality of his dad whom he had never known and the fictitious family his mom created for him.

"What did he do?" Jamie inquired.

That question always challenged Robin more than any other. She had no idea what Clay did for a living. He rode a bike with near obsession she gathered from their discussion the one night they spent together. Beyond that, those few hours did not allow time for such detail. However, what they did allow time for she cherished. Her son had given her purpose in life as well as endless pleasure.

"Your dad was a salesman. He sold bikes and sometimes he fixed them, too." To her that made sense, remembering Clay's adamant attachment to cycling.

Jamie dropped his feet to the floor. Sadness clouded his bright eyes. "How did he die?"

Guilt again gripped Robin, talking about the death of someone with whom she had no contact for ten years. How many lies could she impose on her son? For now, she determined that the story she created would have to do. Softy, Robin explained how riding on a county road, his dad was struck by a passing motorist. Severely injured, he suffered in the hospital for several days before he died. At the time of his dad's death, she explained, Jamie was only an infant.

With eyes wide, Jamie stared at his mother. "Do you think he sees me, sees us?"

"If you believe he does, then he does." Though Robin ensured that her son attended both Sunday school and church service, she did not pursue questions of life after death. In her own mind, she wavered in her acceptance of Biblical promises. If her son wished to believe his dad could see him, she would not interfere.

She smoothed her son's ruffled hair. She placed her hand under his chin, urging him to look at her. "Jamie, did something happen today in school that made you want to hear about your dad again?"

He glanced down at the floor, at first reluctant to talk about others picking on him. "Two kids made fun of me on the play ground."

Hearing this always incensed Robin. She refused to accept that kids naturally enjoyed persecuting others their age. She believed, instead, that it reflected a lack of guidance from home. Kids who picked on others lacked confidence and self-respect.

She reached toward her son, placing her hands on his shoulders then asked, "What did they say?"

"Oh, they asked where my dad was. Why he didn't come to school yesterday. They said I hatched from an egg or something."

Robin's arms encircled her son. "You just ignore kids like that. You lost your daddy when you were just a tiny baby. Remember, he loved you dearly. I love you dearly. You are a wonderful young boy. I'm so proud of you."

Jamie buried his face in his mom's stomach. She held onto him firmly until he leaned back to say, "Thank you, mom. I think I'm hungry. Can we go to Mac Donald's now?"

They shared a brief moment of laughter.

His mom responded, "Maybe later."

In the quiet of her bedroom, Robin thought about her son, about herself, and even about Clay, the father her son would likely never know. In her mind she traveled back over ten years. She recalled the excitement the RAGBRAI, "Register's Annual Great Bicycle Ride Across Iowa," brought to her small town of Packwood, Iowa, population about three hundred. The annual ride, the longest and the oldest in the country, brought through her small town riders from across America and even a few from other countries. Churches, restaurants, and bars cherished the business that came with the cyclists. The three churches in the community offered inexpensive dinners for the hungry and tired riders who for the day had ridden over seventy miles. Furthermore, Packwood marked the last stop before the conclusion of the ride in Dubuque, Iowa, the following day.

Robin retained vivid images of this handsome rider who sat at her table in the lower level of the United Methodist Church. Over the years when the bike route came through Packwood, the church served a delicious, home cooked dinner that appealed to hungry riders. Her job included making certain all guests at her table received prompt attention. She still see the handsome, young man who sat by himself quietly eating the famed pork chop dinner.

Perhaps, wishing to justify her standing off to one side of the long table or perhaps, just an excuse to meet the young man, Robin had stepped behind him.

"Everything okay?" she asked.

The young man turned to face her. "Everything is delicious. Thank you."

She briefly caught her breath. The guy, just sitting there, exuded sexuality. His smile involved his entire face, especially his alluring, brown eyes. "If you need anything, please let me know." She moved, self-consciously, back to her post at the far end of the table.

When the young man completed his dinner, he walked over to Robin to thank her again. She asked where he lived, the beginning of a conversation that concluded with his promise to stop back at the completion of her duties. That evening ended with their moment of ecstasy on the soft grass in Friendship Park.

The next day she winced at the thought of what happened in the park. Never had she imagined that she would have sex with a man whom she hardly knew. She dated all through high school, none of the dates leading to sex in the park. What happened that night shocked and yet pleased her. Life in small town Iowa included activities far less stimulating then what she engaged in the previous night.

In the days that followed, the image of Clay Pennell dimmed. Robin's classes at the Indian Hills Community College located in nearby Ottumwa, Iowa, captured most of her time and attention. Living at home allowed her to spend time learning rather than working at some menial job in Packwood. Missing her period changed her life instantly and drastically.

When her family doctor confirmed her pregnancy, she suffered immediate despair. What should she do? Should she tell her parents? Should she contact Clay, whom she knew lived some place in the Twin Cities? Should she consider an abortion? Her relatively conservative life definitely did not prepare her to face an unwanted pregnancy.

As the weeks passed and her stomach stretched out, she made the decision to reject abortion and to carry the baby full term. Not an antiabortion zealot, Robin, still, valued life, even the life of a fetus. Eventually, with encouragement from her doctor, she informed her parents of her pregnancy. An initial shock gave way to impressive parental support which proved vital as her delivery date approached, and she could no longer hide her condition.

The excitement of Jamie's arrival far exceeded the guilt and shame Robin or her parents may have harbored. The lively, seven pound boy added for Robin and her parents another dimension to life in placid Packwood.

With help of her parents, Robin completed her degree and certification as a LPN. After graduation she had taken a job at the local community hospital where after over eight years she continued to work.

Grateful for the continued help and support of her parents, Robin flourished as a nurse and mother. Jamie flourished as a vibrant, intelligent boy. Occasionally, during the quiet moments before sleep descended, she considered attempting to contact Clay Pennell. Aware of the potential disruption to his life as well as hers and Jamie's, she dismissed those thoughts as she drifted off to sleep.

CHAPTER 10

Tension filled the examination room located on the third floor of Rochester's Mayo Clinic. Details of the confrontation of a few days ago faded as the future of Clay's right leg transcended petty differences between Vicky and him.

"We should have done this weeks ago." Vicky sat rigid in the chair squeezed between Clay and the tiny desk attached to the corner of the examination room.

Clay reached for her hand. "I agree. I just wanted to get out of the cast and back to some kind of normal life."

"I don't blame you for that. Confinement is not your thing." Vicky pressed Clay's hand.

"I know. I probably shouldn't have tried riding as soon as I did. It didn't help me at all." Clay sat up straight in his chair, tenderly flexing his damaged right leg.

"I should remember this, but when did you first find out about the infection?"

Clay fixed his eyes on Vicky's face, searching for when Dr. Martin, his personal physician at home, first informed him of the infection. "I don't know exactly. Probably not long after he removed the cast. I remember that the incision still hadn't totally healed."

A soft knock at the door announced the arrival of the doctor. The door opened to a tall, thin man, probably in his early forties with thick blond hair and a precisely trimmed mustache. "Hi, I'm Doctor Lawson." He stepped toward Clay and Vicky with hand extended. Clay moved to stand up to shake the doctor's hand. He quickly motioned Clay to stay seated. With a firm grip, he shook hands with both of them. "You are Clay Pennell and this must be your wife Vicky. Nice to meet you and welcome to the Mayo Clinic."

"Thank you." Clay and Vicky responded in unison.

Dr. Lawson positioned himself at the small corner desk. He opened the file he carried, studied it briefly, then looked up at Clay. "You're, apparently, having some problems with your leg?"

Clay nodded. He forced a smile. "Yes, for a long time."

"I've checked the records submitted by your doctor back in the Twin Cities. I believe a Dr. Martin. But why don't you tell me yourself about your leg."

Clay thought for a moment. He turned to face the doctor. "Over six months ago I went on a morning bike ride. I'm a cyclist. Clay proceeded to describe, briefly, to Dr. Lawson the accident, the white pickup, the shoulder and leg injuries, the surgeries, the months of rehabilitation, and finally the insidious infection.

"Apparently, you continue to have discomfort in your right leg. How about your shoulder? Dr. Lawson closed the file, keeping his attention on Clay.

"The shoulder has given few problems. It seems all right now, maybe a minor twinge once in a while. Nothing like my leg."

"What about the infection? When did you find out about that?"

Clay gazed straight ahead sifting through his memory. "I guess about the time the doctor removed the cast. They did surgery on the broken bones. I'm not sure which ones, but they're in the calf area. The incision hadn't healed. It oozed something."

"Your body is obviously fighting the infection. What did your doctor do about the infection?" Dr. Lawson knew what the doctor did. The file contained a detailed description of the treatment. He, however, wished to learn of Clay's familiarity with that treatment.

"Well, he hooked me up to an intravenous dose of antibiotics. For a couple hours it dripped into me. He also prescribed an oral antibiotic."

"Have you been taking the medication regularly?"

"Yeah, I have." Clay folded his hands in his lap, staring down at the floor. "I've taken too many of them and too many pain killers."

"Which pain killers have you been taking?"

Clay looked at Vicky for help in remembering the name. "Vicodin, I think."

"Does the pain killer help?" Dr. Lawson gazed steadily at Clay.

"Most of the time." Clay shifted in his chair, exhibiting a reluctance to talk about the Vicodin, and what for him went beyond.

Dr. Lawson sensed this reluctance. "Have you had any adverse reaction to the Vicodin?"

Clay looked at the doctor, then at Vicky. Should he even mention his recent introduction to marijuana? Clay ran his hands through his hair, stalling while he decided what to say. "No, not really. It's just that, I think, I've come to depend on it too much. Taking the pain killer doesn't solve the basic problem. It only covers it up." Clay breathed deeply, drooping his shoulders.

"I understand. Powerful medications can have powerful effects." Dr. Lawson turned his attention to Vicky. "What do you think? Has the injury adversely affected you?"

In her mind, no question that the accident affected their lives and their marriage, if the two even existed separately. However, Vicky did not wish to pursue their personal problems at this time. "Of course, it has had an affect, much more for Clay than for me. We both simply want to get beyond the accident."

Dr. Lawson looked briefly at the young couple sitting before him. "Thank you for your honesty and your willingness to talk about the problem. In many cases merely talking through a medical problem can hasten the recovery. Though the antibiotic hasn't helped much to cure the infection, it has very likely prevented it from spreading."

Dr. Lawson turned to face the desk then reached for a pad of paper in the rack above the desk top. As he wrote, he explained, "Today I want to x-ray the leg and administer a couple blood tests. That won't take long. But it will tell us where we stand with the fracture and the infection. Right now I want you and your wife to wait right here. I will send in a technician, first, to draw some blood and then take you for an x-ray of the leg." Dr. Lawson stood, and walked to the door. "When you are done with those procedures, I will see you back here." He looked at Clay and Vicky. "Any questions right now?"

Clay glanced at Vicky, who shook her head. He asked, "Where did the infection come from?"

A troubled expressed crossed Dr. Lawson's face. "It can come from any number of sources. Sadly, one of the main sources is the hospital where you had the surgery. Bacteria live in hospitals, too. We can't always sterilize the environment in the operating room or in other areas of the hospital. Exactly, where yours came from, we will never know. We can only speculate."

Clay nodded in acceptance of the explanation. "Thank you."

In slightly more than an hour, Clay and Vicky resumed their places in the examination room. As directed, they waited for the return of Dr. Lawson and expectantly some word about the infection.

Soon, they heard the soft knock on the door followed by Dr. Lawson's entrance into the room. He smiled and headed directly to the chair in front of the small corner desk. Opening the file he carried, he turned to face Clay and Vicky. "I don't think I'm telling you anything you don't already know. The blood test revealed a very active infection in your right leg. The oral antibiotics don't seem to carry enough impact to fight the infection. The bone fractures have healed, but the incision has not, mainly because of the infection. The antibiotics have prevented the infection from moving out of the leg. That's a good thing. So far they can't seem to overcome the infection itself, though."

Clay and Vicky listened intently.

Dr. Lawson continued. "We're going to duplicate what your doctor in the Twin Cities did upon discovering the infection. We're going to try a more powerful assault. I'm going to send you to a more comfortable exam room. For about two hours a strong antibiotic will flow directly into your blood stream. I will then prescribe an oral version of the antibiotic that I want you to take twice a day. I also want you to stay off that leg as much as possible. Absolutely, no biking. In one month I want to see you again. Then we can determine who's winning the battle." Dr. Lawson paused. "Do you have any questions?

"Can I go to work?" Clay asked.

"What exactly do you do?

"Manage a bike shop." Clay sat rigid in his chair in anticipation of the doctor's answer.

"Go to work. Try to stay off the leg when possible. Remember, conquering this infection will require every weapon in our arsenal. Giving the leg plenty of rest is part of that arsenal."

Vicky cleared her throat. "What happens if the antibiotics don't work?"

Dr. Lawson closed the file. With both hands firmly on his knees, he faced Vicky. "Ultimately, the situation could require amputation to prevent further advancement of the infection."

Clay uttered a groan.

"I know that sounds drastic. I do want to be honest, though. This is a serious infection which allowed to exist could endanger other body organs. Let's, for now, go with the treatment I've prescribed. I will see you in about a month."

Mildly stunned, Clay and Vicky sat alone holding hands while they waited for another round of a more powerful antibiotic.

CHAPTER 11

The trip to Rochester and the Mayo Clinic, for both Clay and Vicky, produced a paradox. That they now knew definitively the source of Clay's problem satisfied them. That they also knew the potential for an amputation shocked them.

In the two weeks since the appointment, Clay adhered faithfully to the doctor's insistence that he stay off the leg as much as possible. The pain medication as well as the oral antibiotic at times rendered him incapable of work. Ross understood Clay's status, ensuring him that he could come to work only when he felt strong enough to do so. When he did attempt to work, he found abundant time to elevate the right leg while he rested in the office.

Since the appointment, Vicky had departed for Orlando and the international trade show at the convention center. Upon their return from Rochester, Clay and Vicky debated the question if she should now leave Clay alone for nearly a week. He insisted that she attend. She insisted that she stay home to attend to her husband. Their positions on the trip essentially switched from a few days ago when she first introduced the chance for her to travel to Florida. At that time her argument centered on her responsibility as an executive of the company. His argument centered on her responsibility as the wife of a husband who needed her help.

Now, she confessed her responsibility to her husband. She could not leave him to take care of himself when he needed to stay off his leg. He admitted that she did have a responsibility to the company for which she worked. Besides, Clay's parents lived only minutes away. They certainly could monitor Clay in Vicky's absence.

Clay eventually won the argument, or, perhaps, Vicky won. Whoever would claim the victory, Vicky departed for Orlando three days ago, leaving Clay in the hands of his boss and his parents.

Rarely during their marriage had Clay and Vicky spent time away from each other. Most of their time away from work they devoted to each other. In her absence, for Clay, usually with his right leg elevated, the time passed slowly, especially in the evening when he and Vicky often shared moments of conversation about each other's day at work. Never had Clay found any enjoyment in sedentary activities, such as watching TV unless he happened to find some sporting event, especially one dealing with cycling. Presently, his aversion to TV persisted, except now he had few options. He could only read so much before restlessness trickled through his body.

Each day since her departure, Vicky called to check on how Clay handled his solitude. Each day, also, Clay's parents checked on him to ensure he was okay. All of this attention bothered him since he always considered himself independent and capable of taking care of himself.

Clay had spent the entire day at home, resting his leg. The previous day he spent at the bike shop hobbling around attempting to do his job. By the end of the day, with energy depleted, he accepted Ross's suggestion that he stay home for the next couple days.

For the day he accomplished little else besides resting his leg and gradually falling victim to a spreading restlessness. Even his sound left leg twitched with impatience to move. Clay threw his head back on the large sofa chair, his refuge during this period of recovery. He pressed his eyes tightly closed, the image of mounting his bike for an evening ride vivid in his mind.

Since the visit to the Mayo Clinic, the Vicodin controlled the pain. It didn't, however, control his need for activity. Concerned for his potential addiction, Clay avoided any more marijuana. Nonetheless, he had not discarded three joints that remained of the supply he received months ago from a college friend.

Cautiously, Clay removed his leg from its resting place on top of the ottoman. He reminded himself that Dr. Lawson of the Mayo Clinic did not prohibit him from walking on his right leg. With his hands on the arms of the sofa chair, he eased himself up to stand mostly on his left leg. From there, he slowly walked to the bedroom dresser where he had concealed the marijuana. With one joint in his hand and another in his shirt pocket, he made his way to the kitchen where he lighted up.

He inhaled deeply, the miracle of marijuana rapidly finding its way into his blood stream. Soon, he could feel a lightness flow through his body, chasing away the restlessness and the tedium. He leaned against the kitchen counter, savoring the growing euphoria this one small joint generated, the combination of pain medication and antibiotics likely serving to enhance the impact of the marijuana. The earlier image of his mounting his bike for an evening ride returned, even more vivid in its realism. Clay swayed from side to side, his attention diverted from his damaged leg. He continued the deep inhalations until the joint burned down to a mere stub. He tossed it into the sink. He lighted another.

With each subsequent drag on the joint, Clay drifted farther away from reality. He felt no pain. He felt only elation, a spreading sensation, a freedom that eluded him for months. Oblivious to his physical condition, he allowed the image of a bike to lure him toward the garage. He walked slowly without a limp, without pain. He entered a world of pure, pleasurable sensation.

In the garage, Clay pressed the button to open the garage door. In the light, he braced himself against the garage wall to gaze at his bike parked where he left it weeks ago.

With steps carefully measured, he approached the bike. Placing his hand on the handle bar, he tipped the bike away from the wall. With complete disregard for his leg or for anything else not related to his singleminded obsession with a bike ride, Clay swung his leg over the bike to settle onto the seat. His instability served as no deterrent. His left leg rotated the pedal. He pushed off.

The medication, the marijuana, and now the raw thrill of riding his bike carried him through the garage and onto the driveway. Dusk covered everything with a haze, magnified by mood altering substances flowing through Clay's body. Not in firm control of the bike, he swerved over to the driveway edge. The bike's front tire slid off the driveway causing him to lose his limited control. The bike tipped over, tossing Clay into a flower bed bordering the driveway. A sharp, steel spike used to secure a tall flower protruded ominously from the flower bed.

As Clay crashed to the ground, the sharp spike ripped through his leg, tearing open the incision that for months struggled to heal. He felt no pain. He lay entangled in flowers and his bike. He lay there as he drifted off into semiconsciousness, his blood flowing onto the flower garden.

"What in the hell were you thinking?" Harold Pennell looked down at his son resting comfortably, attached to an array of tubes and wires monitoring his status. "My God, you could have died out there in the yard if Josh hadn't heard the noise of your fall."

Clay lay unresponsive, suffering from the trauma as well as feeling the after effects of his plunge into the world of controlled substances.

"The doctor tells me that your blood contained generous amounts of something more than pain killers." Clay's father stepped closer to the bed. "What's going on with you? You're not involved in that stuff, I hope. It's illegal. You could end up in jail."

Clay and his father enjoyed a close relationship beginning when Clay first displayed an affinity with biking. When Clay would rather venture off on his bike, his dad encouraged him. Often his mother expressed concern over what she interpreted as antisocial behavior. His father saw it as mature independence. Clay saw it as a chance to spend time away from the demands placed on him by an overprotective mother.

While Harold Pennell gave his son freedom to make his own decisions even when Clay was still in middle school, he did expect him to abide by family rules, home before dark, eat well balanced meals, mind his mother, complete homework, and keep his room clean. That Clay would even consider the use of drugs like marijuana never entered Harold's mind. It simply ranked high on the list of things Clay rejected. Until the suffering and frustration that came with the delayed healing of the leg, Clay, at over thirty years old, still rejected it. Now, to discover Clay used marijuana shocked his father.

Harold persisted questioning Clay, who wished only to rest and to sort out the events of that evening. Finally, Clay turned to look directly at his dad. "I don't want to talk about it now, Dad," his voice barely audible.

"Well, the doctor wants to keep you over night. They will assign you to a hospital room. You're in good hands here. The bleeding has stopped and the incision closed. Your mother and I will stay until you are settled in your room. Then we'll come back in the morning. I guess, if all goes well in the morning, you can go home."

Nurses woke Clay early to continue the monitoring of his condition as they did periodically through the night. All of his vital signs suggested he faced no danger. However, what happened cast serious doubt on his leg's ability to heal. Still, quick action by Josh Ditmer, Clay's neighbor, brought an ambulance in minutes after Clay's fall. Josh just happened to look out his front window when he thought he saw Clay's garage light come on. He knew Vicky had traveled to Orlando for a convention of some kind. Though no one requested that Josh watch out for Clay, he, nonetheless, assumed some responsibility to do so.

Quick action by the emergency room staff stopped the bleeding and mended temporarily the incision so violently reopened. A simple blood test established the presence of marijuana. To the emergency room staff the presence of marijuana in patients they treated had long ago ceased to amaze them. Of course, the emergency room doctor would have to know.

"How you doing this morning, Mr. Pennell?"

"Okay, I guess." Clay mumbled, a night of interruptions depriving him of a restful sleep.

"I'm Dr. Zebrow. I saw you last night. You have quite a gash in your leg."

Clay raised himself to look at the doctor. "I'm sorry. It was stupid. Risking everything."

"According to your records, you've had quite a time with that leg. We've stopped the bleeding but not the infection. Infections like the kind that has settled in your leg can put up a formidable battle against an attempt to control them. Your records indicate, for you, the fight has lasted several months. I'm sure you don't have to be reminded of that."

"No, I guess not." Clay answered with emphasis.

Dr. Zebrow checked the file he held in his hand. "Whatever the reason, your body contained a heavy dose of marijuana. Though it has its medical uses, I don't think you had that in mind last night. If you did, you definitely over did it. You do know that smoking pot is illegal?"

Clay smiled. "I know. I was stupid."

"Of course, I don't intend to report you, privacy rules. I would advise, though, that you exercise great care with that stuff."

"For sure, I will. My dad gave me the same advice. At my age, I should know better. No excuses but it's been a bad few months." Clay announced.

The emergency room staff released Clay the next day. Dr. Zebrow echoed the advice of Dr. Lawson, "Stay off the leg as much as possible."

Clay sat in his living room facing his parents, his leg elevated. They had checked him out of the hospital and brought him home.

"Clay, what's with the marijuana?" The muscles in his mother's face tightened as she touched on this subject.

"Mom, look. I made a mistake. These last few months have given me pain in more ways than just in my leg. You know that. A while ago, an old college friend thought it would help with the pain and the frustration. It did. I hadn't touched it for weeks until last night. As I said, it helped. I just didn't want to get involved."

"I certainly hope you've learned something from last night." Harold exercised his role as father.

"I know." Clay looked down at his elevated leg then up at his parents. "Do me a favor. Please don't say anything about this to Vicky. She has suffered enough because of me. I don't want this to add to it."

His parents looked at each other then nodded their acceptance of his request.

"Won't she know something happened when she sees the condition of your leg?" Agnes asked.

"I can deal with that part. It's the marijuana part."

When his parents left, Clay rested his head back on the sofa chair. He thought about the last twenty-four hours. Instead of him on a bike, this time he envisioned his wife as she biked next to him all those years ago on the ride which brought them together.

CHAPTER 12

Brian Tarlton smiled, his eyes following Vicky's every step as she walked out of the small employee lounge. A company the size of Wagner Electronics needed no separate areas for employees and executives to take a break or to eat lunch. The single lounge encouraged employee contact away from the pressure of customers. It also gave the company executives the chance to relate more closely with other employees.

Vicky Pennell attracted the attention of more than just Brian Tarlton. Most eyes followed her wherever she went. However, not all those eyes looked at her with the desire that burned first in Brian's throat then spread downward to his stomach. From the day she entered the door of Wagner Electronics, Brian saw her as a charming challenge.

Vicky was not the first object of Brian's desire. His career as a small company executive included numerous instances of thwarted relationships with attractive fellow employees. At fifty-nine years old, Brian's career had taken him from meager jobs selling door to door to executive positions with several companies. His tenure at each one depended on his performance, his career ambitions, and his relationship with other employees, particularly other female employees. Throughout that career, he exercised restraint in most relationships, realizing the danger of incurring the reputation as a lecherous old man.

Brian possessed a remarkable talent for selling just about anything including himself. It wasn't the product that sold. It was Brian's marvelous talent to engage prospective buyers. He could quickly convince customers of a need that they didn't even know they had. Of all the products he sold during his career, selling himself stood out as the most important. To young attractive colleagues, he often exploited that personal salesmanship.

Prior to his assuming the position of vice president of sales at Wagner Electronics, Brian narrowly escaped criminal prosecution when a young woman with whom he worked at his former company accused him of sexual harassment. Attempts to establish consent proved successful. Rather than pursue the case in court, the young woman withdrew her accusation. Surprisingly, a significant raise in pay followed her conciliatory action. Brian enjoyed significant influence in that company's personnel policies.

Though Brian avoided prosecution for the alleged sexual harassment, he did not escape the ire of his wife of over thirty years. She had tolerated her husband's affinity with young women long enough. This time his pleas for forgiveness failed to give him a reprieve. His wife filed for divorce, the first step in a lengthy battle over property rights. The prolonged, contentious divorce had another adverse effect on Brian's career. His influence in the company failed to preserve his job. In weeks after the settlement of the sexual harassment case, Brian was released from his position in the company. His resume recorded the release due to a desire for further career opportunities.

Brian's talent in sales, his personality and his connections in the corporate world all played a role in his acquisition of a position with Wagner Electronics. Hired as the vice president of sales, he soon distinguished himself as a valuable asset to the company, inspiring his sales staff to increase sales over fifteen percent. Combined with this success, Brian struggled with his major weakness, a propensity for young, attractive women. Aware of what inappropriate behavior with female employees can do to a career, Brian disciplined himself, careful to restrict his fantasies to only that. His first sight of Vicky Pennell intensified that struggle.

When Brian arrived at Wagner Electronics, Vicky already was a veteran of five years. She first met him at an executive committee meeting where Madison Wagner introduced him to the other executives. At that time, Madison served as the company president, his father the CEO. Brian took the job formerly held by Madison.

In a few months, Madison's father retired, making room for Madison to assume the position of CEO. Brian's success with the company rewarded him with the position of president, the highest corporate position of his career. Since that time, Vicky, herself, had viewed the company president as a goal worth striving for.

Vicky tipped back her seat, rested her head and closed her eyes. Only with reluctance had she decided to make the trip to Orlando. Clay did need someone to look after him. However, she finally agreed with him that his parents could assume that responsibility. They lived only minutes away. Besides, Clay insisted he was no invalid. He just had to stay off his leg "as much as possible," an admonition he heard too often.

Traveling with three men made Vicky slightly self-conscious. She dealt with seductive stares since even before high school. Nonetheless, this trip placed her in near constant contact with her male colleagues. In the years since joining Wagner Electronics, she rarely confronted any thing like sexual harassment. Frequently, she could feel the stares of others as she made her way around the office or around the sales floor. Those experiences only added to her history of adapting to the frequency with which she attracted the attention of others. In reality, she didn't mind. It all came with just who she was.

About three years ago, at an annual, company Christmas party, Brian Tarlton made suggestive comments to her. She quietly ignored them. Beyond that, she faced no violations of propriety.

Of course, on the flight to Orlando, it was her misfortune to be seated right next to Brian Tarlton.

Though they exchanged a few idle comments after boarding the plane, both elected to rest during the over three hour flight from the Twin Cities to Orlando. Vicky dozed off for a short time, falling victim to the tedium of flying. About half way through the flight, Brian asked, "You awake?"

Vicky turned her head to see Brian looking at her. "Yes, just resting my eyes."

"How's your husband doing?"

Vicky smiled, hearing that question again. "He's doing okay."

"It's his leg, isn't it?" Brian intended to take advantage of sitting next to the prettiest woman in the company. He needed to prolong the conversation.

"Yes, a bike accident." Vicky believed that by now everyone in her office knew about Clay's accident. She didn't know what else to say.

"Was the leg broken?"

"Yes, but now infection has set it." Vicky explained, her comments directed more to the seat in front of her than to Brian seated next to her.

"I'm sorry to hear that." Brian shifted in his seat. "Is he able to work?"

"Kind of part time." Vicky leaned back on the head rest hinting at the end to the conversation.

Brian persisted. "What do they do about infections like that?"

"A heavy dose of antibiotics is about the only thing."

"Has it worked?"

"No, not yet. He returns to the Mayo Clinic soon to find out any progress."

A flight attendant came by to ask if they wanted a beverage. Brian ordered a coffee; Vicky ordered nothing.

Gently spinning his coffee cup on the pull down tray, Brian asked, "What are your plans for the future?"

Vicky turned to face him, a troubled look crossed her face. "What do you mean?"

"Do you have any special career plans? Do you intend to stay with Wagner?"

Vicky frowned, wondering what prompted his question. "Right now, I have no intention of leaving. Why do you ask?"

Brian shifted in his seat to face Vicky. "I see you as a woman with goals. Until you reach the top, you're not satisfied."

Had her aspiration to greater things been that obvious? Vicky said nothing for a moment, puzzled by Brian's assessment. "I guess I find enough challenge in the position I have. I haven't really thought much beyond that."

"I just thought I would ask. I'll be retiring in a year or so. That will leave the president's chair empty." Brian studied Vicky's reaction to his revelation.

With renewed interest, Vicky asked, "When did this come up?"

"Oh, I don't know exactly. Probably in the last few months. I guess I've worked long enough, time to take a rest and do some of those things I've put off all these years."

"Have you discussed this with Madison?" Vicky inquired.

Brian nodded his head. "More than once."

The captain's announcement that they had begun their descent into Orlando ended the conversation, leaving the thought of president of the company lingering in Vicky's mind.

Upon landing, a tram whisked Vicky and her three traveling companions to baggage claim. From the airport, a thirty minute taxi ride took them to the Orlando Convention Center complex which included the Hilton Hotel where they would spend the next four nights. Vicky couldn't seem to get away from Brian Tarlton, who, as on the flight, found his way next to her in the taxi.

Each, of course, had separate rooms, Madison and Tom Morgan, vice president of sales on the fifth floor, Brian Tarlton and Vicky on the sixth. A barely audible sigh disclosed Vicky's displeasure upon learning of the floor arrangement. She briefly considered the next three days and what she would have to do to escape Brian's attention. With confidence, she knew she could handle his ingratiating behavior. She didn't wish to have to confront it so often.

Madison proposed they meet in the lobby after getting settled. He would treat them to a late lunch. Vicky chose to stay in her room to rest in preparation for the busy days ahead. Besides, she worried about Clay at home by himself, not really by himself, but no one was there full time. He probably needed more full time attention. She felt guilty having left him for the trip. Still, she was here now, and she would make the most of it.

At 8:00 the next morning, Vicky and the three other executives stood in mild wonder as they looked out over the vast interior of the Orlando Convention Center.

"My God, this place must cover several acres under one roof," Tom Morgan exclaimed as he stepped up to the security personnel checking convention credentials.

"It looks like every electronics firm in the world is here." Brian added his description of what they observed.

"Yeah, next to Las Vegas, this is supposed to be one of the biggest trade shows in the country," Madison added.

Standing in awe of the vast expanse of the vendor displays, Madison and his staff moved to one of the numerous lounge areas set up around the exhibit hall. Madison suggested they sit down to plan their strategy to ensure the greatest coverage of the dozens of displays. They gathered around Madison who took out the convention program of events and vendor lay out. "Why don't we each select those areas we wish to visit? That way we won't duplicate the effort."

A half hour later, each had made a schedule that, at least, partially satisfied Madison's plan. Vicky made certain that her schedule did not coincide in any way with Brian's.

CHAPTER 13

Three days of discussions with vendors, of struggling with massive crowds, of long walks between the convention center and the hotel exhausted Vicky. On this, the last night of the stay in Orlando for Wagner Electronic's executives, she stretched out on her room's generous sofa chair, resting her feet up on a small desk chair. She paged through the accumulated literature and brochures piled on her lap. Would she ever assimilate all of it? Over time she would review it selectively. Most of that she could do at home. She placed the stack of material on the small table next to her sofa chair, reached for her cell phone, and punched in Clay's number. To her relief, nothing had changed at home, Clay purposely avoiding any mention of his bike venture in the driveway.

Vicky graciously declined Madison's invitation to have dinner with him, Brian and Tom. She preferred spending the evening quietly in her room. With her light, room service dinner completed, she sat back to watch TV until she went to bed in preparation for the group's early morning flight home.

With local news just starting, a soft knock on her door startled her. For an instant, she debated whether to open the door. She considered what could threaten her safety in a Hilton Hotel? Besides, security personnel stood guard at the lobby entrance to the elevators. Slowly, she eased herself out of her chair, pushed aside the room service cart and tray, and walked to the door. She looked in the peephole. Outside her door with arms imperiously folded across his chest stood Brian Tarlton.

To herself Vicky asked, "What could he want now?"

For a fleeting moment, she considered ignoring him. If she didn't answer the door, perhaps he would assume she had already gone to bed inducing him to leave. But that would amount to her admitting a minor defeat with this guy. She could handle Brian Tarlton if it came to that.

Vicky slid off the chain lock, opening the door only a few inches.

Brain broke into a huge smile, "How about some company?" he asked, placing his hand on the door, prepared to push it open.

Vicky hesitated before responding. She couldn't believe his audacity. "I'm really tired. We do have an early flight tomorrow morning. Can it wait?"

Brian continued his move through the door, backing Vicky deeper into the room. "Can we talk a bit?"

Vicky turned to walk back to the desk positioned near the room's window, reluctant to make Brian sense any welcome.

"About what? What do you want to talk about that can't wait?" Vicky's voice strained with irritation.

Brian boldly walked to the large entertainment center, leaned against it, and folded his arms across his chest in a gesture of command. "On the plane flying here, I mentioned my intention to retire in a year or two. I think you have an interest in my position at Wagner Electronics. I've admired your ambition and competence, among other things," his lips spread into a smirk. "I wanted to tell you I think I could help you get a promotion to president of the company."

Vicky reached for the small desk chair, placing it between her and Brian. "Thank you for your kind words. I haven't really thought much about advancement in the company. I've had other things on my mind." She stood firm and confident, masking nascent apprehension.

Brian persisted, stepping away from the entertainment center. He approached Vicky still standing behind the chair. "I have an influence with Madison. It could make a difference in his decision about my replacement. All I ask is a small favor." The smirk reappeared.

Vicky stiffened; fear flashed through her body. "What kind of favor?"

Brian rushed toward Vicky, pushing the small chair aside. He reached with both arms to grab her by the shoulders. Before she could respond, he pulled her toward him smothering her lips with his, hands groping under her top.

Vicky pushed back against his chest with a violence born of outrage. She jerked her head away from the revulsion of his mouth and lips. Brian yanked her body closer. She managed to free her right arm. She reached back to deliver a solid slap to his face. He jumped back with a jolt, a trickle of blood seeping from his mouth.

"You fucking bitch!" he bellowed. "I know your type! You don't fool me, throwing those tits of yours around the office every day!"

"Get out! Go right now before I call security!" Vicky demanded, controlling the outrage that surged through her body. "I don't need yours. I don't need anybody's influence. Now, leave before you get into serious trouble."

Wiping the blood from his lip, Brian backed two steps, then turned and rushed for the door. Vicky stood rigid, watching him leave. She reached for the sofa chair. Carefully, she sat down, trying to control the trembling that invaded her body.

She slowly relaxed. She laid her head back on the sofa chair. She breathed deeply. The trembling in her body subsided. Vicky leaned forward in the chair burying her face in her hands. Tears trickled through her fingers. Years of dealing with eyes following her every move could never prepare her for the humiliation of an assault on her body, on her dignity. Gaining control over her emotions, she considered briefly how much her behavior, perhaps, encouraged aggression like that displayed by Brian. Quickly, she dismissed that thought as certainly no justification for what he attempted to do.

Vicky relaxed in the sofa chair, reached for a tissue to dab her eyes, then leaned back, resting her head on the softness of the chair. She shook her head in an attempt to erase the memory of Brian's attempted assault. A faint smile spread her lips. She would delight in seeing Brian retire. Perhaps, she could hasten that retirement by a brief discussion with Madison. She would welcome the chance to assume the title of president of Wagner Electronics.

CHAPTER 14

Travelers carrying brief cases or pulling small carryon bags on wheels spilled from the escalator descending from the arrival and departure gates to baggage claim. A relatively quiet time for a Friday afternoon at the Minneapolis/St. Paul International Airport, business travelers were ending their week with a return home.

Clay stood with his parents at the bottom of the escalator waiting for sight of Vicky, whose flight from Orlando landed minutes before. His leg discouraged Clay from driving. His parents eagerly joined him in greeting his wife on her return from the five day trip to Orlando.

"You will explain to her what happened the other night." Clay's dad nudged his son reminding him that he needed to tell Vicky what happened on the driveway.

"I know, Dad. I'll tell her when the time's right." Clay moved unsteadily from one leg to the other, favoring his right leg.

"She needs to know what damage was done that night."

"Yes, I know she does." Clay gritted his teeth in irritation.

"What about the pot?" His mother joined in.

"What about it?" Clay answered sarcastically.

"Well, you should explain that too."

"Mom, I know what I have to do. I'm not a kid any more."

Clay's dad coughed. "You're not?" He said with a grin.

"Okay, It was stupid. How many times do I have to say it?" Clay stepped back to sit on the plastic bench stationed in the middle of the baggage claim aisle.

Harold joined Clay on the bench. He placed his hand on Clay's leg. "We only want you to do what's right."

"Don't you think I know what's right?" Clay snapped.

"Of course, we do. Don't take offense." Harold patted his son on the knee.

"Oh, I'm sorry. Look, I appreciate everything you've done including picking up Vicky with me. I know how serious this leg of mine is. It's serious for Vicky, too."

"Hey, guys, I see her. She's at the top of the escalator." Agnes announced.

Clay and his dad got up from the bench to stand beside Clay's mom watching Vicky descend to baggage claim. Approaching the bottom of the escalator ride, Vicky spotted her husband and in-laws. Her face broke into a huge, sparkling smile. She waved vigorously. As she stepped off the escalator, she rushed through the security doors into Clay's waiting arms.

"I've missed you, sweetheart." Clay whispered into her ear.

"I've missed you, too. How's the leg?" Vicky released her hold on her husband as if suddenly aware of his vulnerable, right leg.

"About the same," Clay affirmed.

Vicky turned to her mother and father-in-law to greet them and to thank them for helping Clay and for picking her up. The four made their way to the carrousel where Harold rescued Vicky's one bag. They quickly located the proper exit that would take them to the parking ramp and Harold and Agnes' car waiting to take them home.

During the forty minute ride to their suburban home, Vicky answered questions about her flight and about the trade show. She emphasized the vastness of the Orlando Convention Center as well as the hundreds of vendors there to display their merchandise. She confessed to being a bit overwhelmed by the show but also acknowledged the value in her exposure to products that reflected advanced technology. Only for an instant did the last night at the hotel flash through her mind. An incident that would remain imprinted in her mind for a long time, she felt no need to discuss it at this time with Clay and certainly not with his parents. Someday she would share it with Clay. Right now, the outrage hovered too close to the surface. Their conversation did shorten the ride home where Vicky again would reclaim its familiar comforts.

Preparing for bed, Vicky and Clay discussed in greater detail her experience in Orlando. He, playfully, inquired about traveling with three men.

"Really, I hardly saw them except on the plane." Vicky turned from her closet where she hung up clothes she unpacked.

"How did that happen?" Clay asked.

Vicky explained how the four of them divided up the special sessions and exhibits. She pulled from her carryon the stack of material she collected. "This is how it worked for me." She laughed, plunking the stack on the bed. "Did you get to work much?"

"No." Clay uttered.

"Oh, the leg worse?" Concern etched on Vicky's face.

Clay sat down on the edge of the bed, unbuttoned his belt, and carefully slipped out of his trousers. Doing so exposed the large bandage on his leg, slightly stained with drainage from the damaged incision. Clay placed his hands under his right thigh lifting his leg onto the bed. Pointing to the bandage, he said, "This is the reason."

Shock registered in Vicky's eyes as she stared at the messy bandage. "What on earth happened?" she breathed in a near whisper.

Taking a deep breath, Clay said, "It's a long, sad, stupid story."

Vicky's eyes widened with alarm. "What happened?"

Clay invited his wife to sit down next to him on the bed. Grasping her hand in his, he told her about the nightmare that landed him in the hospital. He included his foray into pot.

When he finished, Vicky sat staring at her husband, first his bandaged leg then his face. "Sweetheart, I wish you would have told me more about your pain. I'm so sorry. I didn't realize the agony you most have suffered. Too much of my time goes to my job. I know that now."

Clay touched his wife's cheek. "Vicky, it has nothing to do with what you did or didn't do. It has nothing to do with your job. It's just . . ." Clay paused searching for the right words. "It's just I fell for an easy fix, pardon the pun."

"I should have been here, not traipsing around a convention center."

"Honey, don't say that. What you did was right. I was just stupid. I'm going to have to live with it. Besides, I learned a valuable lesson. Pot can give a glorious high, but it does nothing about the fall to the bottom."

Vicky reached for her husband, bracing his head between her hands. "I love you, Clay." Her words nearly smothered as her lips covered his. They gently settled back on their bed, Clay's leg even now a concern. With clothes scattered across the bed, they allowed their passion to take them to their private Shangri-La.

CHAPTER 15

Clay's revelation, the encounter with Brian, her ambivalence about discussing the Brian incident with Madison, the impending appointment at the Mayo Clinic, all conspired to keep Vicky awake. Reluctant to disturb Clay, whose rhythmic breathing hinted at his sleep, she carefully pushed back the blanket and quietly slid out of bed to walk to the living room.

A late autumn, harvest moon partially illuminated the street as Vicky stood before the living room window gazing into the darkness. A collection of thoughts collided in her mind, ignited by Brian Tarlton's brash intrusion into her life. Like a scab torn away from the sore, that nightmare renewed old pain.

Only when most deeply troubled would Vicky remember the hours she spent at home, in the privacy of her room, suffering bouts of despair over a personal failure, a failure only in her mind. When those desperate moments occurred, she remembered how oblivious her parents were to her secret life. She avoided blaming them for her pain; however, she refused to exonerate them completely.

The years since had given Vicky a more realistic self-concept. She learned to accept her successes more readily rather than always demanding more of herself. Her performance at Wagner Electronics, overall, offered her gratification. She was doing all that her talent would allow. Nonetheless, that did not preclude her ambition for the future.

Mixed up with these thoughts were fears about Clay's future. Vicky moved away from the window to sit on the sofa, stretching her legs out onto the carpet. What would amputation mean to him, to them? Like Vicky, Clay, too, possessed a determination for success that drove him to seek, perhaps, beyond himself. How would amputation blend with that characteristic?

Brian's face, distorted by anger, pushed its way back into Vicky's mind. The encounter produced a profound effect on her, more overwhelming than, perhaps, justified. The thought of surrender Vicky found deplorable, a blatant violation of what she valued most, her integrity as a woman. For her, surrender under any circumstances was a form of failure. Nothing stood as more anathema to her sense of value than failure. The encounter with Brian removed another scab from the memory of a moment of weakness when Vicky did surrender.

Vicky swung her legs up onto the sofa, leaning back on the sofa arm. She followed as her memory took her back several years. She was a freshman at the University of Wisconsin, Stout located in Menominee, Wisconsin. Adjustment to life in college proved difficult for Vicky. Throughout high school, she competed with a much smaller world of academic and athletic talent. In college, she discovered competition from students who shared her commitment to success, to winning.

Vicky peered into the darkness of her living room. A faint smile formed on her face. Visions of guys both in high school and college whose eyes followed her as she walked by appeared in her mind. That had happened to her since middle school. In the intervening years, she developed a resistance to their, often, seductive stares.

In the spring of her freshman year, a long, arduous period of adjustment ending, Vicky agreed to join an upper class man for a beer in one of the popular student pubs adjacent to the college campus. A young Chicago native of obvious Italian descent, Salvador Costa persisted, during the year, in talking with Vicky, of seeking a date, and of making no excuses for his attention to her.

Rarely, did Vicky have a beer. She really didn't even like it. However, visiting a bar constituted a part of adapting to college life, at least college life in small town Wisconsin. Anticipating the ending of an occasionally troubling year, Vicky submitted to Salvador's entreaties.

They sat across from each other in a booth, one of many lining the wall of the small bar, reviewing the highlights of the year. Six tables occupied the center of the room separating them from the bar where several, presumably students, sat upon the high bar stools.

"Well, what do you think of your first year at Stout?" Salvador took a long drink of his beer.

Vicky played with her glass of beer, moving it around on the flimsy coaster. "Okay, now that it's almost over."

"Has it been that tough?"

Vicky tried to avoid his eyes which never left her face. "At times, yes. It's not like the high school I attended last year."

"It shouldn't be, right?" Salvador affirmed.

The sudden unexpected seriousness of the response gave Vicky pause. "I understand that and agree with you. It wasn't like my high school." She answered mildly insulted by his intimation that she didn't distinguish between high school and college.

"And where is that high school?" Salvador kept the conversation going.

"A little community north of here that you've never heard of." Vicky settled back on her side of the booth, folding her arms across her chest, a move which diverted Salvador's attention from her face to her breasts.

He ordered another beer. She declined. The conversation dragged on, gradually marked by long pauses. Finally, Salvador suggested they go for a walk around the campus. The early spring evening offered a hint of the romantic, a clear sky, a gentle breeze and a bewitching, tea cup moon.

Vicky hesitated before answering. She felt confident in her ability to take care of herself. She did for several years already. She agreed. They left the bar heading for the path that encircled the campus. They walked side by side absorbing the freshness of the evening.

Half way around the campus path, they came upon a bench placed for the less energetic who may wish to rest. They sat down. Salvador nudged closer to Vicky.

"A great night, don't you think?" He asked, turning to face Vicky.

She sat unmoving, a sparkle visible in her eyes even in the semi darkness of the path. Salvador inched closer, placing his arm around Vicky's shoulder. She made no move in response to his inching closer, but she also did not reject his encroachment. At this time, the circumstances caught Vicky in their grip. In the past, she avoided potential compromising situations she now faced; she would never have allowed herself to come this close to surrender. The evening, the end of a trying year, and the natural attraction to a handsome male combined to render Vicky vulnerable to the forces of nature.

Suddenly, Salvador grabbed Vicky. He pulled her toward him, his mouth frantically searching for hers. Still, she offered no resistance. She also offered no submission. His hand found Vicky's breast. She stiffened. He ignored it. He roughly pushed her down on the bench, forcing her legs apart. He positioned himself on top of her, pressing his hard manhood against her virgin crotch. His hands pursued her body, first her breasts, then her stomach, finally her crotch. His fingers ventured where no other person's had. Vicky's body tingled with sensations she never before experienced. Thoughts of resistance vanished in the rush of released hormones, locked all these years in Vicky's dread of surrender.

Salvador fumbled with the zipper of her jeans. He unbuckled his belt, obviously maneuvers he experienced before. His trousers he kicked off. His hand slid around her back. He pulled down her panties as she arched her back in response to sexual desire long suppressed, all sense of integrity and chastity obscured by flowing passion.

Vicky sat up with a start, emerging from a shallow sleep, her neck stiff from resting on the sofa arm. She remembered vividly the crushing realization of having lost her virginity to a man she hardly knew on a bench on the campus of the University of Wisconsin, Stout.

She had violated one of her fundamental principles, never surrender. She had surrendered to the power of passion. In her mind, she had failed. Falling victim to Salvador constituted surrender. For weeks, following that dramatic event, she struggled to cope with this, her greatest failure.

Now, as she reflected on Brian Tarlton's futile attempt to lure her into surrender, she felt a renewed sense of revulsion. After the moment of failure at Stout, Vicky vowed that it would never happen again. Only out of love would she ever again submit to a man.

Vicky stretched, rubbed her eyes, then quietly walked back to the bedroom. She slipped under the covers to rest next to the man she loved.

CHAPTER 16

Vicky moved quickly from beneath the covers. Clay slept soundly, his leg protruding from under the covers. Events of the last two days combined to deprive Vicky of a restful night. She entered the bath room, last night's return to the past vivid in her memory.

She stood in the shower much longer than usual, delighting in the feeling of home. She faced a busy day of cleaning and reorienting to her weekend routine. An absence of only five days made a remarkable difference to her and her duties around the house. She never stopped to think about how only five days could make her house so in need of cleaning.

Standing before the large bathroom mirror over the double sinks, she looked tired; she was tired. Small puffs under her eyes told the story of a sleepless night. Despite that, Vicki took great pride in how she looked even without the magic touch of makeup.

"Good morning sweetheart." Clay peeked around the partially open bathroom door. "You're up early." He braced himself against the door frame, reaching down to examine his bandaged right leg.

Vicky turned to look at his leg. "Does it drain a lot?"

"Yes, it does." Clay started to remove the bandage.

"Has it gotten worse?" Vicky asked.

"Yeah, it has since my dumb ass rumble in the flower bed." Clay limped to the vanity where he stored the bandage supplies.

"Do you need help with that?" Vicky reached for a roll of gauze.

"No, I can manage. I've had plenty of practice."

Vicky watched as Clay meticulously removed the old bandage and applied a new one, a task he'd performed at least twice a day since the driveway incident. He would have to forgo a shower for now until the wound on his leg healed much more than it had.

Vicky watched the slow process of changing the dressing on his leg. "Do you really have to work today?" she asked.

Clay glanced up as his wife. "I don't have to. I just want to. I can't stand sitting around doing nothing." Clay confessed.

"Remember what the doctor said about staying off the leg." Though serious about that admonition, Vicky smiled, knowing that her husband would not likely abuse his leg again.

"Don't worry. Ross lets me do what I can. Sitting by the checkout counter won't hurt me."

Through the day Vicky swept and cleaned much longer than the house required. Frequently, she paused to consider her dilemma: telling Madison about the encounter with Brian and risking dissension in the office or saying nothing and allowing Brian to escape responsibility for unacceptable behavior. She would have to decide what to do. More important, however, was the impending appointment at the Mayo Clinic, an appointment that took on much greater importance since the accident in the driveway during her absence.

Clay's 11:00 a.m. appointment required them to leave for Rochester about 9:00 a.m., allowing for the one and one half hour drive. They checked in to the clinic at 10:45 a.m. A nurse escorted them to a small examination room similar to the one they sat in over a month ago. The nurse took Clay's blood pressure, asked a series of questions about allergies and pain, the same questions he answered during the last appointment, then drew blood for testing. She left the room stating that Dr. Lawson would see them shortly.

Seated in the small chairs in the examination room, Vicky squeezed Clay's hand. "You all right?"

Clay reached for her hand. "Yeah, don't I look all right?" He moved his right leg to a more comfortable position.

"How does the leg feel now?"

"About the same. Not much has changed in several weeks."

Silence spread through the room. The passage of fifteen minutes made them restless. They both were eager to hear the doctor's assessment of the leg, particularly in view of the damage done in the flower garden. The rustling of paper announced the arrival of Dr. Lawson, who tapped on the door before entering.

"Good morning." Dr. Lawson stepped into the room extending his hand to both Vicky and Clay.

"Good morning." They replied in unison.

Sitting in the chair located in front of the small corner desk, Dr. Lawson opened the folder he carried. "How have you been?"

Clay looked over at the doctor, wondering if he knew about the driveway episode. "About the same, I guess."

"'The same' doesn't sound like we've made much progress." Dr. Lawson studied the report. Clay and Vicky sat quietly. He looked up at Clay, then at Vicky. "Do you want to tell me about your ride in the driveway?"

Clay shifted his position again. He looked down at the floor. "It's probably all there. It was stupid but unless I have to, I'd rather forget about it."

Dr. Lawson turned to face Clay and Vicky. "I don't think it's something we can forget about. It certainly was stupid, but that's irrelevant now. We have to deal with an even more aggressive infection. Tearing open the incision, the way it looks, did serious damage to the lower leg and foot. Blood tests reveal no decrease in the infection. We're going to need to examine that leg more thoroughly to find out what's going on."

Without comment, Vicky and Clay sat looking at the doctor.

"We're going to x-ray the leg and foot first. Then we'll have to decide our next move. In a couple minutes, the nurse will take you to x-ray. After that we'll talk more."

In less than half an hour, Clay sat with Vicky back in the examination room. Dr. Lawson placed the x rays in the lighted viewing panel attached to the wall. He explained. "Notice this area just below the ankle. It's starting to decay. Tissue there is basically dying."

Vicky gasped. "What has caused that?"

Clay concentrated on the x ray.

"Lack of nourishment." Dr. Lawson answered tersely. "The prolonged infection has impeded blood flow to the foot. Unchecked, parts of the foot would die. The driveway thing didn't help. But rest assured that isn't the cause of what's happening to your lower leg."

Clay stared at the x-ray then at his right foot. A strange feeling stirred in his chest, moving to his stomach. "What do I do now?" his harsh voice reflecting the strain of uncertainty.

"Well, we have a couple choices. We can increase the antibiotics in a further attempt to control the infection. So far that hasn't worked very well."

Vicky and Clay waited in anticipation for Dr. Lawson's explanation of the other alternative, one which they thought they already knew.

"The other alternative is amputation of the foot."

Despite the expectation of hearing that alternative, Vicky gasped, placing her hand over her mouth to shield the sound. Clay closed his eyes, breathed deeply, and shook his head. How could he live without a foot? His whole life he depended on his legs, both of them, to give him exercise, to give him an occasional escape from reality. He was not a sedentary person. This last year reinforced that.

Clay leaned forward, bracing his arms against his knees. Staring at the floor, he asked, "That's it? The only options?"

"I'm afraid so, given the potential danger to the rest of your leg as well as to major organs." Dr. Lawson paused. "Look, let's give a strong dose of antibiotics one more try along with serious rest. Wait one more month to see what has happened. Then we can make a decision."

Vicky and Clay turned to face each other. Vicky took Clay's hands in hers. Tears formed in the corners of her eyes. She looked into his eyes, hers blurred by tears. "We'll make it." She affirmed. "I love you." She leaned forward resting her head on Clay's shoulder.

CHAPTER 17

Since the accident on County Road #19, while Clay suffered from a formidable infection in a broken leg, Miles Hunter pursued his pointless life performing petty tasks at his father's law office. Little had changed in his life. Only rarely did he reflect on the incident that sent a worthless cyclist into the brush. When he did, the thought gave him some satisfaction. His disdain for cyclists persisted, even increased. He simply could not tolerate sharing the road with sissies on bicycles.

Late afternoon in the law office, Miles sat at his desk in a corner of the large room serving his father and his two partners. A long day was ending and Miles had nothing to do but attempt to throw paper wads into a waste basket ten feet away.

"Miles, can't you find something better to do?" His father stood before his son.

"Not right now." Miles refused to look his father in the face. He balled up another wad of paper and hurled it at the waste basket. "This office is a drag." He grumbled.

For years, Chester Hunter, Miles' father, had tried to encourage his youngest son to apply himself in a constructive way. His efforts only produced more belligerence and hostility. Over the years, Miles developed the reputation as a bully. As early as grade school, he faced disciplinary action after taking advantage of younger kids.

Chester stood facing his son. "Miles, look at me." Miles turned his head with a sneer. "If you don't like it here, you are free to go any time." Chester's voice carried throughout the office.

Miles stood up before his father, defiance distorting his face. "What the hell do you want me to do?" He growled.

Chester breathed heavily. "I want you to do only what I've wanted for years. Grow up and show some ambition."

Miles kicked the chair where earlier he sat. "Why don't you get off my back? I do what I have to do around here. If you don't like it, fire me!"

Miles turned and stomped out of the office. His dad watched him go, shaking his head in frustration and sadness. Miles hurried across the small parking lot that served the law office to where his gleaming, white Cadillac Escalade was parked. He climbed in, slammed the door, and roared out of the lot, wheels squealing.

His violent temper rendered him incapable of rational behavior. Anger raced through every fiber of his body. He hated when his dad treated him like a kid, always talking about ambition and making something out of himself. What in hell did he expect, some dammed Einstein? He didn't need to hear that shit every other day. At thirty-one years old, he could do with his life what he pleased. Right now, the only thing that pleased him was what he did so well—drive around in his precious pickup.

As he drove, his anger subsided. He had no particular destination. He just needed the joy and relaxation driving afforded him. The numerous county roads and semi-residential streets carved throughout western Hennepin County gave him space to do all the driving he desired. To add to his pleasure, he stopped to buy a six pack of beer, always an asset as he drove.

Back in his pickup, Miles snapped open a can of beer, placing the rest of the pack on the floor under his leg. That drinking and driving were an illegal combination made little difference to Miles. What he wished to do, he did.

His drive took him around a part of Lake Minnetonka. Approaching an intersection with another county road, Miles noticed a group of four cyclists nearing the intersection on his left. His contempt for cyclists had only intensified over the last few months. One of those bastards, Miles reminded himself, scratched his Escalade.

Miles faced a red light at the intersection. The cyclists raced to make their green light. They didn't. As they neared, they ignored the changing light, racing through the intersection in front of Miles.

Nobody cuts off Miles Hunter, especially not a cyclist. The cyclists' dash through the intersection required Miles to delay the gunning of his pickup to unleash its inordinate power. The delay ignited Miles' temper. He grabbed his beer from the console cup holder, drained the can and turned right in pursuit of the cyclists.

Dressed in matching riding clothes and helmets, the cyclists raced on, oblivious to the white pickup that followed them. Riding single file, they stayed outside the white line allowing enough room for motorists to pass. Still, their audacity at the intersection incensed Miles.

He pulled up next to the four cyclists who still ignored him, intent on watching the road ahead. Miles rolled down the passenger side window. He yelled, "Hey, you pussies. Do you know what a stop light is?"

The front cyclist looked over at Miles. He said nothing nor did any of the other three. That they didn't respond only added to Miles' anger.

Miles maintained a position next to the four. "Why don't you assholes get off the road?" He yelled. "Can't you hear either?"

Finally, the third cyclist looked over at Miles and declared, "Get lost. Mind you own business."

Something inside of Miles erupted. He sped ahead a few feet before pulling off the road directly in front of the cyclists. All four of them stopped behind the pickup. Though not big, muscular men, they did enjoy trim, agile bodies that allowed them to take care of themselves. Besides, the four of them constituted formidable opposition. Anyone in his right mind would avoid the four to one odds. Not Miles. He intended to show these pussies who owned the road.

Miles jumped out of his pickup and hurried around to the back. Confronting the one who had told him to mind his own business, he threatened. "Look, you wimp, driving on the road is my business."

The four cyclists gathered to face Miles, who stood undaunted. The cyclist replied, "Then do your business and leave."

Nobody ever talked back to Miles Hunter and got away with it. He pushed the cyclist back into his bike causing him to fall to the ground, his bike on top of him. One of the other cyclists spoke up. "We don't want any trouble. Why don't you just leave before someone gets hurt?"

Miles glared at the cyclist. "If anyone's gonna get hurt, it's you!" He punched the cyclist in the face.

Instantly, the remaining two pushed Miles, knocking him to the ground. He jumped up quickly with fists clinched, eyes wide and nostrils flared. "Come on, mother fuckers! Let's see what you have!"

The four cyclists accepted Miles' invitation. In just minutes, he lay on the side of the road dazed, blood draining from his nose. The four cyclists rode away.

After a few minutes, Miles staggered back to his pickup, wiping the blood with his arm. He stood for an instant watching the cyclists fade in the distance. With his shirt, he wiped more blood from his nose, determined not to stain the interior of his Escalade. He climbed in behind the wheel, snapped open another beer, vowing that next time he would run over the bastards.

CHAPTER 18

Vicky sat back in her office chair and turned her attention away from the computer. On her desk, the pile of purchase orders expanded. She couldn't concentrate on purchases right now. Her office did give her privacy to concentrate on whatever she chose. For the last few days since the appointment at the Mayo Clinic, she could think of little except Clay's leg.

The appointment concluded with another hour long intravenous treatment of an especially potent antibiotic. During the drive home, Vicky and Clay sat in silence most of the way, each digesting Dr. Lawson's pessimistic prognosis in his own way. Vicky did the driving while Clay stared at the nondescript winter landscape. She attempted to divert attention away from his leg. Clay didn't want to talk about anything.

At home, Clay sat somber and unresponsive. His inability to work dragged the days out endlessly. He tried to read. He tried to watch TV. Nothing could take his mind off his leg. Yet, Vicky sensed that he really failed to grasp the full reality of what could happen to his right leg if the antibiotic treatment did not control the infection.

Vicky tried to discuss that reality. Clay refused to discuss it. Instead, he depended on the antibiotics to solve the problem. That they had failed in more than a year was irrelevant to Clay. Losing part of his body, he found nearly impossible to grasp.

Each day before Vicky departed for work, she helped Clay to prepare for his lonely, aimless day at home. She could do only so much, make his lunch, position the TV, lay out a book or magazine. He would have to decide what he wished to do. Lately, he wished to do virtually nothing. He was not completely immobile. However, he believed he could hasten the healing by strictly adhering to the doctor's advice: "Stay off the leg as much as possible."

Vicky's office was one of four provided for the company leadership team. Though small, it did afford privacy from the distractions of a vibrant company with a growing work force. Vicky needed that privacy, not as vice president for purchasing but for Mrs. Pennell, Clay's wife.

She stood behind her desk to stretch, her body stiffened by too much sitting. She walked around to the front of her desk and reached for the stack of purchase orders. Madison needed to see them. Several contained improper coding which compounded payment. She flipped through the stack, noting the numerous high lighted pages. Glancing up at the back of her computer positioned on the top of her desk, Vicky, decisively placed the orders back on her desk. She walked around to her chair, sat down to study the image on the computer screen.

For much of the morning, she could not resist searching the internet for information related to amputation. The recent conversation with Dr. Lawson of the Mayo Clinic did not guarantee such drastic action; however, he suggested that it could be a definite possibility if the last massive injection of antibiotics failed to subdue the infection. Clay responded differently to the conversation. To Vicky, her husband suffered from denial. He currently refused to consider his life without a right foot. His life depended too much on his engagement in physical activity, the kind offered through cycling. In Vicky's opinion, if Clay refused to accept the reality of a potential loss of his right foot, at least she should learn something about what to expect. So far she had learned a lot, some of it mildly alarming, some of it not.

What she discovered on the computer reinforced what Dr. Lawson said about infection leading to loss of blood flow and tissue decay. That the surgery could require up to a three week hospital stay alarmed her. Few medical conditions, any more, demanded long hospital stays. She learned that the wound following surgery healed quickly, assuming the absence of infection. She wondered how the doctors would gain control over an obstinate infection.

Of particular interest was the information about the psychological impact on the patient. Some suffer more than others over the loss of a part of their body and the fear of disability. Clay, definitely, would have a struggle with that. All the information, the caution, and the awareness of complications would fade in importance if the patient adapted well to a prosthesis. That adaptation could take months. Vicky looked away from the computer. Gently, she rubbed her eyes. She asked herself, Would Clay ever ride his bike again?

A knock at her office door dragged her back to reality. Often, at times too often, other office staff or sales staff came to her door. Still, she welcomed those who came. Generally, her office door stood partially open. Today, the urge to learn something about amputation persuaded her to close the door.

"Come in." She invited as she let the computer fade to screen saver mode.

The door opened. In it stood Brian Tarlton, a smile spreading his lips. "May I come in?" he asked in a voice unusually soft.

Vicky inhaled audibly. Not since their return from Orlando had she confronted Brian one on one. What happened there carried little importance now. Clay's situation dominated her attention. However, Brian's standing in the door way revived visions of the hotel room and his audacity to think that she would surrender to his advances.

"Yes, come in." Vicky replied in monotone. "Leave the door open."

"How's your day?" Brian asked as he entered Vicky's office to stand in front of her desk.

"Like all the others, I guess." The tone of Vicky's voice signaled her reluctance to engage in idle conversation with Brian Tarlton.

"I won't take much of your time." Brian folded his arms across his chest, a gesture he commonly used to establish some degree of superiority. At least that's how Vicky interpreted it. "About the last night in Orlando." Brain paused, dropping his arms to his side, flexing his hands, his eyes bearing down on Vicky. "You would be well advised to keep it to yourself."

Vicky's body tensed as she stood up behind her desk. "What's that supposed to mean?"

The smile vanished from Brian's face, replaced by a twisted sneer. "Just what it says. I don't think you would do yourself any favors by blabbing rumors around the office."

Vicky cleared her throat, incensed by Brian's attempt to control what she did or did not do. With eyes locked on Brian, her voice harsh and strained, she uttered, "Are you threatening me?"

Brian stepped back to push the door closed with his foot. He turned to face Vicky. In a voice scarcely above a whisper, he snarled, "Look, bitch, I know your kind, throwing your body at anyone who looks. You're not going to fuck up my retirement by

crying to Madison. I can make life damned tough. Just try me!"
The muscles in Brian's neck bulged; his cheeks flushed.

Vicky resisted the urge to scream. Instead, she breathed deeply and sat down in her chair. She placed her hands, palm down, on her desk. Looking up at Brian still standing in front of her desk, an intimidating glare narrowing his eyes, she uttered calmly but definitively, "Don't ever come in here to threaten me. You disgraced your position, yourself, and this company. No, I have not told anybody about your transgression. I'm ashamed of what happened."

Brian started to say something. Vicky held up her hand. "Don't say any more. Just remember, if I feel discussing the incident with anyone would accomplish anything, I will not ask for your permission. Now, Mr. Tarlton, please leave my office. Close the door behind you."

Brian turned and stomped out, slamming the door as he left.

Vicky's body trembled with emotion. She gripped the arms of the chair, breathed deeply, and picked up the phone. She punched in Clay's cell phone number. He answered after only two rings.

Vicky smiled. "Hi, sweetheart. How you doing?"

Chapter 19

The valiant effort to control the infection failed. A three hour surgery removed Clay's right foot just above the ankle. Restricted blood flow had added to the decaying tissue in the foot. Though Clay resisted the decision to amputate, Dr. Lawson, Vicky, and finally, Dr. Robinson, the surgeon, convinced him that amputation was his only option if he wished to avoid further complications caused by the infection.

Now, in the Mayo Hospital's room 340, Vicky sat watching her husband still under the influence of the anesthetic. He lay with his right leg suspended by apparatus extending from the ceiling of his room, much like another hospital visit nearly eighteen months ago when a desperate cell phone call from Clay marked the beginning of months of pain, suffering, and frustration. With multiple tubes and wires monitoring Clay's condition, Vicky sat, feeling helpless to do any more than the latest in electronic monitors. She, therefore, waited while Clay emerged from the anesthetic.

According to Dr. Robinson, who performed the surgery, the amputation should eventually return Clay to a life similar to the one he once knew. He advised Vicky of her vital role in helping her husband make the transition from the hospital bed to the walker, the cane and ultimately to whatever form of locomotion he chose, including a bike. He reminded her of the critical psychology that accompanied the loss of a limb, especially for someone like Clay, who enjoyed a life of physical activity.

In his office, before the surgery, Vicky had spent considerable time with Dr. Robinson. "How long before he can get around on his own. Maybe on crutches?" She asked.

Dr. Robinson confronted that question with most of his surgeries. Not exactly the same context but similar in that spouses or relatives always wished to know when their loved one could return to something like a normal life. "Mrs. Pennell, each person responds differently. Your husband's active life style should shorten recovery. Generally, for an operation like his, several weeks or perhaps even a few months will return him to his former life style. You should remember, though, his life may never return completely to its former style."

Vicky anticipated that and discussed it briefly with Clay and with Dr. Lawson. "I understand that, doctor. What might be his limitations?"

Dr. Robinson folded his hands in front of him on his desk. "That will depend on Clay and on you. Patients who devote themselves to their therapy and do what the therapists tell them to do, in situations like Clay's, they ultimately can reenter life with few problems. Adapting to an artificial foot should not require the time and commitment a more drastic amputation would. It really depends on the patient and honestly," he looked directly at Vicky, "on his wife."

In a brief conversation with Dr. Robinson following the surgery, he reported that serious tissue decay in the right foot certainly justified the decision to operate. He did caution Vicky that the next few days would determine the status of the infection. He expressed confidence that the surgery would, at last, eliminate the infection, but only time would confirm it. Dr. Robinson would offer no estimate on the length of the hospital stay. That depended on the wound and the status of the infection.

Clay moved in his bed, restricted by his elevated leg as well as the monitoring devices. Vicky quickly stood up and moved to the side of the bed. She touched Clay's left arm, the only one free of needles and intravenous tubes. Clay opened his eyes.

"Hi, sweetheart." Vicky leaned closer to her husband.

Clay managed a faint smile but said nothing.

"You okay?" Vicky asked, fully aware that after a three hour operation to remove his foot, he probably wasn't okay.

Clay nodded his head to supplement the faint smile.

Vicky tenderly squeezed his arm. As she did, a light tap on the door announced the arrival of Clay's nurse to check on his vital signs and to ensure the free flow of intravenous pain medication. A petite, young woman, Vicky estimated about her own age with "Barb" printed on her name badge, the nurse, without hesitation, inquired about how Clay felt. Vicky smiled to herself, feeling less guilty of asking Clay if he was okay. The nurse checked the elevation of his leg, the monitoring devices and asked about anything he might need at this time.

Clay smiled again. "How about a right foot?" He whispered in a voice weakened by the many hours he had not spoken a word along with the anesthetic and pain medication.

The nurse emitted a short laugh. "I don't think I can come up with that right now, but I'll see what I can do.

Vicky took delight in Clay's sense of humor at this stage in his recovery. To her it represented a good sign that maybe he was ready to accept the reality of his condition.

"Anything you need right now?" Barb asked.

Vicky looked at Clay before answering. "I don't think so."

As she moved toward the door, Barb assured them that she would be back to check on Clay periodically.

In the days that followed the surgery, a parade of nurses and doctors maintained a close watch on Clay. Dr. Robinson stopped in on a daily basis. On one of those visits just days after the surgery he informed Clay that the latest blood tests revealed no infection.

Clay clapped his hands. "God, it's about time." He declared.

Still, Dr. Robinson wanted Clay to remain a bit longer in the hospital to confirm the accuracy of that test.

Of course, the news regarding the infection was a cause for celebration. Clay celebrated with an ice cream sandwich, smuggled in by a cute, young LPN, a gesture that would stick in his mind as he worked to regain something of the life he once knew.

Another cause for celebration followed word from Dr. Robinson that Clay could begin discussions with the people who would fit him with a prosthesis. For the first time in days, maybe months, Clay felt that maybe the nightmare of the last eighteen months would soon end.

CHAPTER 20

Clay gripped the rails of the guided walkway. Perspiration formed on his forehead and upper lip. He shivered as he gazed at the tread in front of him. Previously, he sat in the same large rehabilitation room while limb fitting staff secured exact measurements of his leg and the stump that once ended in a foot. This time, however, he tried out the temporary prosthesis.

Eight weeks had passed since the surgery to remove his decaying foot occurred at Rochester's Mayo Hospital and Clinic. Six weeks had passed, many of them crowded with tedious days and sleepless nights, since Clay hobbled out of the hospital on crutches. Over the weeks he gained proficiency on the crutches, restless as he waited for the stump to heal.

Before Clay even left the hospital, Dr. Robinson, his surgeon, approved discussion with limb fitters. For this discussion, the Mayo Clinic transferred Clay's records to the Methodist Hospital Rehabilitation Center in suburban Minneapolis. This would facilitate the rehabilitation Clay faced over the next several months. For his appointments, he would not have to drive to

Rochester. Clay did, indeed, meet with the limb fitters. However, he believed that too much discussion only delayed the day when he could walk without crutches.

Earlier in the day, the staff of the rehab center fitted Clay with a temporary prosthetic foot. This prosthesis he would use until his stump stabilized sufficiently to tolerate a permanent prosthetic foot. As Clay looked down at the prosthesis, it had the shape of a normal foot. However, it certainly did not feel like a foot as he slowly applied weight on it.

Two rehabilitation staff, Carrie and Stephanie, stood one on each side of Clay.

"You feel all right?" Carrie asked as Clay's body tensed.

Clay took a deep breath. "Yes."

"We are here to help you, but we also want you to take some control of yourself." Stephanie advised.

Clay nodded his head in understanding, eager to get on with it.

"Hold the bars with both hands and step forward with your left foot." Stephanie touched Clay on his upper arm,"

Clay did as directed.

"Now step forward with your right foot."

Clay grimaced as he learned heavily on the guide bars, took his first step wearing the prosthesis, then stopped. He took another step without hesitation, then stopped again. He turned to look first at Carrie then at Stephanie. He exclaimed, "I'm walking!" A huge smile lighted his face, perhaps his happiest moment in the past year and one half.

Not only did that day include his first physical step on the path to recovery, it also included a first psychological step in restoring his confidence in leading, again, a normal life. Prior to the moment when he took that step, he suffered periods of despair, of thoughts of giving up, of a vision of leading a life of an invalid, a cripple who needed help to perform the simplest of everyday tasks.

Sadly, his parents didn't help to dispel these moments of distress. When Vicky went off to work each day following Clay's release from the hospital, his parents would arrive to fulfill his every need. He tried to explain that he wasn't an invalid. He could serve himself on his crutches. He didn't need them to wait on him.

"Son, you have to be careful about the stump." His mother cautioned, not unlike she cautioned him about threats to his safety when he was yet a little boy.

At least he and his family had adjusted to using the term "stump." At first, it sounded so crude and offensive they tried to avoid using it. However, the staff at the Mayo Clinic as well as at the Methodist Hospital rehab center used the term freely. "Call it what it is." They advised.

Clay's parents insisted on fixing his lunch, making sure he had water near by, or adjusting the TV. Soon Clay refrained from objecting to their insistent help. He tolerated it until they were satisfied that he could make it through the day until Vicky came home from work.

After that first momentous day at the rehab center, Clay received detailed instructions about what he should do and what he should avoid doing with his leg. Spending time exercising the right leg and applying pressure on the temporary prosthesis foot was good provided he used caution and his crutches to give him support. He most definitely needed to avoid a fall. Vicky also expressed her opinion on what Clay should or should not do. With Clay's increased confidence and more tolerant mood, these expressions stopped short of contention.

With the acquisition of the temporary prothesis, Clay determined that he would return to work on some part time basis. Ross displayed impressive compassion and understanding during Clay's extended ordeal. He even hired more part time help to compensate for Clay's absence. It was Clay's desire to begin to repay Ross for his kindness.

Clay's parents along with Vicky joined in the opposition to his returning to work. This time Clay's determination combined with his impatience to recapture some of his former life rejected their caution. He was adamant. He would return to work at least for a few hours each week. His only admission, he needed a ride.

With dedication to his goal of returning to his former life, Clay worked hard getting used to the prothesis. Each day he applied a bit more pressure to the artificial foot, still bracing himself on his crutches. He counted the weeks since that first glorious step, now five weeks ago. His stump had adjusted to the prothesis. At least he believed it had. He rarely felt any pain. At times he did feel an itch inside his big toe, the one that joined his amputated foot. That phantom feeling, the rehab staff explained, was normal. His frequent visits to the rehab center confirmed the impressive progress he made.

On a Friday afternoon at the end of the fifth week with his prosthetic foot, Clay relaxed in his living room chair, one that served him well during his lengthy recovery. He had worked a short shift at the bike shop. Ross persuaded him to take off early. The TV carried nothing that interested him. He looked at the screen but saw nothing. His mind took him back almost fourteen years to a small town in south eastern Iowa where he met a young girl named Robin Foster. How rarely he thought of her and of their brief time together. Why he did now, he couldn't explain, nor did he need to.

He leaned back in his chair, closed his eyes, and envisioned the long ago, ride across Iowa. For months he dismissed ever having the chance to do that again. Now, he wasn't so sure. Recent progress in his adaptation to his artificial foot gave him hope that maybe someday. He smiled to himself. Perhaps that hope fueled the thoughts of Robin. Certainly, she would always serve as a connection between him and the ride across Iowa.

Clay shifted in his favorite chair, the status it achieved only in the past several months. His crutches rested close at hand. He needed to use the restroom. Having to rely on the crutches did, at times, dissuade him from moving. Now his bladder insisted. He shifted his weight to the edge of the chair. He reached for his crutches. At the same time, a thought rushed through his head; nerves twitched at the base of his neck. Rather than reaching for the crutches, he gripped the arms of the large sofa chair. Determination stretched the muscles in his neck and face. He pushed himself to a standing position, most of his weight resting on his left leg, his eyes fixed on the wall behind the TV, his mind concentrating on his next move.

He gingerly shifted more weight onto the artificial right foot. He pushed on the foot, testing the feeling. He felt no pain. Next, he stepped forward on the right foot. He did it. He had taken a step unaided on the right foot. He took one more, careful to maintain his balance. He felt nothing but jubilation. All alone in the house, Clay shouted, "I did it! By God I did it!"

CHAPTER 21

That one step two weeks ago led to two steps, then three, then more. The jubilation generated by those steps encouraged Clay to spend even more time on the prosthetic foot. Careful to avoid a rush to walking on the foot, he combined much of his exercise with his crutches, then with just one crutch. He did not work on his walking alone. Twice a week he returned to the Methodist Hospital Rehabilitation Center where the staff guided him and advised him on his accelerating pace to recovery.

Both Carrie and Stephanie generally supervised his visits. They guided his progress from the very first time he tried a prosthetic foot.

"When do I get my real foot?" Clay asked Stephanie as she observed his walking with only one crutch.

"Soon," She answered evasively.

Clay stopped and turned around to face Stephanie, who stood ten feet away. His face assumed a serious expression. "What does that mean? I think I'm ready."

Stephanie dropped her arms to her side. "I guess I think so, too. I can appreciate how you feel. You have done all we asked of you. Your progress shows it, too. But we have to make sure your stump is ready for the permanent prosthesis. Going ahead too fast can only delay that permanent foot." She studied Clay, who listened to her every word.

Clay stepped closer to Stephanie. "What has to happen that hasn't happened?" He asked.

"Why don't we sit down over on that bench?" Stephanie reached for Clay's free arm. Seated next to Clay, Stephanie resumed her explanation. "The conditioning of the stump is critical to fitting the permanent prosthesis. Without that, delicate nerves running through the stump could be damaged which would only cause more delay."

"It's been weeks since I've worn this temporary thing. I don't feel any serious pain when I apply pressure on the foot." Clay explained.

Stephanie tapped Clay's arm. "Yes, you have made great progress. I would say you're going to be ready, as I said before, soon."

Clay shook his head but smiled.

"Really," Stephanie continued. "Your surgeon is the one who decides. I think it's time that you see him."

Clay sat, a pensive mood engulfed him. He rubbed his hands together then nervously wiped them on his trousers. He turned to look directly into Stephanie's eyes. "Tell me. Do you think I'll ever ride my bike again?"

Stephanie returned the serious look, reaching for Clay's hand. She squeezed it gently then smiled. "Mr. Pennell, returning to your bike will be your decision. It will not happen in a few days or even a few weeks, but if you want it to happen, eventually it will. Nothing about a prosthetic foot should prevent your biking." Her smile widened. "You have made marvelous progress these last many weeks. Your determination and your dedication have paid off for you. Now you simply need a bit more patience until that stump of yours has reached the point where the permanent foot will not cause any damage. After that I would suggest you spend time on a stationary bike before even trying a regular bike."

Clay's eyes brightened; he breathed deeply. He now reached for Stephanie's hand. "That's the best news I've heard since I learned about the end to the infection. Recently, I've thought about riding my bike and couldn't imagine why at some point I couldn't try. Your confidence in my recovery has given me the assurance that sometime soon it will happen."

"Remember, though, don't rush things. Take your time and listen to directions from the doctors who will decide about the permanent prosthesis. The stationary bike is a good thing too."

Clay laughed out loud.

Stephanie looked puzzled by the outburst. "What's so funny?" she asked.

"I'm sorry," Clay confessed. "I was just thinking that I work in a bike shop that carries dozens of bikes. Not one of them is a stationary bike."

Stephanie joined Clay in a moment of levity. "I guess you're not in the business of providing fitness equipment, at least not that kind."

"It is kind of interesting to think that a bike that runs on wheels isn't considered fitness equipment in the same way that a stationary bike is." Clay started the slow process of standing up.

"Yes, that is interesting but also very true." Stephanie stood up to assist Clay if he needed it. "You will have to find a fitness center where you can workout on a stationary bike to reacquaint you with what sitting on a bike feels like."

"Yes, I certainly can do that. A fitness center is located only a short distance from the bike shop where I work. I definitely will use its facilities as soon as I get the clearance to do so." Clay stepped closer to Stephanie embracing her in a soft hug. "Thank you for all you have done to make my life real again."

"You are so welcome. It's been rewarding just watching your progress. Please keep in touch."

As he slowly walked toward the exit, carrying the one crutch that served him so well during his recovery, he paused and turned to look back at Stephanie. "Thank you, but I think I got a lot more rewards than you did."

The next week Vicky drove Clay to Rochester where they saw Dr. Robinson, who performed the amputation. He examined the stump, poking and squeezing to detect sore spots or tenderness. He found none. At last, he asked Clay to sit up on the examination table. He replaced the temporary foot. He then asked Clay to step off the table, walk to the door of the examination room and back. Dr. Robinson observed Clay's every move. As Clay turned to walk back toward the examination table, the doctor proclaimed, "Mr. Pennell, I think you are ready for the final step." He laughed. "I don't mean that literally. You are ready for the permanent foot."

Clay raised his arms in victory, opening them to Vicky, who jumped up from her chair to join her husband in celebration.

As Dr. Robinson stood by smiling, Vicky and Clay held each other in a tight embrace. Words proved inadequate to express their joy.

Dr. Robinson requested they sit down for just a minute. "I will forward to the people at Methodist my recommendations. You can arrange with them to be fitted with your permanent foot which, literally, will become a part of you.

Driving back to the Twin Cities, Vicky and Clay spoke excitedly about the future, their mood in sharp contrast to that after previous visits to the Mayo Clinic.

The next week, Vicky and Clay watched as the fitter, a muscular, young man named Roberto, meticulously determined the measurements for Clay's permanent prosthesis. When Roberto completed his measurements, Clay asked, "When will I get the final foot?"

Roberto sat back on his knees. "This will take only a few days. By next week at this time, I can meet you back here for the final fitting."

"We will be here." Clay announced.

They were back the following week with excitement growing as they waited for Roberto's arrival. The final fitting took just minutes. "Please," Roberto stated after completing the fitting. "Would you stand up and walk to that wall over there and back?" He pointed to a wall several yards away.

At this point in his adaptation to an artificial foot, Clay, at times, used a cane for support. He had discarded the crutches some time ago. He stood up, testing the new prosthesis. He glanced at his cane leaning against his chair. He did not reach for it. Instead, he stepped forward, carefully, looked over at Vicky, then at Roberto. Without further hesitation, he walked confidently to the wall and back, only a slight limp a reminder of the artificial foot. He returned to the applause of Roberto and Vicky. Clay only grinned.

"There you go, Mr. Pennell. Please remember, though, that everyday is a learning day with any kind of prosthesis. Be careful for a while. Don't push yourself. Always remember that this is not a natural foot. It does a good job of replacing one but isn't one. In time, though, you will hardly tell the difference as you adapt and as the prosthesis adapts."

Clay stretched his hand out to Roberto. Shaking hands, Clay choked for an instant. "Thank you, sir. You don't know how happy this makes me and my wife."

That night Clay and Vicky celebrated another plateau in his recovery. They ordered a pizza, rolled back the large oval rug in the family room, and turned on soft, instrumental music. For the first time since living in their home, they did something they had never done before on the floor of that family room. They danced.

CHAPTER 22

With the fitting of the permanent prosthesis, Clay now revisited the discussion with Stephanie about working out on a stationary bike. A fitness center recently opened only blocks from Clay's bike shop. Never before did he feel any need to workout at a fitness center. Of course, over the past two and one half years, he concentrated on much more important things than working out. Now, though, so many hurdles had fallen before him that he looked with anticipation to preparing himself to return to his bicycle.

In only minutes Clay completed the registration at the fitness facility. Exactly one week after the fitting of the permanent prosthesis, Clay sat on a stationary bike testing his artificial foot on the pedal. His concern centered on the effect on the foot of applying pressure on the pedal. For twenty-two minutes he pedaled without a hint of soreness in his lower leg that ended with the prosthesis. With delight he worked out on the bike for a full thirty minutes before concluding he had enough for the first time.

Changing to his street shoes, one for each foot, he left the fitness center proud of his accomplishment for the day and only a bit tired from his time on the bike. Clay smiled as he considered how much time elapsed since the last time he pedaled a bike. He cringed with the thought of his foolish venture on the driveway. Since he last seriously rode his bike, leg and back muscles had softened and stamina decreased. He realized he needed time to regain his strength before he seriously considered riding a bike with wheels.

Clay stepped out into the late afternoon sun and stood for a moment, remembering where he parked his car. As his eyes traveled over the parking lot, he suddenly noticed a bright white pickup located in a remote corner. A vision of the white pickup that paused following his accident flashed through his mind. For an instant he thought if that could be the one that knocked him off the road. He shook his head, dismissing the thought as ridiculous. In this area of the Twin Cities one could find any number of white pickups. Despite a slight limp, Clay walked with confidence and pride toward his car, taking one more furtive look at the gleaming white pickup.

Weeks before, Clay returned to work, virtually full time. At first after his return, he performed those functions that permitted him to sit or lean upon something. However, he did use the time at work to practice walking, first with a crutch, then with a cane, and finally with neither. On those days he spent longer periods of time on his feet, his stump did remind him that he wore an artificial foot. For Clay, the practice walking made the minor discomfort worth it. Approximately six months following the amputation, Clay regained a part of his life he, at times, feared he had lost forever, his ability to walk without pain and without assistance.

Despite the excitement over his progress he shared with Vicky, Clay still knew he had yet to recover an important part of his life, his biking. Since the disastrous ride on the driveway the preceding fall, the ride that could have cost him more than his foot, Clay only thought about cycling. Learning to walk again assumed much more importance. Still, during those long days when confined to the house and Vicky at work, his mind returned to the days when biking played such an important role in his life.

How could he forget that biking was how he met Vicky? How could he forget the countless times he turned to biking to escape his mother's insistence that he clean his room, empty the dish washer, or do his homework? These quiet moments, recently, also returned Clay to a small, Iowa town named Packwood and a sweet, young girl named Robin with whom, in a careless, passionate moment, he plunged into the world of sexual gratification.

Even before he received his permanent prothesis, Clay would walk into the garage to look at his bike, still parked where his neighbor, Josh Ditmer, left it after the incident on the driveway. Resisting the temptation simply to sit on the bike, he would grasp the handle bars, resting some of his weight on them, then walk slowly around the garage using the bike for support. Never did he consider doing something stupid like he did months before.

Now, standing in the garage looking at his bike, Clay decided the time had arrived. His recovery wasn't perfect. He still suffered a noticeable limp along with occasional tenderness. Nonetheless, biking took most of the weight off his foot. His workouts at the fitness center near the bike shop confirmed that. There he discovered, among other things, his prosthetic foot made very little difference in his ability to pedal a bike. He found out after thirty minutes on the stationary bike the only soreness he felt was in his butt, one of the more vulnerable parts of a biker's anatomy.

Following several sessions at the fitness center, Vicky and Clay discussed his progress, a topic much less contentious than discussions months ago regarding her hours spent on the job. Clay's recovery diverted attention away from many of the petty arguments that before his accident threatened to disrupt their marriage. She agreed what he accomplished in the past weeks to strengthen his body and adapt to his new foot deserved praise, but always, qualifications clouded the conversation.

"Sweetheart," Clay pleaded as he sat with his wife on their front step, taking in the freshness of the late summer evening. What else has to happen?"

Vicky snuggled against her husband, squeezing his arm. "I just don't want something to happen to set you back."

Clay wrapped his arm around Vicky's shoulder. "What could happen riding my bike around the block? I have kind of tested my foot on the fitness center's stationary bike. I've even checked with my trusted allies, Carrie and Stephanie, both agreed. I'm ready."

"Yes, but they're not married to you. They don't live with you. Besides, look what happened last fall right here in the driveway."

Clay moved his arm off Vicky's shoulder. He folded his hands with elbows resting on this knees. "Things happened that night that won't happen again. Most of it had nothing to do with biking."

Silence enveloped the two. They sat lost in their own private thoughts, their own private opinion of the risks involved in Clay attempting to ride his bike.

"Look," Clay turned to face his wife, "it's got to happen some time. You know I'm not going to risk hurting myself. Let's think about it over tonight and decide tomorrow."

Tomorrow was a Friday, the end of another work week. At the breakfast table before they left for work, Clay studied his wife, who sat across from him. "Well, honey, what do you think?"

Vicky looked up at her husband, that enchanting smile brightening her beautiful face. "I think you should go ahead."

Clay jumped up, walked around the table, and reached down to give his wife a firm hug and a tender kiss on lips that tasted of corn flakes. "Thank you. Let's have a party. I'll invite Ross at the shop, Josh next door and my parents. Maybe, we could have a couple snacks and a beverage."

Vicky looked at Clay in mild alarm.

He laughed. "No, not that kind. Just coffee, soda or some ice tea, something like that."

For Clay, the workday passed quickly. Most of the time he envisioned that return to his bike. He felt confident that the time he spent on the stationary bike as well as the time he spent walking around the bike shop prepared him for this crucial test. He made sure to talk to his parents, his boss and his neighbor Josh, whose alert action last fall saved Clay from even further injury.

The plan involved gathering at their home about 6:00. Day light savings time extended the day, making evenings more amenable to outdoor activities. Vicky prepared a few snacks and made coffee. Clay brought home soda for the non-coffee drinkers.

When he returned from work, Clay tested the bike tires. He wheeled it around the garage checking on the gear alignment. He wiped the bike clean after its many idle months.

"Are you sure you should be doing this? Clay's mom stood at the head of the driveway nervous about what could happen.

Clay smiled, placing his arm around his mother's shoulder, "Mom, I'm not three years old any more. If I didn't think I could do this, believe me, I wouldn't." For just an instant, Clay pictured in his mind that little, three year old boy he heard so much about who jumped on his bike to ride for the first time without training wheels.

Clay's mom moved away from his arm. She turned to face her son. "I suppose you know best." She shook her head. "All those months that you've suffered."

"Now, Mom, we can celebrate that they're over."

Clay's dad joined in to reassure his wife that all was under control. How many times during the last thirty years had he strived to allay his wife's fears over their only son? "Let's get this over with." He declared.

Not in months had Clay worn one of his biking outfits. Not in months had he squeezed into his special biking shoes. This time, however, was very different. He did not have a clip-less pedal for his right foot. He would use the simpler toe clip that would hold his prosthetic foot in place.

His parents, Ross, his boss, Josh, and Vicky stood to one side of the driveway. Clay approached his bike leaning against the garage door frame. He moved the bike out into the middle of the driveway. He tightened his helmet and snapped his gloves. He placed his left foot on the pedal, nudged the bike ahead, and swung his right leg over the seat.

Instantly, his body responded to the bike as it rolled slowly toward the street. Clay turned left, pushed on the pedal with his left foot followed by his right. He felt as if he hadn't missed a day of riding. It all seemed so natural. He turned to look back at his audience. He rejoiced in their applause as he rode, jubilant, down the street in pursuit of the past.

CHAPTER 23

Robin Foster sat with her parents in the modest but comfortable family room she tastefully decorated with a collection of new and old furniture. Jamie biked to a friend's house to kick around the soccer ball. While her parents relaxed on the sectional sofa, she tended to the coffee and peanut butter cookies she recently baked.

Over the years, Robin enjoyed a close relationship with her parents, Charles and Neena Foster, her father now retired from his job as a superintendent in Packwood, Iowa's construction industry. Particularly with the birth of her son, Jamie, Robin looked to her parents for support during those critical first years of motherhood. Even as Jamie grew older, his grandparents occupied a critical place in his young life. Of them, as well as of his mother, he often inquired about his dad. He searched for information about him that, perhaps, his grandparents possessed that his mother did not. Charles and Neena carefully avoided even a hint at never having met Jamie's father.

"Why don't you sit down? We can take care of ourselves." Robin's dad advised his daughter. In their world, others didn't wait on them. They took care of themselves.

Robin stood facing her parents, holding another small tray of cookies. "I will in a minute. I want you to sample my cookies."

"Thank you," her mother answered. "I really don't need to sample any more cookies."

Like Robin, her mom was a small, petite woman, blessed with the strength to resist temptation of high caloric foods, but one who still enjoyed the flavor of home made peanut butter cookies.

"You could use a little of the padding cookies give." Charles joked. He, too, possessed a youthful appearance despite his sixty-eight years.

Robin's parents joined her in planning for Jamie's twelfth birthday party. The occasion was the dominate one of several to awaken in Robin the memory of that night twelve years ago when she and Clay Pennell conceived a child. Not often did she discuss the memory with her parents or with anyone else. However, the image of Clay frequently drifted through her mind. Was he still the handsome man she remembered? Did he still live in the Twin Cities? Did he still have this obsession for biking? Did he even think about her? Did he ever imagine he was a father? Would Jamie ever learn the truth about his father? Would she ever overcome the guilt she felt when she talked about Jamie's father?

Though she thought about these questions, she refused to search for their answers.

"It's hard to believe that twelve years have passed already." Robin's mom reached for another cookie. She sat back in the sofa, studying her daughter. "Have you heard anything about Jamie's father?" The question had arisen before, many times, but not recently.

The topic of Jamie's father no longer made Robin uneasy. She resisted discussing it for months following the discovery of her pregnancy. Jamie's birth, the demands of caring for him, and her job at the local community hospital occupied too much of her time to dwell on the past.

"No, I have not. I guess there's no reason to. He must have a successful life as I do." Robin reached down to pick up her cup of coffee. "Besides, he knows nothing about his son."

"Will you ever try to contact him?" Her father asked.

Robin smiled at the futility of such a contact and took a swallow of coffee. "I can't say I'll never contact him or try to contact him. I really can't think of any reason to, especially for Jamie's sake."

"He is your son's father." Her mother injected.

Robin breathed deeply, sensing the intensity of her mom's comment. "Mom, I know that. Nobody knows that better than I do. But Jamie doesn't know that. No one has spent more time thinking about telling him the truth. All he knows about his dad is that an accident caused his death. What do you think would happen if he suddenly found out that was a lie?"

The potential repercussions of that becoming a reality spread silence through Robin's family room.

Robin's mom reached across the coffee table to grasp her daughter's hand. "Your right. Of course, you're right. We have to think first about Jamie. You have done a marvelous job in doing that and in being both mother and father to our grandson."

Robin closed her eyes to prevent tears from seeping through. "Thank you. I've tried."

A few more moments of silence ended with her dad's question, "Have you ever thought about getting married?"

Robin laughed out loud at that question. She glanced down at her coffee cup. "Sure I have, many times. Not much available for husbands in Packwood," she admitted over a muted laugh.

"Have you ever tried?" He persisted.

"Dad, I'm not going to go man hunting. I did that once. You know what happened." She paused. "Seriously, I don't have time to get into a relationship at this stage in my life. Jamie and my job take up most of my time. Our lives right now don't have room for a third." She sat back in her chair signaling the end to the discussion.

Silence returned. Each took another bite of a cookie then a sip of coffee, attempts to cloak a sensitive subject.

Robin's's mom broke the silence. "We came here to talk about our grandson's birthday party. Let's do it."

That discussion concluded with plans to invite three of Jamie's friends for a small party at a local fast food restaurant. Not a very assertive boy, Jamie didn't have a wide range of friends. However, his friendly disposition, always with a ready smile, his willingness to cooperate with what his friends wished to do, and his just plain good nature did have appeal.

Though small in stature, Jamie possessed a promising talent for his favorite sport of soccer. Quick on his feet, resilient and elusive on the field made him a first choice when others his age gathered for a game. Soccer gave him the chance to interact with other boys his age. The interaction worked to combat some of his innate shyness. To his birthday party, he invited just three of his soccer buddies.

The party started at Jamie's home hosted by his mother and his grandparents. Opening his presents, his eyes shined with excitement and happiness. The most important gift came from his mom, a new pair of soccer shoes. From his home, the party moved to a fast food restaurant in the heart of Packwood's business district where the young boys indulged in hamburgers, French fries, and soda. They concluded the feast with chocolate sundaes.

Two weeks later, Jamie missed school, complaining about stomach pains and cramps. Robin, in her role as a LPN at the local community hospital, frequently confronted symptoms like those. Assuming her son suffered some form of the flu, she ensured he drank plenty of water and ate only bland food. She also contacted the other three boys to discover that one of them suffered similar symptoms.

In three more days, Jamie had not improved. He had gotten worse with the onset of diarrhea. Robin delayed no longer. She took him to the family doctor who, following an examination and tests, concluded that Jamie suffered from an E. coli infection. The news shocked Robin, who knew of the dangers of E. coli getting established in the intestines. She also knew about the possible adverse effects on the kidneys if the infection did not respond to treatment.

Robin contacted the fast food restaurant to alert them to the plight of her son as well as that of his friend, both of whom had gotten sick after the birthday party. She plunged into research on E. coli, colitis, and the threat of a kidney condition termed hemolytic uremic syndrome which could do irreparable damage to her young son's kidneys.

With resolve she acquired over the years as a single mother, she vowed that she and Jamie would beat the insidious infection.

CHAPTER 24

Miles Hunter snapped open another can of beer. Another senseless, Friday day at his dad's law office ended early with Miles confronting his dad about a raise. He took a generous swallow before planting his feet on the sofa cushions and leaning back against the sofa arm.

Clashes with his dad happened far too often. Of course, Miles assumed no responsibility for the animosity that blistered the relationship with his dad. For him, his dad just didn't understand that at thirty-three, Miles needed more money to support his meager life style, meager in Miles' opinion. Today, as in recent days, the discussion of duties and pay collapsed into shouting when Mr. Hunter rejected his plea for more money. Over the years Miles nurtured the conviction his family owed him a living. Beyond that he believed society also owed him something. Any explanation of why, he ignored. He just believed he didn't have to contribute, only receive.

Burdened with a volatile temper, Miles often exploded at his dad who long ago gave up trying to reason with his youngest son. Approaching anger that could produce physical harm, Miles, only hours ago, blurted out, "You're a fucking cheap skate! What the hell do you do with all your money? Shove this place up your ass!" He charged out the door, raced to his pickup and pealed out of the parking lot, nearly clipping another car as he bullied his way onto the street.

Though he considered himself independent, in charge of his life, Miles worked in his dad's law office or, more accurately, he put in time at his dad's law office doing menial tasks. On two previous occasions, Chester Hunter, Miles' father, secured apartments for his son. Twice the arrangements ended in eviction. Miles ignored paying rent or utilities. With no other option available at the time, Miles returned to the spacious home his parents owned on heavily wooded Lake Minnetonka property, the home in which he grew up. That arrangement lasted only a few months, Miles' constant hostility toward his parents creating impossible living conditions.

Again, with his dad's help, Miles found a small apartment in a quiet Lake Minnetonka community called Long Lake. Ironically, Long Lake also served as the home of the bike shop where Clay had worked for several years. Miles did his best to ignore the bikers who frequently rode by his apartment or who gathered around the bike shop that served a large area around Long Lake.

Modest without qualification, with one bedroom off a combined kitchen-living room and a bath barely big enough for

Miles' six foot, two hundred pound frame, the apartment gave him the freedom he required away from intrusion by others. The apartment also provided everything he needed, a place to sleep, a place to shower, a place for his forty-two inch, flat screened TV, a fridge for his beer, a place for solitude away from nagging parents, and a place to park his treasured pickup.

The drive to his apartment cooled Miles' temper. He parked in his own private parking space. Since his apartment was one of only four in the building, each tenant had his own spot in the adjoining parking lot. Miles stomped up the stairs to his second floor apartment, pushed open the door, and tossed his keys on the kitchen table.

Miles spent very little time performing house cleaning duties. He washed dishes when the sink would hold no more; he vacuumed rarely; he hung up his clothes when he no longer found a place to sit. Shoving aside yesterday's jeans, he sat down on the sofa which took up nearly one wall of the living room.

He pushed the remote to catch the late innings of an afternoon Twins' game. With the team trailing 11-4 in the eighth, a brief search for something better to watch proved futile. Nothing interested him.

"To hell with this shit!" He shouted out loud. Standing up before the sofa, he drained his can of beer, then walked to the fridge. Grabbing four more cans, he stuffed two in his rear pockets and carried the other two.

Squeezing the beer cans into his rear pockets produced more resistance than before. Not one to concern himself about a healthy life style, Miles, nonetheless, noticed recently that his pants fit tighter than before and that his stomach protruded a bit more. Standing before the fridge, Miles thought about his physical condition. A bulky man with powerful arms and legs, with big hands, and with a big head draped with hair reaching his shoulders, he always viewed himself as an intimidating person, one that others respected. Maybe he should do something to regain the physical condition that formerly gave him pride.

The only recent physical clash was the one some time ago with the four cyclists who humiliated him at the edge of the road. That would not happen again, but Miles decided he would check into a workout place. He knew one was located not very far from his apartment, only a short distance from the bike shop serving all those pussies who believed biking reinforced their virility. A sneer crossed his face as he thought about bikers. Soon he would check into the workout place whatever it was called.

Right now, though, he was bored, bitter, and trying to erase the confrontation with his dad. Whenever Miles faced boredom or whenever life agitated him, he turned to the one outlet, his overwhelming pride, the most important possession in his life, his white Cadillac, Escalade pickup. With the beer cans bulging from his rear pockets, he hurried out to his pickup. Placing the cans in the center council, he ran his hand over the smooth contours of the dashboard and the soft touch of the steering wheel. He could never get beyond his fascination with his vehicle.

His anger temporarily quieted, Miles backed out of the driveway and onto Brown Road that extended south out of Long Lake. He grinned, reaching for another can of beer. Feeling the power of his Escalade respond to the pressure of his foot, he accelerated, oblivious to the forty mile per hour speed limit.

Less than a mile ahead on the same Brown Road, Mildred Hughes looked both directions before she stepped onto the shoulder. With her followed an aging golden retriever, Max, her friend and companion. Since the death of her husband two years ago, Max's companionship became even more vital. At sixty-eight years old, Mildred retained her commitment to physical exercise. Twice each day, every day, she and Max went for their walk along Brown Road which fronted the home where she lived for over thirty years.

As she and Max walked on the shoulder of the road, Mildred heard a firm, "On your left." She and Max moved over to allow a single cyclist ride by. Brown Road served many of the Twin Cities' cycling clubs. Its quiet hills and gentle curves made for a perfect training route for serious cyclists who spent many summer weekends in competition. Mildred thanked the cyclist for announcing his presence. Much too often bike riders passed her on her walks without the slightest indication of their passing. She watched as the rider grew smaller, blending in with the late afternoon shade bordering the road.

Mildred and Max walked several minutes along this familiar, residential road which rarely attracted much traffic except for the local residents. Suddenly, from behind, Mildred heard an approaching vehicle. In an instant a white flash shot by her and Max. She shook her head in disgust over reckless drivers. Too often she witnessed speeding and recklessness on her road. She threatened to note license numbers and call the police, but invariably the chance to do so vanished in a wink. This time she did catch a part of the license. She thought she saw an "L" and, at least, a "9" and "6." She wasn't absolutely sure, but maybe it would be enough for the police to go on. She looked down at Max. "Max, old boy, maybe we can offer a little help on this one."

Miles assumed wherever he drove was his territory. The residential road carried only light traffic, allowing him to unleash his Escalade. He whizzed by an old lady walking her dog, showing little concern for her rights as a pedestrian.

In the distance, he could see a cyclist. He gripped the steering wheel, letting his foot relax on the accelerator. In his mind he reached back a short time when four bikers left him on another road roughed up and bleeding. He despised cyclists, an attitude he fueled by frequent personal reminders of their skinny legs, effeminate, tight pants, flashy shirts and ugly helmets. He resented having to share the road with them. They should keep to the miles of bike paths traversing the Twin City area.

Miles reached for another beer. Bracing the steering wheel with his knees, he snapped open the can. Drinking and driving laws applied to sissies like those who rode bicycles. He drew closer to the cyclist riding on the road's edge, just short of the gravel shoulder. That image of the four cyclists expanded in his mind, provoked by too many beers and too much defiance.

He accelerated again, rapidly approaching the bike rider. With little thought of consequences, with hatred and revenge controlling his actions, he inched his pickup closer to the road's edge. He'd for sure scare the shit out of this dude. He heard only a dull thud. He paid no attention to it, completely devoid of any concern for the safety of the bike rider. He drove on, ignoring the fate of the cyclist who careened wildly off the road, crashing through a decaying fence and tumbling into a flower garden at the edge of adjoining property.

Several blocks back, Mildred saw what happened. She saw the floundering biker. She saw the speeding white pickup. She stood in shock as she tried to recall that license number, something with an "L" and a "9" and a "6." She never walked without her cell phone. She dialed 911.

A dispatcher asked, "How can I help you?"

Shaken by the horrible scene she witnessed, Mildred strained to find the words. "There's been an accident, a guy hit on his bicycle." She talked slowly into her cell phone. Max stood obediently by her side.

"Where are you calling from?" The dispatcher asked.

Mildred still struggled to calm herself, to control her breathing. "On Brown Road, almost to the intersection with Fox Street."

"Are you injured?" The dispatcher asked.

Mildred hesitated, catching her breath. "No, I wasn't involved. I saw this pickup run a biker off the road."

"Is the biker injured?"

"I don't know. I saw it all from a short distance away. He was thrown from the bike.

"Stay there. I'm sending help." The dispatcher advised.

Thinking of what could have happened to the cyclist sent shivers through Mildred's body. She pulled Max along as she hurried to the scene of the accident. She could see a car had stopped, and the driver hurried to the aid of the cyclist. She heard sirens screaming in the distance. She couldn't control the trembling in her body. She didn't know how she could help when she got there. However, she did know that she had, at least, part of the license number of the white pickup she was certain hit the cyclist. That might help.

CHAPTER 25

One of four children of Harriet and Chester Hunter, Miles never fit in very well. The youngest of the four, from an early age, he resented everyone telling him what to do or supervising anything he did do. Miles resisted contact with other kids. He preferred playing by himself. He despised sharing anything.

Harriet and Chester worried about their youngest child. He displayed unusual habits completely inconsistent with his siblings. One of those habits which troubled them deeply was Miles' propensity for indifference to the feelings of others. Almost as if he lacked a conscience. He showed no emotion when his brother, for example, came home with a broken collar bone sustained on the football practice field. He showed no emotion when a neighbor's dog ran out in front of his father's car, got run over, and lay writhing on the roadway. The poor animal died in pain. Miles, only eight years old, shrugged his shoulders and walked away.

This indifference to the suffering of others, this near absence of a conscience, manifested itself in several ways. One of those ways involved small animals. Miles gained a twisted delight out of torturing small animals and watching them suffer. Blowing up frogs with fire crackers or smashing a turtle's shell satisfied some ghoulish proclivity derived from some gene combination that failed to function.

This deliberate assault on innocent creatures included a particularly brutal ordeal imposed by Miles, age ten, on a squirrel. With some ingenious snare, Miles captured the squirrel which made its home in one of the several trees shading the Hunter, lake property. For several days, Miles inflicted excruciating pain on the poor, helpless creature. From poking its eyes out, one by one, with a sharp stick to dipping a rag in gasoline, lighting it and spreading it over the squirrel, Miles celebrated each gruesome trick until the squirrel mercifully died.

As birthdays passed, Miles found less and less fascination with torturing helpless animals. However, the tendency for indifference to others persisted. His hatred of cyclists, likely, derived from his indifference. His defiant, belligerent attitude also played an important part of this contempt for bike riders using his roads. That contempt culminated two years ago with his brushing a cyclist off the road. He never stopped nor had he heard anything about the rider, if he lived or died. Miles concluded he got what he deserved, riding on roads designed exclusively for motor vehicles like his cherished Escalade pickup.

Miles raced through the intersection with Fox Street. Anger, beer and his indifference to others compelled him to drive on. Miles did glance in his side rear view mirror only to discover it damaged by the impact, its remote control inoperable. Through his interior, rear view mirror, he did catch a brief glimpse of activity across the road and into the trees beyond. He also saw the lady walking her dog.

For an instant, the reality of hitting another cyclist settled down upon him. For an instant, he thought about consequences. Was he seriously injured? What if he died? Miles ran his hand through his hair. The potential consequences gave him a brief shiver. His lack of conscience quickly gave him reason to worry only about himself. What to do now and where to go acquired more importance than the fate of the cyclist.

He dismissed potential consequences. He accelerated, a smile revealing his delight with the power under the Escalade's hood. He headed west away from the city, seeking peace in what he loved most, driving his pickup.

At his first opportunity, he pulled off the road, shifted into park and stepped out to assess any damage to the right side of his pickup. The side mirror had sustained minor damage. He straightened it as best he could. A scratch on the rear fender marked where the pickup struck the rider. Miles walked to the front fender where a faint blemish remained from the previous encounter with a cyclist. He climbed back into the driver's seat, mildly disturbed over the slight damage to his dream vehicle, damage that he could very likely repair himself. He reached for another beer and pulled back onto the road.

Reaching Interstate I-94, Miles drove, but his mind was occupied not with driving but with his need, maybe, to protect himself from identification. He reflected on what recently happened to further complicate his day. Did the old lady see him brush the biker? Two years ago that wasn't a concern. That incident with a sissy cyclist went unnoticed by anyone else. This time he wasn't sure. In his mind, he briefly retraced his drive before brushing the biker off the road. He could see the image of a woman walking along the side of the road. He remembered nothing else. Approaching the exit that would take him back to his apartment, Miles dismissed any more attention to bikers or witnesses.

On the way to his apartment, he avoided driving by the scene of his latest accident with a biker. To Miles, it was an accident. Pulling into his driveway, he parked his pickup and jumped out to check once more the minor damage it sustained. A little rubbing compound and a little wax would do a good job of concealing the damage. The side, rear view mirror he would work on later.

Miles stepped into his apartment and tossed his keys onto the cluttered kitchen table. He pulled open the fridge. His cell phone rang. Reluctantly, he answered. "Yeah?"

"That you, Miles?" His mother asked.

"Yeah." Miles grumbled.

"Where have you been?" His mother's voice reflected the tension she felt when talking to her son.

"No place." Miles still resented questions from his parents.

His dad spoke next. "Miles?" He asked.

Miles kicked a pair of jeans lying on the floor in front of the sofa. "What do you want?" He mumbled.

"Did you see anything near you at the intersection of Brown Road and Fox Street?"

Miles' body stiffened; he shook his head. "No. Why?"

"We heard on the TV about a biker seriously injured by an apparent hit and run driver." Chester Hunter paused waiting for a response.

Miles paced around his apartment holding the phone to his ear. "I heard nothing. I saw nothing. Good bye."

"Wait a minute." His dad pleaded.

"What do you want, now?" Miles growled.

"According to eye witness reports, the cyclist was hit by a large white vehicle."

Miles threw his arms into the air. "What the hell are you saying? Am I the only guy who drives a white vehicle? Right away you think I'm guilty. It never ends with you two. Anything bad happens, it's my fault. I've heard enough of this nonsense. To hell with that bull shit!" He shoved the phone into his pocket.

Miles opened the fridge, grabbed a beer and walked the few steps to his bedroom. He flopped down on his bed. There was a witness, he thought. The old lady squealed to the cops. Consequences resurfaced in his mind. "God damn those bikers!" He muttered to himself.

His cell phone sounded again. He ignored it. Soon he heard his dad's voice leaving a message. Miles sat up on the edge of his bed and punched on the phone. "What do you want, now?"

"Will you listen for a minute?" His dad persisted.

"Okay, what've you got to say?"

Chester cleared his throat. "The eye witness reported seeing part of the license plate."

Miles clinched his fists and blinked his eyes. "So what?"

"The eye witness remembered part of the plate. Something with an 'L' and a '9' and a '6.'"

Miles caught his breath. The impact of his dad's revelation struck a glancing blow to Miles' confidence. Silence filled the phone connection. "So what? Does that mean I hit the bastard?" Miles snarled into the phone.

In a calm voice, his dad replied. "Son, I don't know what it means. I do know those are some of the numbers on your plates. I would hope to God if you were anyway involved, you would have the courage to stop to help."

"I wasn't there! I did nothing. I don't want to talk about it! I'm fed up with you and mom always accusing me of something." This time he hurled the phone against the wall.

Early the next morning, Miles got out of bed, dressed and left. In the parking lot, he stood behind his pickup studying the license plate which read "LOT 926." The damned witness had remembered some of the numbers but not the letters. Miles concentrated on the numbers, especially the number "2." Increasingly, anger, hatred, and defiance crowded Miles' mind, making rational decisions elusive.

He fired up his pickup to drive to a paint dealer in Long Lake. At the paint store, he bought a can of black, enamel paint and a stiff brush. With his purchases, he drove to the privacy of a quiet, secluded driveway which led to an abandoned marina. Parking the pickup, he grabbed the paint and the brush and walked around to the back of the pickup. With a hand as steady as he could make it, he altered the "2" in "926" to an "8." When he finished, he did the same to the front plate. He walked around his pickup, a sneer revealing his satisfaction with his work. That what he had done constituted a crime completely eluded Miles. The need to protect his identity assumed a far greater importance than the simple act of altering a license plate.

The art work accomplished, Miles turned his attention to the alleged eye witness. The only person he could think of was the lady he passed walking on the side of the road. He remembered seeing no one else. He debated what he should do. If she was the one, she already shot her mouth off about what she saw. But she wasn't real certain about what she saw.

What could he do about it? He sat in his pickup, staring out into the trees that lined the abandoned driveway. Of course, the police had only part of the license plate identification. Now, he altered that. Maybe with a little persuasion, the lady's memory would falter, discrediting her eye witness claims.

Miles turned the ignition, backed around and left the isolated driveway. Maybe he should watch for the lady who walked Brown Road the evening of the accident. She apparently didn't live too far from where he did. A little intimidation might cloud the trail to him and his pickup.

Alone again in his apartment, Miles sat forlorn in front of the TV searching for something of interest, something on TV that could divert his attention from the agony of the day. The implied accusations of his parents combined with the recent verbal collision with his dad created more complications in Miles' life. No longer working for his dad, at least temporarily, left Miles with virtually nothing to do. Taking another swallow of beer, he considered again that woman who walked with her dog along Brown Road. She must be the eye witness. He thought more about the intimidation that occurred to him before.

Suddenly, Miles tossed the near empty beer can toward the kitchen sink, beer splashing on the floor. He jumped up, resolved to get out of the confinement of his apartment and away from the troubles that clouded his life. Instead, he fulfilled the promise to himself to do something about his sagging body. With resolve Miles displayed infrequently, he rushed out of his apartment to drive to the fitness facility just beyond the bike shop.

At the fitness center, he registered and paid the small fee for an hour's workout. An attendant gave him some advice as to which machines to use depending on his purpose for working out. Miles explained he wanted to tone and tighten up his muscles. He regretted the sag taking over his body.

Miles worked diligently on several of the machines before giving up. For the first work out, he very likely over did it. He would suffer for it in the morning. Still, the workout gave him a release from the anger and bitterness he carried with him most of the time.

Dripping with perspiration, Miles rejected taking a shower. He could do that at his apartment only minutes away. Feeling more refreshed than he had in a long time, he stepped out into the parking lot where his white pickup sat alone in a far corner. Miles paused when he saw a young man who appeared to be studying his cherished pickup. Walking toward his vehicle, Miles dismissed anything serious about the man's intentions here in clear light of day. Besides, his pickup very often attracted attention. Miles was proud of that.

Climbing into his pickup, Miles looked around to watch the young man walk across the parking lot, his progress slowed by a distinct limp.

CHAPTER 26

Clay rode cautiously, his eyes attentive to the route ahead as well as that behind. All the weeks of therapy and exercise, at last, enabled him to try riding to work, a distance of fewer than five miles, a distance at one time considered not even worth the effort. Now it represented an overwhelming achievement in view of the pain Clay suffered for more than two years.

He and Vicky discussed at great length his attempting to ride his bike the short distance to work. The route included a few, heavily traveled streets around their house as well as gently rolling almost rural, blacktop roads lightly used near the bike shop. Clay continued to ride short distances around his neighborhood. He also spent time riding the stationary bike at the fitness center. Their discussion touched on all the possible problems Clay could face, Vicky bringing them up, Clay striving to dismiss them. Eventually, Vicky consented to his riding to work. However, first she wanted to follow him in her car just to make sure he faced no difficulties. Clay agreed to her demand for one ride. After that he would ride on his own.

On this late autumn morning with a crispness in the air, Clay biked toward the quiet of Brown Road which would take him to the bike shop. He smiled as he rode in the relative quiet of the morning, only an occasional song from a bird interrupted the silence. Since his return to biking, Clay discovered something he had not considered, the psychological effects of the accident. Despite his history of biking, he found his confidence on the bike eroded by thoughts of the accident. He now gripped the handlebars tightly, wary of what might approach him from behind or what he might face ahead. Attention to matters like this never before followed him on his bike. In amazement he faced these insecurities. How could they be? After all, he had biked for almost thirty years. How they could haunt him he couldn't figure out. He simply knew they did.

Approaching a person on the side of the road diverted Clay's attention from the mystery of the psychology of biking. An older woman appeared to struggled with a package attached to a bank of mail boxes. Next to her stood a large black dog.

Closing in on the lady, Clay stopped, balancing his bike between his legs, only the tips of his feet touching the ground. "Good morning. Could I give you a hand?"

Leaving the package lodged between two of the mailboxes, the lady, in mild alarm, turned, smiled, and repeated, "Good morning. Thank you. I guess the mailman was a little careless this morning."

Clay dismounted his bike, leaning it against the bank of mailboxes. "Here, let me try to get it loose." With a little tug, Clay released the package. It wasn't very heavy, just bulky. He set it down next to the road.

The lady smiled again. "Thank you so much. I really appreciate your help. I think I can handle it from here. I live just down that road a short way. You can see my name on the mail box. I'm Mildred and this is Max." With mention of his name, the dog stood up straight, wagged his tail vigorously, and rubbed his nose in Clay's outstretched hand.

Clay reached to scratch the dog's ears. "I'm Clay, and I work at the bike shop just up the road in town. I'm riding to work now."

Mildred tugged on Max's leash. She nudged the package a few inches away from the road, looked at Clay, and smiled again. "You know, you bikers are such nice people. I walk here with my dog at least twice a day. Very often I see bikers like you on this road. Regularly, they let me know they are coming behind me. I appreciate the 'On your left.'"

Clay smiled. "Why, thank you. I know some of us don't always show that kind of courtesy. I do expect that most of us do."

Mildred leaned against the mailboxes. "I don't want to detain you, but just a few days ago a biker was hit by a white pickup down the road near the next intersection." She pointed to the intersection of Brown Road and Fox Street.

For an instant the reality of Clay's accident flashed through his mind. "Yes, I heard about it. A hit and run, right?"

"Yes, I saw the fancy, white pickup brush by the biker and not even slow down. I called 911. I also caught part of the license plate number."

Clay shook his head. "Sometimes there's just not enough room for everyone on these roads. Seems silly but true." The white pickup reference sparked anew that fateful moment when a white pickup knocked him off the road in an area not too far from where he talked to this friendly lady. How many people owned white pickups? How many people who owned white pickups would deliberately force a biker off the road? How many times did these questions pressure their way into Clay's mind?

Clay thanked the lady for the compliments and the information about the hit and run. He apologized but informed her of his need to get to work. She thanked him for helping her with the package and watched as he rode north toward Long Lake and the bike shop.

Clay propped up his right leg on the ottoman he used frequently to relax the stump after extended periods of wearing his prosthetic foot. His days at the bike shop had returned to something similar to the pre-accident days. For many cyclists the season was ending. For others, the biking season never ended. Even the often harsh winter conditions of the Twin Cities failed to dissuade some cyclist from almost daily rides. Each day at the bike shop found Clay spending most of his time on his feet. His artificial foot gave him good support. He assigned some of the credit for his adjustment to the prosthetic foot to the time he spent on the stationary bike. Still, after a sometimes ten hour day, his right leg reminded him it no longer retained the same capacity for abuse that his left leg did. The moments of relaxation in his favorite living room chair served to reduce the tension that often gripped his lower right leg.

Reading the morning paper, Clay suddenly paused to read over a headline in the suburban section. "Hit and run driver still at large" captured Clay's attention. He perused the article which described the accident and the possible eye witness he spoke with on his ride to work. The cyclist, though in critical condition, was expected to survive. The reference to the white vehicle or pickup as the article described it caught Clay's attention. He recalled Mildred's(He was sure he remembered her name.)account of the accident and the speeding pickup.

"Honey," Clay called to his wife who had just returned from her long day at Wagner Electronics. "Can you come here?"

"Sure. Give me a minute. What is it?" Vicky answered from the bedroom where she changed into something more comfortable.

"A very interesting story here in the paper."

Vicky walked into the living room wearing her familiar cut off Jean shorts and a T-shirt with "Cyclists Rule" printed across her chest. She leaned down to give Clay a light kiss on the cheek. "What about this story?"

Clay pointed to the article about the injured cyclist. "Remember we heard a few days ago about another hit and run accident involving a cyclist and a pickup out near the bike shop? I told you about the older lady I met on my ride to work. She saw the whole thing. Simply reading that the rider was hit by a large white vehicle of some kind gives me a shiver."

Vicky eyes widened. "I understand completely."

Clay handed her the paper. She read the brief description of the incident. "Apparently, they haven't found the driver yet, right?" She looked down at Clay.

"No, apparently not. It says in the article and confirmed by the lady I talked to that she remembered part of the license of the vehicle, the paper thinks but she knows, was responsible for hitting the rider." Clay reached for the paper. "Here, let me see it again." He scanned the article. "Yes, here it is. The eye witness remembers seeing a couple numbers, a '9' and a '2'." Clay shook his head. "Not much to go on there."

Vicky sat down on the arm of Clay's chair. "How's the rider?"

"Probably will make it, according to the article." Clay reached down to massage his stump. "I pity what the guy is likely to face all because some jerk didn't have enough room for his damned big truck or whatever." Since his accident, Clay had even less tolerance for reckless, inconsiderate drivers, many he met almost every time he biked.

For a few moments, both Clay and Vicky sat in silence. Vicky grabbed Clay's hand. "Are you thinking what I'm thinking?

Their eyes met.

"If you're thinking that this might be the guy who hit me, then yes." Clay, again, studied his stump.

Silence settled over Vicky and Clay, their attention focused on the same question. What should they do if anything?

Clay looked up at Vicky, who now moved to stand before the living room window. "Do you think I should call the sheriff's office?"

Vicky turned to look at her husband. "Do you really want to get into that again?"

Clay shrugged his shoulders. "I don't know. In one sense, no. But in another, I just hate to see some bastard, excuse me, get away with driving over cyclists."

"I agree. It's your decision. I'll support whatever you want to do."

For the rest of the evening, Clay's attention kept returning to the question of his contacting the sheriff's office or just forgetting about it. After all, he had regained control of his life. His prosthetic foot served him extremely well, much better than he ever expected. All his careful exercising, his workouts at the fitness center, and his compliance with directions of the staff at the rehab center had paid remarkable dividends.

Clay had returned to something very close to his old routine. Frequently, his morning ride, depending upon the weather, took him five-ten miles, nothing like the twenty-thirty he formerly rode but still an impressive accomplishment considering what he faced with his leg. On weekends, both he and Vicky sometimes rode together for a few miles before returning home for a brunch, combining their culinary talents. He now worked his usual ten-twelve hour days at the bike shop which recently realized a delightful increase in customers, thanks in part to the exorbitant cost of gas.

Yes, the long days did impose demands on Clay's energy which, he confessed, did not quite compare to what he once enjoyed. He didn't blame that all on his amputation. Part of it he placed on his flirting with the mid thirties. In his favorite sofa chair or in bathroom's steamy whirlpool bath tub he did find relief from the occasional soreness and twinges that developed in the stump that ended his right leg. When he considered what he faced for all those months of pain and frustration, he, now, rejoiced in his life and that of his marvelous wife.

Indeed, Vicky definitely qualified as a marvelous wife. Earlier in Clay's futile attempts to deal with his injuries, he questioned her commitment to his elusive recovery as well as her fidelity to their marriage. He recalled clashes over petty, inconsequential matters that should never have divided two people presumably in love. Clay recalled his suspicions regarding the long hours at her job. At times, he would return from the bike shop to wait for her arrival much later. Her attempts to allay his suspicions Clay dismissed, particularly when waiting for his right leg to heal confined him to their home.

He remembered his apprehension when Vicky announced the trip to Orlando. Though he had not noticed it immediately, Vicky's attitude toward her work underwent a subtle change after that trip to Florida. She seemed more attentive to his frustration. At least from his perspective, she devoted less time to extended hours at work. Gradually, they spent more time together, maybe because of his need for attention or maybe because, and this explanation pleased Clay the most, she displayed her innate compassion and devotion to her husband. Whatever the explanation, Clay's life included more gratification then at any previous time in recent memory. That evening Clay went to bed ambivalent about contacting law enforcement people about the recent hit and run.

In the morning, early, Clay awoke with resolve. He jumped out of bed into his prosthetic foot. A small room off their bedroom served as a den or office for both Clay and Vicky. Clay hurried into the room to look for the name of the officer he had contacted following his accident nearly two years ago. He saved all the records that pertained to his extended recovery including the call he made to the Hennepin County Sheriff's department. Vicky's organizational skills had rubbed off on Clay, who knew just where to find the information he sought.

Stewart Cook was the name of the officer he spoke with numerous times while the department worked diligently to identify the driver of the vehicle that hit Clay. Of course, their diligence failed to turn up the culprit. Perhaps, this recent incident might have a connection to his accident. Clay realized that evidence linking the two was pure speculation on his part. Still, the accident occurred not far from where his did. Also, how many large white vans, pickups or SUV's clutter the streets and roads of western Hennepin County?

Before even taking his morning ride, Clay dialed the office of the Hennepin County Sheriff not even sure Mr. Cook still occupied the office or even served on the sheriff's staff.

A sweet, young voice greeted him. "Hennepin County Sheriff's office, how may I help you?"

A little unsure how to proceed, Clay cleared his throat. "Is there a Mr. Cook at this office?"

"Yes, of course. Can I ask who's calling?"

Some of the tension faded with this discovery. "My name is Clay Pennell. About two years ago I reported an accident, a hit and run, involving me on my bike. I reported the accident to Mr. Cook, who spent much time searching for the driver of the

185

vehicle that hit me." He paused, waiting for some response from the sweet voice.

"Do you wish to speak with him?"

"Yes, if I could please." Clay waited for the transfer.

"Mr. Pennell, good to hear from you. How are you?" Mr. Cook spoke in a friendly tone, giving Clay the impression that he must remember him.

"I don't know if you recall the accident I reported to you a couple years ago."

Mr. Cook answered instantly, "Of course, I do. You suffered some severe injuries, as I recall. How are you?"

"I'm fine now, thank you." Clay wished to avoid telling the long story about his infection, amputation and prosthetic foot. "I'm calling about an accident that happened not far from where mine did, I believe at the intersection of Brown Road and Fox Street, just south of Long Lake."

"Yes, I know what you're talking about. The department right now is doing all it can to locate the driver of the vehicle involved in that hit and run."

"That's why I'm calling. I read in the paper about an eye witness and the recording of part of the license plate on that vehicle, I believe, described as a large white pickup."

"Yes, that's right, Mr. Pennell. I must remind you, though, that since this case is under investigation, I can't divulge too much about it."

"I understand, officer. I just want to ask if there might be any connection between my hit and run and this one?"

For a few seconds silence filled the line. "That is an interesting question, ah . . . Mr. Pennell."

"Clay." Clay inserted.

"Yes, Clay. Look, Clay, why don't you let me take out the records of your case to bring us up to date. Certainly, we will keep your suspicion in mind as we pursue the investigation of the more recent accident."

"Thank you, Mr. Cook."

"Clay, why don't you leave your name and number. I will get back to you when we have something to report.

Clay gave the officer his number, both cell and land line. "Thank you, again, Mr. Cook. I know how busy your department is, and I really appreciate any thing you can do to find the person responsible for both these accidents."

"You are welcome. Will talk with you later."

Clay closed his cell phone, walked in to the bathroom to prepare for his morning ride, one that he dearly missed for all those months his body battled an insidious infection and adjusted to an artificial foot. He smiled into the mirror noting the tiny gray hairs in his temples. "Maturity," he commented to himself. As he walked out of the bathroom, his thoughts did not include anything about maturity. He thought only of justice, finally justice.

CHAPTER 27

Without hesitation, Vicky supported Clay's decision to contact the sheriff's office. She suffered along with her husband through the long months of uncertainty including agonizing decisions related to his infected right leg.

As did Clay, Vicky privately rejoiced in the renewed harmony of their marriage. Neither she nor Clay could identify a time, a discussion, or a decision that marked the return of more domestic tranquility. She realized, nonetheless, that over the previous months a new calm had settled over their home and their relationship. Even despite the tortured decisions they faced or maybe because of them, a fresh relationship gradually emerged.

Not so at work. Since the dreadful incident in Orlando combined with Brian Tarelton's threats in her office, for Vicky a disquieting tension hung over the office. She hardly spoke with Brian, only when she absolutely had to. After all, he served as president of the company. Even when company business compelled her to speak with him in person or by phone, she felt intimidated, a feeling she rarely experienced. Brian sensed her unease and took advantage of it, only exacerbating the crumbling relationship of the two executives. The animosity between the two compromised the quality of Vicky's work performance. Several times she threatened to talk to Madison. She didn't, in part because she always believed she could take care of herself and in part because of Brian's belligerent warning delivered in her office.

Each Monday, Madison conducted a meeting with his executive team to review the past week's performance and to address company practices and polices which might need revision. At the conclusion of this week's meeting, Madison asked Vicky to join him in his office. Not an unusual request, it had to do, Vicky assumed, with a large shipment of flat screen TV's.

First, Vicky retreated to her office to gather materials related to the shipment and, as usual, check her hair and makeup. She knocked lightly on the door to Madison's office.

"Come on in." Madison announced.

Vicky entered. She motioned to Madison to remain seated. She reached for the chair positioned in front of his desk, a chair with which she had acquired a distinct familiarity.

"Thank you for coming on such short notice." Madison chuckled softly. The small Wagner Electronics office complex made frequent contact among the executives routine.

"When the boss calls, I answer." Vicky smiled, always feeling comfortable in the presence of the CEO. With dignity she settled into the chair before his desk.

"I know that about you, Vicky. I've valued your dedication through the years. How is Clay getting along?"

Would this question never end? Vicky asked herself. "He's doing extremely well, biking nearly every morning, working every day." She answered with obvious satisfaction and relief.

Madison studied his attractive vice president for purchasing. "I know both you and Clay have had to face frustration and ambiguity these past few months. Sometimes that can make it tough on both husband and wife." He paused, shifting position in his chair. "You don't have any problems at home, do you?"

The question surprised Vicky. What had prompted it? Had she done something wrong? She retained her composure. "No . . . no problems. Why do you ask?"

Madison again shifted in his chair. He sat up straight, reluctant to display any intimidation. He did not lead that way. However, he did seek candor and honesty in dealing with his employees. He wished to encourage his employees to seek the same.

"Vicky," he held her attention with his eyes. "I've always admired your composure. You have an impressive ability to stay calm whatever the circumstance. It's a sign of self-confidence and a confidence in your relationship with others."

Vicky sat, intent on what Madison said, curious as to just where it would lead.

"Recently," Madison continued. "I've detected some tension in your interaction with certain members of the staff. Though I've noticed it before, just this morning at our weekly meeting, I sensed something between you and Brian. Maybe I just misinterpreted what I sensed, but is there some conflict between the two of you?"

Vicky stirred in her chair. Was her contempt for Brian Tarlton that obvious? No question, she attempted to avoid contact with him unless absolutely necessary. Apparently, she hadn't concealed her hostility toward him as well as she thought.

Not often did words fail Vicky. At this moment, they did. Caught between exposing Brian Tarlton for the degenerate that he was and risking his threatened retaliation, Vicky stared at Madison, saying nothing.

Madison could see Vicky's momentary search for a response. "Look, I'm sorry to intrude into your personal life. It really isn't my business except when it has some impact on office relations. Office compatibility is essential for a company to prosper. We have prospered. You've helped to make that happen. We don't want to mess with what makes us better as a company." Madison paused, leaning his arms on his desk in front of him. "If something bothers you, maybe I can help."

Vicky sat silent, looking first at her hands folded in her lap, then at the space above Madison. In her mind she wrestled with the decision to share her secret with him. If it adversely influenced office compatibility, perhaps the time had arrived. To hell with Brian's threats.

Vicky rose from her chair to stand facing Madison. She took a deep breath. "Mr. Wagner, if I may be so formal, I've never been so happy with my marriage or with my husband, who has faced heart breaking decisions this past year." She hesitated before going on. "I will confess that the situation here in the office has changed. That change happened last year on the final night of our stay in Orlando."

In discreet detail, Vicky related what happened the night Brian made his humiliating advances in her hotel room. She also told of Brian's threats, later, in her office. When she finished, Madison sat speechless. The search for words was now his.

Madison broke the silence. "Vicky, I'm terribly sorry to hear that. I apologize for Brian's behavior." He hung his head. "I know apologies don't make it any better, but thank you for telling me."

Finally, telling someone about the incident relieved for Vicky a part of the guilt that shadowed her for months. Repeatedly, she considered discussing it with Clay. She concluded that at this time it would serve no purpose. Much of the petty contention that dulled their marriage during the long period of Clay's battle with infection and the threat of amputation was vanquished by his near miraculous recovery and return to a normal life. Still, Vicky determined that until a time when revealing the incident to her husband would make no difference in their relationship, she would refrain from talking about it. The memory lingered of Clay's suspicions about her late hours at work. Someday, she realized, that discussion should take place. She always believed in complete honesty with her husband. Keeping the truth of the incident to herself violated that belief.

Madison moved back in his chair and stood up behind his desk. He causally leaned against the back of the chair. "You know, of course, that Brain intends to retire sometime in the next year." He looked into Vicky's eyes.

Vicky nodded her head in acknowledgement.

"I can hasten that retirement." Madison expressed with firmness. "I will not tolerate that kind of behavior from people in this office. Don't worry. I will deal with Brian. If he issues any more threats, just let me know."

Vicky stood rigid, absorbing Madison's every word. She trusted him. He would do what he said. She could feel tension drain from her body. Until Brian no longer worked at Wagner Electronics, however, she could never feel completely at ease in the office. Perhaps, by the end of the year, that would happen.

Madison moved around his desk to face Vicky. "I'm sorry you've had to carry this around so long. I promise you that by the end of the year Brian will be gone."

Vicky smiled. "Thank you. I appreciate your understanding."

Madison guided Vicky to his office door. Before he opened it, he stopped. "You know, Vicky, when Brian leaves, the company will need a new president." A smile accompanied his final comment. "Think about it."

Vicky's face lightened in a marvelous smile of her own. Yes, she would think about it. She had thought about it for quite some time.

CHAPTER 28

Miles stumbled over his shoe left in front of the TV. A quick kick sent the shoe banging into the wall. With hands on his hips, he stood rigid in the middle of the small living area of his apartment. He could give a shit less about these damned bicycle riders. Why did he think about the pussy who got in his way? In his idle moments, currently there were many of them, his mind carried him back to the scene of a few days ago on Brown Road. That scene included the lady walking her dog and who had since assumed the title of eye witness.

Miles plopped down on the sofa which supplied the only seating in the living area. He ran his hands through his hair, breathed deeply, and uttered to himself, "Those God damned bikers." an expression he uttered far too often. He couldn't clear his mind of what happened at the intersection of Brown Road and Fox Street and the complications it created.

Since the confrontation with his parents the night of the incident with the biker, he refused to return to work. His dad pleaded with him to return, trying to allay his son's anger with an increase in salary. Even that failed to lure Miles back to work. Instead, he prowled around the limited space afforded by his apartment when he didn't find some escape in his pickup. Even then he didn't find the release that driving his pickup previously rendered. That an alleged eye witness reported, at least, a part of a license plate disturbed him. This partial license number implicated him. Even if true, the eye witness account carried no credibility. That he altered his plate gave him no reason for guilt. That the whole affair disrupted his life no one except him seemed to care. Whatever it would take, he intended to regain the life he once enjoyed.

Since the accident, to Miles it was an accident, he searched for the lady who, he assumed, had earned the title of eye witness. At least, he intended to find out something about this lady and her walking habits. Several times he drove the route he took that early evening days ago looking for the lady walking her dog. Each time ended in frustration. Even altering the times that he searched made no difference.

Miles pushed himself up from the sofa. He made the few steps to the fridge, opened it to view the supply of beer which left room for little else. He grabbed a can, snapped it open, and tossed down a generous swallow. He lowered the can, exhaled deeply, wiping his mouth with his sleeve. From the nearby cupboard he reached for a bag of chips. He returned to his place on the sofa, chips and beer his nourishment for now.

Staring absently at the darkened TV screen, Miles pushed more chips into his mouth, followed by another healthy swallow of beer. The cool rush of beer always made him feel good. It did again. It helped distract his attention from parts of his life that made him angry.

Placing the bag of chips on the sofa, Miles rose to seek another can of beer. Again, he returned to the sofa, more relaxed and more attentive to those parts of his life that pissed him off. His siblings who plastered their perfect lives all over every family gathering and his parents who constantly reminded him of his failure made his life miserable. Nobody understood him. He had to live just like his siblings. Yet, he deplored living like his siblings. He gulped more beer. He wasn't like his siblings. His parents never could accept that.

He studied the blank TV screen, his mind churning with thoughts about his life and about what angered him. He shook his head to pull himself back to reality. "To hell with all this bull shit," He uttered, jumping up, throwing the empty beer can in the sink. With a fresh beer in hand, he pushed through his apartment door, heading for his pickup.

On a perfect summer evening, Miles opened wide the windows of his Escalade, backed out onto Brown Road, and headed south out of Long Lake. With no particular destination in mind, he drove, relishing his favorite past time, his pickup. He approached the intersection with Fox Street. For only a moment, the events of that late afternoon skipped through his mind. Much to his dismay, he couldn't rid his mind of that damned biker crashing into the brush along the road. He drove on, willing himself to ignore the images.

A half mile beyond the intersection with Fox Street, Miles spotted a person walking toward him on Brown Road. He tensed. Could this be the lady he'd searched for, on this stretch of road, several times the last few days? He slowed as he approached. The walker was a woman walking her dog. A tingling flickered in his stomach. Of course, he had not seen the woman close up the evening of the incident. But how many women walk their dog on this quiet section of Brown Road?

Miles slowed to a near stop. He glared at the woman walking on the opposite side of the road. She looked over at him, eyes wide. Did her expression reveal recognition? Miles accelerated. Thoughts of what he should do raced through his mind. Would confronting the woman only make matters worse? Would she confirm what she only partially knew about his identity? The need to protect himself along with his intense defiance when he sensed a threat produced a quick decision. Of course, he knew what to do. Why did he even hesitate?

He approached a driveway. He pulled onto the driveway, skidding to an abrupt stop. He backed out onto Brown Road to pursue the woman walking her dog. In minutes, Miles pulled onto the shoulder and stopped in front of the woman. She stood perplexed, watching Miles climb out of his pickup.

Mildred Hughes thought about this moment often since the day of the hit and run. She used great care in choosing times to take her daily walks. Though she only caught a glimpse of the white vehicle that afternoon, she sensed a recognition of this pickup that sent chills from her neck down her spine. With her dog by her side, she stood, nervous, on the shoulder watching this large man approach her.

Miles walked up to Mildred. "Do you walk here often?" He asked without introduction or preface.

Mildred stepped back, her dog filling the space between the two. She cleared here throat. "Yes, why?"

"Did you see an accident the other day just up ahead?"

Mildred now with certainty believed the hit and run driver stood before her. She nodded her head.

Miles closed the distance between them, ignoring the dog that guarded the space in front of Mildred. He raised his hand to point his finger at her, a snarl distorted his face. "If you know what's good for you, you'll forget about what you saw or thought you saw. You really don't know what the hell you saw anyway." Miles placed his hands on his hips to emphasize his command of the situation. "I don't want to hear another fucking word about what you thought you saw. It's screwing with my life." Miles glared at the helpless woman who stood with mouth open and hands trembling. "Do you understand?" Miles screamed.

Mildred stood motionless. Miles turned back to his pickup. He slammed the door and pulled out onto Brown Road, in his wake spewing gravel from the shoulder. Mildred kneeled down to accept the affection of her dog. He licked the tears that dripped from her chin. The trauma of the last few minutes prevented her from even thinking about checking the license plate of the huge white pickup.

Miles' foot on the accelerator producing that feeling of power drained some of the intensity of the encounter. Nearing Long Lake, he relaxed; his shoulders slumped; a grin spread across his face, satisfied that the woman would take his threats seriously. They would prevent her from spreading bullshit about what she thought she saw. He'd nearly convinced himself of his innocence, taking offense with Mildred's inaccurate witness. He did not intend to suffer for an accident that wasn't his fault. He didn't give a shit what the walking woman thought she saw.

When he or his dad secured Miles' apartment, neither knew of the irony that placed Miles in the same community as Clay's bike shop. Of course, Miles discovered the bike shop shortly after moving in to his apartment. Located just blocks from that apartment, the bike shop did remind Miles of his animosity toward cyclists. Still, except to drive by the shop on his way to his dad's law office, he had nothing to do with it.

This late afternoon drive did take him passed the bike shop. On the window, Miles noticed some poster likely advertising, perhaps, a biking event for the collection of sissies who used the many roads around the lake for practice. He ignored it to head to his apartment. Before he reached his apartment, he pulled into the gas station located at the corner of Highway 12 and Brown Road. He drove up to the pump, filled the tank of his Escalade, then went inside to buy a snack and pay for the gas.

Reaching the entry door, Miles stopped. Attached to the door, he saw a poster that resembled the one attached to the bike shop window. The muscles in his neck tightened when he saw the words "hit and run." He stared at the poster which exhorted the members of the Long Lake community to contact the sheriff's office with any information about a hit and run accident which left a young cyclist in the hospital fighting for his life.

Miles' body tensed. That recurring sensation of suffering abuse by others ignited his anger. "Those chicken shit people protecting the damned biker who shouldn't have ridden on the road in the first place." Miles mumbled as he pushed open the door to the station. Inside, he grabbed a box of donuts then slammed his credit card on the counter. "Who put up the damned sign?" He grumbled.

The young, female cashier looked up at Miles. "What sign?"

"The one on the door, right there." Miles pointed to the door.

Intimidated by his obvious hostility, the cashier explained in a weak voice, "I don't know. I just got here. I didn't even notice the sign."

Miles signed the receipt and left the station, ripping away the poster as he stormed through the door.

CHAPTER 29

Clay leaned against the main counter of the bike shop studying the latest catalogue of biking apparel. With winter approaching, the shop needed to increase its stock of cold weather biking clothes. Unlike previous winters when he would ride in nearly all winter weather except, perhaps, blizzards, Clay now recognized the limitations his new foot imposed on his biking. He didn't mind. His foot permitted him to bike enough for his satisfaction even though that amounted to only a fraction of his former biking routine.

With the reduced biking, Clay devoted at least three days a week to working out at the fitness center near the bike shop. Those workouts retrieved some of the strength that vanished during the long, gruesome months of battling the infection in his right leg. More important than that, the stationary bike he rode for weeks helped him blend his new foot with the stationary bike pedal, a major step toward the return to his bike on wheels.

Clay closed the apparel catalogue, pausing to study the splendid riding jacket displayed on the cover. He smiled. He had one like that, a gift from his parents in recognition of his virtually complete recovery from his accident of two years ago. The quiet morning at the bike shop enabled him to replay the exciting events of the previous evening.

An appointment at the Methodist Hospital Rehab Clinic made Clay late to arrive home following a full day of work at the bike shop. Since acquiring his prosthetic foot, he visited periodically with his therapy friend, Stephanie, who declared her admiration for Clay's impressive progress back to a normal life.

Approaching his house, in his car this time, he noticed his parent's car parked in the driveway. Visits from his parents occurred frequently and at most any time during the day or evening. Consequently, he thought nothing of seeing their car. In the garage, Clay shut off the engine, climbed out of the small Mazda he called his own, and walked by his bike parked off to one side of the garage. Only a tender tap on the rear tire displayed his affection.

Stepping into the entry leading to the kitchen, Clay heard a strained chorus of "for he's a jolly good fellow." He stopped suddenly to witness first Vicky then his mother followed by his father march from the living room to the kitchen. They all three stopped directly in front of Clay, who stood with mouth partially open, eyes in a squint trying to determine the cause of all the celebration. What had he done now?

"Sweetheart," Vicky stepped forward to embrace her husband. "Congratulations on the second anniversary of your accident." She reached up to kiss him softly on the lips.

"We are so proud of you son," his mother announced as she too gave Clay a kiss on the cheek.

His dad stood back a few steps to allow the women to share their congratulations. "Son, I never doubted you for a minute." He paused. "Well, maybe for a minute after your brilliance in the driveway. Seriously, you've shown all of us real courage and determination to overcome the odds you faced. Now, look at you, back to normal and speechless." His dad concluded with a brisk handshake and a burst of laughter.

Indeed, Clay stood speechless. Finally, he found a few words. "Thank you, but I never thought what happened deserved any celebration."

Vicky reached for her husband's hand. "Honey, I guess our celebration is not so much to remember the grim reality of that Saturday morning. It has much more to do with you." She moved closer to snuggle against Clay's shoulder. "You faced horrible odds for months as the infection held at bay all the antibiotics the doctors poured into you. Still you faced it all with courage and strength to continue fighting back, not giving up. That's worth celebrating."

"Son," his father stepped closer, "these last few months have seen you come to life. The glimmer in your eyes that evening you mounted your bike for the first time since the amputation reminded me of that little boy who entered the world of cyclists on a tiny bike with no training wheels. Your mother and I join Vicky in celebrating you."

In his search for words to express his thankfulness, he, again, struggled to hold back tears. He moved forward to embrace the three most important people in his life. All he could find to say, all he needed to say was "Thank you."

Finally, from the entry, the small group moved to the living room where a large package lay next to the sofa chair that served Clay so many weeks as he fought the infection or recovered from the amputation. He walked with pride and dignity to that chair and bent down to inspect the package and to note the wrappings came from his bike shop. He kneeled to touch the large package, turning his head to look at his wife and parents standing in the middle of the living room.

"What have you done now? You didn't buy some silly thing at the bike shop?"

"Yes, we did," asserted his mother. "It's not silly either."

"Come on. Open it," his dad commanded in his most authoritative voice.

"What do you think, Vicky? You must be a part of this."

Vicky simply shrugged her shoulders.

Clay reached down to grab a corner of the wrapping paper. Under that he found a box representing one of the bike shop's most expensive suppliers of fine biking clothing. He eyed his family with suspicion, ripped off the wrapping, and slid his fingers along one edge of the cover. Opening the cover, he sat back with a gasp. Inside lay one of the most expensive riding jackets his shop stocked. Costing nearly three hundred dollars, the jacket served a cyclist with convenience and comfort for those late fall and early spring rides.

Clay sat back on haunches, looked up at his wife and parents, a wide smile lighting his face. "You know I could have used this years ago. I can still use it but not as much. My winter riding I need to cut just a little."

"Try it on," urged his mother.

Standing up, Clay grabbed the jacket in both hands to study it more carefully. It truly was a beautiful garment. He slipped it on to discover it fit perfectly. "Thank you all so much. Over the years I will think about this time whenever I wear it."

His parents stepped close, together, embracing their son in a firm hug. His mom, furtively wiping away a tear, stretched to place a kiss on her son's cheek. "I love you, son. You don't know how happy we are seeing you back to yourself."

Clay's dad gave his son a firm tug on the shoulder. "You, know, Clay, when I think about the stunt you played on the driveway months ago, I doubted you would ever walk normally again. Seeing you now erases all that doubt."

"Thank you both for all the time you cared for me or just listened to my complaints. Things have worked out much better than I could ever imagine."

Vicky stood aside observing Clay and his parents. She smiled, even at a distance, feeling the love and affection emanating from their relationship. When Clay's parents moved back opening the way for Vicky to approach her husband, she moved slowly toward him, a smirk slightly twisting her lips. Standing directly in front of Clay, she grasped his hands, holding them out to each side. The smirk evolved into her classic smile.

"Sweetheart, you can't imagine how proud I am, we all are, of what you have done. What a thrill to watch you walk again and to ride your bike again." She stopped, placing Clay's hands on her shoulders. For an instant she looked away, as if searching for what to say. Turning to look directly into her husband's dark eyes, in a firm voice, she said, "Honey, we have something else to celebrate on this day." Taking a deep breath and releasing it slowly, she announced, "I'm pregnant."

The sound of applause faded as Clay prepared to meet a customer just walking into the shop. Since Vicky's announcement, the applause echoed in his head. He found impossible thinking about much else other than the prospect of becoming a father. His recovery consumed so much of the previous two years simply thinking about fatherhood proved a marvelous diversion and just a little intimidating.

Clay rescued himself from his thoughts, directing his attention to the recently arrived customer. The day moved by fast, as most of them did even though winter approached, and biking for many people would end until spring. At the conclusion of the day, Clay decided he would stop by the fitness center for a quick workout to loosen muscles tightened during a day when he spent so much of it on his feet.

CHAPTER 30

Previously, Miles never worried much about any aspect of his life except, perhaps, keeping his pickup clean and filled with gas. Recently, however, various concerns crowded the narrow confines of his life by himself. After the last argument with his dad about money and about his dad's favorite topic, ambition, Miles refused to crawl back to work in his dad's office, the only job he ever had. His refusal resulted in the near depletion of his money. Besides the money, the damned poster whining about a hit and run accident involving a biker haunted him more each day.

Sitting on his sofa with the standard beer in hand, Miles attempted to analyze the basis for his worry. Had the so called witness shot her mouth off even after his threats? Had anyone in that damned bike shop turned up incriminating evidence against him? How that could ever happen he had no idea. His thoughts just ran unbridled. What about his white pickup? The witness confirmed that she saw the white pickup hit the biker. What occurred to him suddenly was the realization he rarely saw another white pickup around his apartment building or around the town of Long Lake where he lived. Could that cause him problems? Should he get rid of the pick up, the vehicle he admired most of all those he drove over the years? Not used to facing issues like these, Miles did what he was used to doing; he got up to walk to the fridge for another beer.

The several threads of his life that now caused him mild anguish combined with a near paralyzing boredom drove Miles to head for the fitness center to release some of the tension imprisoned in his body. The few times he worked out there did give him a sense of relief and a satisfaction that the work outs were giving him back his body, at least slowing the sag.

Miles stood up from his sofa, stretched, emptied the beer can, and tossed it into the sink. Quickly, he left his apartment, jumped into his pickup for the short drive to the fitness center. Once there, he, as usual, parked where he assumed no one could scratch or dent his Cadillac. He entered the center to discover several men, even a few women working out on the various machines. He signed in on the booklet at the reception desk along with the time. Why the place required that time business, Miles couldn't image. To him what time he arrived shouldn't make any difference as long as he paid his dues. He never considered that maybe someone without a membership would attempt to use the facilities.

Though it made little difference, Miles noticed the name directly above his, Clay Pennell. He probably noticed it because it was not a familiar name to him. Reaching for a towel handed to him by the receptionist, he headed for his favorite apparatus, selecting as a part of his routine that equipment designed to enhance upper body muscles and strength.

As Miles dedicated himself to his workout, Clay sat on the seat of one of the stationary bikes he grew so accustomed to over the past months. The man who just arrived, Miles, caught Clay's attention for no reason other than he qualified as one of the biggest persons in the center. With a bulging chest and muscular arms and thighs nearly the size the Clay's waist, Clay questioned why this guy needed the services of the fitness center. Wasn't he big enough already?

Clay chuckled to himself, attending again to his stationary bike. Only six minutes to go to complete the thirty minute set. He studied the timer embedded in the panel between the handle bars. Time never advanced so slowly than when he rode this stationary bike. Eventually, the digital timer clicked to zero. Clay stepped off the bike, retrieved a paper towel, sprayed it with a special disinfectant, then wiped off the stationary bike on which he just finished his work out.

Clay deposited his towel in the container positioned for that purpose, moved to the reception desk to sign out. He signed his name along with the time. The name Miles Hunter was written just below his. As the name Clay Pennell meant nothing to Miles,

Miles Hunter meant nothing to Clay. Little did they realize how much they shared of each other's life.

Deciding to skip a shower at the center, Clay stepped outside in the very chilly, autumn late afternoon. He stood for a moment searching for his car. Of course, it stood nearly concealed between two big SUV's. Advancing toward his Mazda, he looked up to notice a white pickup parked in a far corner of the lot. His memory told him he saw a white pickup before in this parking lot. Did it make any difference that someone who worked out drove a white pick up? Clay shook his head, thinking he would have to get over this obsession with white pickups. Yes, he would not easily give up the search for his hit and run driver; however, this hang up on white pickups would have to cease sometime.

Sliding behind the wheel of his car, Clay noted the big guy with the muscular arms and legs emerge from the center. Clay sat, watching what kind of vehicle he drove. Would it be a big one for a big man? Clay laughed.

Without hesitation, without a glance one way or another, the man walked briskly to the white pickup parked by itself. As he left, the design of the parking lot forced Clay to drive right in front of the white pickup. Two eyes surrounded by long hair bore down on Clay as he made his way out of the parking lot. He averted the stare. Still, a tiny shiver skipped through his stomach.

CHAPTER 31

"Mom, how come I'm not getting any better?" Jamie lay on the living room sofa, a plastic pail placed beneath him in case the vomiting persisted. For several days, he fought severe cramps that soon produced diarrhea. Another trip to the doctor resulted in a reminder that E. coli infection responded to few treatments. Robin diligently forced him to drink as much liquid as he could tolerate. Dehydration was a sinister companion of E. coli poisoning.

Despite Robin's careful administration to all her son's needs, he failed to improve. She needed to work her regular hours; consequently her mother assumed the responsibility for him during most of the day when Robin worked at the hospital. Even at work, her mind rarely left thinking about her son and how his day was going. Frequent calls told her that not much had changed; the diarrhea rendered Jamie weak and listless. His loss of appetite only compounded his condition.

Robin's position at the hospital and her training made her more aware of the potential dangers of E. coli poisoning. In consultation with Jamie's doctor she reviewed the virulent repercussions of the infection and the damage it could do to the kidneys. Her knowledge of the potential effects only made her more concerned with the passage of each day and no discernible improvement in her son's condition. That condition kept Jamie home from school away from other kids mainly because he was too sick to attend but also because victims of E. coli infection are extremely contagious.

Robin tried to contain her fears, to suppress the panic she felt invading her life. She needed patience to allow Jamie's body to fight the infection. Of course, she took pride in her son's ability to deal with the infection's assault on his body. Rarely did he complain to his mother or his grandmother as they did whatever they could to make him comfortable. His asking if he would ever get better only contributed to their helplessness that grew more pronounced with the passing of each day.

Robin's responsibility as a parent extended beyond her care for her son. She frequently checked with his friend who also suffered from the horrible infection. Though he improved some from the early onset of the infection, he still battled diarrhea and a low fever. She also pursued contact with the restaurant where, she assumed, both boys contacted the E. coli infection. They reported no further knowledge of customers falling victim to the infection and offered to assist her in anyway possible. Sadly, the infection left little to do except trust that young bodies could successfully combat it with time.

That time now stretched to nearly two full weeks. Over the years Robin occasionally entertained the thought of trying to contact Jamie's father. That she lied to her son about his father bothered her. That she had no idea what happened to Clay Pennell always left her feeling guilty. The twelve years she and Jamie shared life included no serious illnesses or conflicts or problems that she couldn't deal with by herself. The current condition of her son forced her for the first time to confront a serious problem. Having the chance to share the problem with his father would spare her some of the strain she experienced. Yes, her parents offered substantial help in watching over Jamie. Still, that did not compare to the influence, she envisioned, the presence of a father would have.

The evening included her parents who prepared dinner for themselves and Robin. Still, Jamie ate very little as the infection tightened its grip on his young body. During much of the evening he rested on the living room sofa where he spent most of his time the last few days. The dinner included a conversation between Robin and her parents about Jamie's prognosis and again about the chance of contacting his father. As for the prognosis, the last visit to the doctor revealed little improvement in Jamie's condition. The longer his body gave in to the infection the greater the chance of adverse effects on the kidneys. Fear and doubt dragged that part of the conversation to a quick conclusion. They simply found no comfort in discussing something they knew little about.

The conversation about contacting Jamie's father generated a lengthy debate with Robin uncertain what to do and her parents convinced that she should make some attempt to contact him if for no other reason than to determine if he still exists. Even hinting about death disturbed Robin, who, in her job as an LPN, confronted death far too often. Eventually, the conversation strayed from issues too difficult to discuss in detail to an attention to the details of the next day which included Robin's mother returning to watch over her grandson while his mother worked.

After her parents departed, Robin kneeled on the carpet in front of where her son lay on the sofa. He opened his eyes to look at his mother.

"I'm sorry, mom. I'm such a bother. I know you don't know." Jamie licked his dry lips. "Does any one know how long this stuff lasts?"

Holding back the tears, Robin reached for his hand made frail by days of little food and abundant liquid. "Sweetheart, you don't have to be sorry for anything. That's what mothers are for. To take care of their big boys."

"I suppose, but you have to work too. It just doesn't seem fair." He weakly squeezed his mother's hand resting on his arm. He moved his head to stare into the ceiling. "Why can't the doctors do something to get me better?"

"Honey, they're doing all they can do. Getting over this might take a long time. We have to try to be strong and patient."

Again looking at his mom, he asked, "When will I get to go to school and play soccer?"

"We have to make sure all the infection is gone first before doing anything like that. Soon, though, maybe you can think about getting back to normal. Now, you need to try to get some rest."

"Mom, all I've done for a last few days is rest."

"I know. But it is the best medicine for you right now." She reached to brush his hair from his forehead.

For a short time she messaged his neck and shoulders, trying to provide as much comfort as she should. In the two weeks since he first got sick, he had eaten little. Vomiting and diarrhea discouraged it. He drank as much liquid as he could tolerate. The rigors of the infection drained Jamie of energy leaving him weak and pale. Gently rubbing his back and shoulders, she thought of the earlier discussion with her parents. Should she attempt to contact Clay? What would learning of a living father do to Jamie's confidence in his mother who over years repeatedly told him a bicycle accident killed his father?

Jamie dosed off into a light sleep while his mother continued messaging his back and shoulders. She watched, the rhythm of his breathing assuring her he had fallen asleep. She then rose from her place on the carpet before the sofa and walked to where a lap top computer sat on a small desk in one corner of the dining room.

She sat down in front of the computer, opened the cover and stared at the screen which contained a full picture of Jamie in his soccer uniform. Should she try to find something about Clay Pennell online? Not well versed in computer searches, she possessed little confidence she could find out anything about a person who did not enjoy celebrity status. At least she didn't think Clay was a celebrity.

Staring at the screen, she decided she had little to lose simply trying to discover if she could find out anything about Jamie's dad from the computer. Online she typed in "identity search" on the Google search line. Immediately, several web sites emerged that all contained something about identity. She selected one of them.

The site popped up on the screen claiming to have the answer to everyone's search. She clicked on the "get started" line. That took her to a screen which included details of what this site offered. For $25.00, the website claimed, a comprehensive search would certainly identify the person looked for. Robin studied the screen. Could she afford to waste $25.00 on something she knew very little about? The countless times she thought of searching for Clay now convinced her she had nothing to lose trying it.

The credit card data completed, she followed the directions printed on the screen. She typed in the name "Clay Pennell." Across the screen appeared the precaution, "Searching. Do not revert to previous screen." She sat captivated by what she attempted to do. In a few seconds a list of names filled the screen, every name the same "Clay Pennell." She muffled a gasp as she stared at the screen. Her eyes studied the list of names which included varying amounts of data for each entry. She started down the list of eleven names with locations from Montana to New Hampshire. She always considered Clay's last name a very uncommon one. Maybe she was wrong. Three listings placed Clay Pennells in Minnesota, only one in Minneapolis.

Robin's heart beat a little faster as nerves tingled at the back of her neck. What would she do if, at last, she found him and his phone number? All the old questions that haunted her for years circled around her mind as she stared at the computer screen. With unsteady fingers she placed the cursor on top of the Clay Pennell listed in Minneapolis.

CHAPTER 32

Driving home, Clay failed to erase that stare from his mind. Could some connection exist between his accident and that particular white pickup? His adjustment to his artificial foot helped return him to a life much like before the accident. It also softened his passion to find the hit and run culprit. Not that he no longer thought about the white pickup, he simply thought about it less frequently and with less intensity. However, the recent engagement with a white pickup renewed some of that intensity.

When Clay entered the house, Vicky greeted him from the kitchen. Vicky's presence when he returned from a day at the bike shop always made his day complete. Since the announcement of her pregnancy, Vicky trimmed the number of hours she spent at work. The excitement of her imminent motherhood spread through the office staff as well as the sales staff. Already during breaks and at lunch time, the conversation drifted toward names for a baby girl or a baby boy. At only two months, Vicky did not know the baby's gender. Both she and Clay were not sure they wanted to know. That didn't quiet the speculation or the suggestions for a name.

"How was your day?" Vicky asked when Clay walked into the kitchen to give his wife a gentle hug. Since learning of her condition, Clay exercised great care whenever he approached her. She laughingly reminded him that pregnancy didn't make her an invalid. It didn't matter. He insisted on treating her like one.

"Busy as usual. I sometimes find it hard to believe how many people bike through the fall and winter."

Vicky moved back to the sink where she washed vegetables. "That's good, isn't it?"

"It certainly is." Clay pulled out a chair from the kitchen table, sat down, and crossed his legs. "When I left the fitness place today, a funny thing happened."

Vicky turned to face her husband. "Really, what was that?"

"I drove right in front of a big white pickup. Now, I know there are many white pickups around here. You also know my thing about white pickups." He shifted his position on the chair placing both feet on the floor. "It was the guy in the pickup which spooked me just a little."

Vicky moved closer to the table. "What did he do?"

"Well, he really didn't do anything except stare at me in kind of a scary way. His look in just those few seconds of eye contact made me feel like some kind of intruder or something."

"What did he look like? Was he a big guy?"

"I'm not sure. I think I know which guy he is from catching a glimpse of him walking to his pickup. If I'm right, yes he is a big guy and working to get bigger apparently."

"Do you really want to get involved like this?" Vicky asked.

Clay leaned back on his chair. "I don't know, probably not, at least until I have more evidence. Just because he drives a white pickup doesn't mean he was the one who ran me off the road." Clay stood up from his place by the table and approached his wife. "We haven't enjoyed that real, daily hug today." He carefully wrapped his arms around Vicky's shoulders, very tentative in how much strength he put into the hug.

Less concerned about her condition, Vicky pulled her husband against her. She tilted her head back smiling up at Clay. "Loosen up. Like I said before, you don't have to treat me like some kind of invalid. I like those strong, reassuring hugs you're so good at."

Clay laughed. "I know. I'm so proud of you, of us. I don't want to do anything to change what we've started."

Standing embraced in the middle of the kitchen floor, Vicky and Clay shared happiness that had nearly escaped them while he battled the infection and subsequent amputation. Now all of that lay in the past, replaced by a bright future that in seven more months would include a baby.

Clay released his arms, letting them drop to his sides. A troubled looked crossed his face. "Another thing about the white pickup, I'm sorry for bringing it up again, is the mystery surrounding the recent hit and run not far from the bike shop. It's just too coincidental for two accidents involving a white pickup and guys on bikes to happen in the same area separated by only a few months."

Vicky placed her hand on Clay's arm. "I agree, but I also think you need to relax a little for now until something comes up that would offer some answers. Right now you need to concentrate on you, on us, all three of us. Let's hope that someday you will find the answers you look for."

Clay reached for his wife, again pulling her toward him and placing a serious kiss on those beautiful lips, to him the most kissable in the Midwest.

CHAPTER 33

In the weeks since that historic moment when Clay mounted his bike for the first ride with an artificial foot, he tried to ride each day or, at least, as often as he could. At times, he did ride the approximate five miles to work at the bike shop. At other times he rode around his neighborhood, a more complicated, more risky ride on streets heavily traveled. With the approach of autumn, weather prohibited the frequency of his rides. While in the past, cold weather offered little resistance to Clay's daily rides. Now, all that he went through with his leg, the amputation and the prosthesis changed that, and it didn't have only to do with his physical condition. More important was the psychological repercussion of the accident and the damage it did.

For over thirty years Clay had ridden a bike with skill and confidence, always feeling in control and always comfortable balancing on two wheels. The excitement of his return to biking shadowed any change in his security on a bike. However, with each successive ride, Clay confronted a slight insecurity when on the bike. Not even long ago when his dad removed training wheels did he experience insecurity. To face it now shocked him.

His rides found him tense about traffic around him, about meeting other bikers, about bicycle or automobile traffic behind him, and about the condition of the road in front of him. He tried riding more often on the many bike trails carved out around Lake Minnetonka and the greater Twin Cities area. However, he found the wide variety of trail users only more intimidating. Though he continued to ride, he did so with increased caution, a condition which reduced the enjoyment he derived from an activity he used as an escape and a major form of exercise most of this life.

He discussed with Vicky the problem with his riding. She suggested that eventually he would overcome the apprehension. Just give it some time. After all he went through with the leg, returning comfortably to biking might take some time. Clay found consolation in his wife's words. Nonetheless, riding with such caution bothered him. Combined with the arrival of autumn weather, this mistrust of his biking skill compelled him to spend more time at the fitness center riding the stationary bike. At least this would help him maintain his physical condition if not help him sooth the psychological one. What at first involved simply testing his prosthetic foot and strengthening his legs, his visits to the fitness center, presently, served as the major source of his exercise.

At least three or four times a week Clay visited the center, usually after his day at the bike shop. Eventually those visits brought him in indirect contact with Miles Hunter and the white pickup. Of course, he did not know Miles Hunter. He knew, though, that this burly man drove a white pickup and commanded a threatening stare which Clay discovered on his last visit to the fitness center.

Two days after his discussion with Vicky about the man in the white pickup, Clay returned to the fitness center following work. He signed in and found a seat in a small changing area of the center. He didn't need to use the locker room or the shower. Consequently, he used the area that provided two large sofas for customer's changing shoes or removing jackets.

Changing shoes for Clay involved more than simply slipping out of street shoes and slipping into athletic shoes. For him it entailed changing his entire foot, the one with the street shoe exchanged with the one with the athletic shoe. Clay made this change quickly and inconspicuously. He wished to avoid an explanation of what happened.

Clay secured his usual stationary bike, set the time, the program, and the resistance. For the next thirty minutes, he pedaled vigorously, giving his legs and his cardiovascular system a strenuous workout. At the conclusion of the thirty minutes, he spent a few minutes on three other strengthening machines. Finally, he walked back to the changing area where he left his coat and street shoes. In one of the sofas sat the burly guy who drove the white pickup.

Clay reached for the athletic bag containing his street shoes and took the vacant sofa. He greeted with a smile the white pickup guy who nodded in response, his eyes locked in a stare at Clay's foot. Undaunted by the guy's fixation on his foot, Clay made the change to his street shoes.

"What happened to your foot?" The abrupt question took Clay by surprise.

Clay looked up from securing his prosthetic foot. "An accident."

Assuming the end of the conversation, Clay stood up to put on his jacket.

"How'd it happen?" The guy asked.

"A biking accident." Clay replied.

The answer produced a noticeable effect. He mumbled, "Sorry," and quickly moved away toward the strengthening machines.

Clay paused briefly, dismissing the guy's reaction as nothing more than curiosity. He grabbed his athletic bag and moved to the desk where customers signed in and out. Signing his name, Clay noticed just below his the name, Miles Hunter. Since he did not notice any other people enter the fitness center while he worked out, Clay assumed that the big guy very likely was Miles Hunter.

Stepping out into the fading light of early evening, Clay stopped abruptly. He recalled the guy's flicker of awareness in his response to Clay's comment about a bike accident. He glanced around the parking lot for the white pickup. In a far corner of the lot it sat nearly isolated. Clay approached the pickup close enough to note the license number, LOT 986. What he would do with the license number he wasn't sure. However, it might deserve some checking with the sheriff's department. Clay walked to his car, considering what to do next if anything.

CHAPTER 34

When Clay pulled into his driveway, he parked behind a gray Lexus with Wisconsin plates. His in-laws had arrived for an unexpected visit, at least unexpected for him. He sat for a moment staring at the gray Lexus, a symbol of a successful farmer. He ran his hand through his hair, smiled, and shook his head.

Vicky's parents from the beginning harbored reservations about the suitability of Clay for their supreme daughter. Hanging around a bike shop all day did not impress them as a career with any future. Vicky's success as a student and an athlete, her drive and determination elevated her in the eyes of her parents to heights far exceeding a normal child-parent relationship. Her quick rise in the corporate world only reinforced their confidence and pride in their daughter.

Stepping out onto the driveway, Clay paused, thinking about the first time he met Vicky's parents. It happened on a bright, warm mid summer day more than ten years ago. Since she and Clay had dated for several weeks, Vicky met Clay's parents frequently due partially to their proximity at the time to Clay's apartment. On this bright day, Vicky convinced Clay they should take the short drive to central Wisconsin to meet her parents. Clay agreed, believing that meeting her parents marked another step in their expanding relationship.

Clay remembered that short drive into the heart of Wisconsin dairy country, that first glimpse of the farm on which Vicky grew up. A beautiful two story house commanded immediate attention with its porch encircling three sides of the house decorated with glistening white spindle fencing. Scattered around the farm yard three large structures served Edwin and Gail Dumont's flourishing dairy business.

As Clay and Vicky pulled up to the parking areas in front of the house, her parents stood on the porch waiting their arrival. A large, imposing man, Edwin Dumont took his success seriously. Following years of hard work on the dairy farm, Edwin stood tall and robust, product of many bright summers either in the fields or tending to his vast herd of dairy cattle. Vicky's mom, Gail, stood proudly beside her husband watching carefully as their daughter brought home the man she might marry someday.

Corrigible welcomes greeted Clay and Vicky, her parents graciously inviting them into the house where Gail prepared a light lunch before Edwin insisted on taking them on a tour of his dairy enterprise. As the four of them walked from one building to the next to observe the milking, the feeding, and cleaning processes, Edwin asked Clay about his career. Clay explained his connection to a bike shop in suburban Minneapolis. From the first moment of explanation, Clay sensed skepticism from both Vicky's parents. Subtle glances at each other conveyed to Clay that they likely didn't approve of their daughter associating with a man who spent his time selling and repairing bikes. Ever since that first experience with her parents, Clay never overcame the feeling that Vicky's parents considered him less than a good match for their daughter.

Since that bright, summer day, Edwin and Gail made frequent trips to Minneapolis to visit their daughter and ultimately to visit her and their son-in-law. They offered their support during Clay's long recovery from the bike accident. However, even then he didn't feel comfortable around them. Now with the impending arrival of their first grandchild, they likely would continue to make frequent visits to check on their daughter and maybe even their son in law.

Again a shake of the head brought Clay back to the reality of his driveway and the need to greet his in-laws. Entering the house, Clay walked into the living room where Vicky and her parents sat. Edwin rose to shake hands with his son-in-law. Clay stepped to where Gail sat, and bent down to give her a slight kiss on the cheek in greeting. Vicky rose to give her husband a hug. He gently responded, again displaying that caution accompanying his movements around his wife.

"Sweetheart, you don't have to be so careful around me. I won't break." Vicky laughed.

"Yeah, okay," Clay turned to find a place to sit next to Edwin on the sofa. "How did your appointment go with Dr. Price?"

Seated again, Vicky moved forward in her chair. "She said everything looks good. The fetus is now nearly seven weeks old. She estimated a delivery date about July 14th."

"Maybe we could shoot for July 4." Edwin announced, looking around the room at each person as if to assess reactions to his humor.

"Not even you have that power." Gail, with a grin, reminded her husband. She then turned her attention to Vicky. "What will you do about your job as you approach delivery?"

"Clay and I have already talked about that. Also I've discussed it with Madison. We agree that I will continue to work as long as I can. After delivery, I can take as much time as I want, within reason, before returning to work."

"Do you ever expect to leave your job and accept the role of a stay-at-home mom?" Gail asks.

Vicky exhaled briefly, looked over at her husband, then at her mother. "We've discussed that too. Definitely, I want to continue with my job." She paused, folding her hands in her lap. "It all depends on what happens after the baby arrives. We just don't know much about the world of parenthood. For now we are taking one day, one week, and one month at a time."

The discussion turned briefly to Clay, his foot, and his position at the bike shop where little had changed. Soon a silence hung over the living room. Clay moved restlessly, considering if he should introduce the subject of Miles Hunter and the white pickup. "Can I get anybody anything, water, beer, wine?"

"Yeah, I'll have a beer," announced Vicky's dad.

To Gail, Clay asked, "How about a glass of wine?"

Gail looked up at Clay, deciding what she wanted. "That's fine."

To Vicky, he said with a chuckle, "You can have only water."

"Thanks," she replied.

With everyone settled with a beverage, Clay introduced the subject of the big muscular guy at the fitness center who drove a white pickup. He explained his suspicions, tracing the several times he came in contact with him. Reference to the brief conversation with the guy about his prosthetic foot produced increased interest from his wife and in laws.

"How did that conversation come up?" Vicky asked.

"He stood near me when I changed shoes. He asked how it happened? I told him." Clay explained.

"What did he say?"

Clay ran his hand through his hair, glanced at the floor in thought. "He seemed a bit disturbed. He made no comment. Just turned and walked away. A few steps away, he turned quickly to look back at me. I don't know. It just seemed a bit suspicious."

"What can you do about your suspicion?" Edwin asked.

Clay hesitated before answering. With a slight shake of his head, he said, "I don't know right off hand. I thought of contacting the sheriff's office. I've talked to people in that office before. I do have a license number." He stared into space, deep in thought. He looked directly at his wife. "Remember, Vicky, I told you about the older lady I met on a recent ride. She described to me an accident she witnessed, the one we read about in the paper, another hit and run involving a white pickup."

"Yes, I remember."

"Well," Clay continued, "she talked about seeing a partial license number. Something she reported to the sheriff's office. She said she remembered a L and a 9. The plate on the pickup in the fitness center parking lot is LOT 986, not exactly incriminating but a start."

Vicky set her water glass down on the small table next to her chair. "If you do call the sheriff, you really need something concrete to report."

"I think a license number is pretty concrete." Clay paused to look at each person in the room. "You know, I just want to find out about this guy. For nearly three years this white pickup has haunted me. This guy where I workout behaves suspiciously in my opinion. I think maybe the sheriff's office might offer some help."

"We understand completely." Vicky's mother echoed the sentiments of the others.

Silence returned to the living room. "By the way, Clay, mom and dad have volunteered to take us out for dinner this evening." Vicky rose to ask if anyone wanted more to drink.

"That's great with me," Clay replied as he, too, rose to assist Vicky in refilling beverages.

Later that night after dinner and good byes to Vicky's parents who insisted on returning home rather than staying for the night, Clay lay in bed unable to fall asleep thinking again about Miles Hunter, the white pickup and the sheriff.

CHAPTER 35

Miles sat hunched over in the tight living room of his apartment. The conversation with the guy at the fitness center who had an artificial foot bothered him. What did this guy know about Miles? Could he have been the one he hit so long ago? He stood up with difficulty, his exercising stiffening muscles not accustomed to strenuous workouts. He reached for the fridge door to secure another can of beer, always a source of comfort for Miles.

Would he have to do something about this guy he met at the fitness center? He never did get his name. Would the ridiculous accident with a stupid cyclist never vanish from his mind? Happily, he had not heard anything about the more recent run in with a biker. Nor had his attitude toward the sissies who rode bikes changed. They simply didn't belong on the same road as pickups.

Slouched back on the sagging sofa, Miles searched for something to watch on TV. Recently, he spent considerable time watching TV since he no longer could tolerate working in his dad's law office. Not even the TV could distract his attention away from the discussion with the footless guy. He would have to talk to him more about the accident and when it happened. Nonetheless, Miles couldn't believe in any repercussions for him even if he was responsible for the guy's lost foot.

Still he worried. What if the authorities connected him to both accidents? What about altering his license plate number? Could that get him into more trouble? Of course, his dad could answer that. He just would not lower himself to ask. Could he eventually lose his driver's license? Could he really spend time in jail? All these questions swirled around his head, questions he thought he would never have to think about again.

With growing anger and resentment, Miles tossed his beer can across the room, beer spattering on the wall and on the floor. He vowed he would talk to this foot guy the next time he saw him at the fitness center.

CHAPTER 36

With her computer curser centered on the only Clay Pennell listed in Minneapolis, Robin breathed deeply and clicked the mouse. She sat transfixed waiting for the computer to acknowledge her command. In an instant the name Clay Pennell appeared on the screen followed by a phone number and a reference to his job in a bike shop. She slouched back in her chair, staring at the computer screen. Did she have the right Clay Pennell? That he worked at a bike shop offered some confirmation.

For just minutes Robin retreated twelve years to that night in the small community park where her son was conceived in one of the most bizarre moments in her life. With extreme effort she tried to visualize what Clay looked like after the passage of all those years. Would he have gotten married? Did he have a family? Did he still just work at the bike shop? So many questions tumbled through her mind already clogged with concern for her sick son.

Robin reached for a pencil and paper on which she recorded the limited information before her on the computer screen. Shutting down the computer, she stood, looking into the empty space above the computer screen. Vivid in her mind appeared the recent discussion with her parents regarding the decision to contact Clay. To her, how could she now confess to her son the reality of a living father? For years she told him that his father perished in a bicycle accident. How could her son ever trust her again if she lied to him about his dad?

Jamie through the years conducted himself admirably, always respectful to his mother and grandparents, always willing to do his homework as well as the few jobs around the house without complaint, always excited about playing soccer, and often inquisitive about the father he never knew. Now Robin faced betraying her son. What would knowing his father lived despite what his mother told him all his short life do to her young son whom she loved deeply?

Deeply distressed, Robin walked slowly to her bedroom. On the way she checked quietly on her son who, for now, slept comfortably in his bed. Before the computer search, learning Clay's phone number or his address, she assumed, would allay some of her concern about contacting him. It had not. She only faced more questions, more indecision. Exhausted, she sat on her bed, tired but reluctant to lie down only to stare into the darkness of her bedroom.

By morning she had captured a few minutes of restless sleep. The night eased none of her concerns about Clay and about her son. She quickly visited her son's bedroom. He lay awake.

"How do you feel this morning?" Robin reached down to touch her son's forehead.

Pale and weak from the many days of his battle with the relentless infection, Jamie managed a weak smile, "About the same, I guess." He raised himself up to rest on his elbow, looked up as his mother, and posed the question he asked frequently, "Mom, will I ever get better?"

Robin kneeled down to take her son's face in her hands. "Of course, you will get better. We just have to be patient. You have a serious infection that will take the body and your medication a while to fight. Tomorrow we visit the doctor again to see if things have changed. Today your grandmother will stay with you while I'm at work. Okay?"

Lying back down in his bed, Jamie replied, "I guess so. I'd rather go to school and see my friends."

"I know you would, sweetheart. Maybe soon you will be able to do that. Right now, though, you need your rest and a little breakfast. What would you like?"

Jamie furrowed his brow, thinking about breakfast. His appetite during his infection had dwindled to a desire for very little. "Maybe a piece of toast and some juice." He paused to look up at his mother again. "Can I eat in the kitchen?"

Robin fought the tears gathering in the corners of her eyes. "Sure you can if you want to." She reached for his arm to help him up out of his bed.

Rejecting the gesture of assistance, he swung his feet over the side of his bed. Sitting on the edge of the bed, he reminded his mom, "I can do it alone."

"Okay, I'll go put the bread in the toaster."

Following his brief breakfast, Jamie returned to his bedroom where he lay back in his bed prepared to spend most of his day there. Shortly after his return to his room, his grandmother arrived to start her day watching over her grandson. Sitting around the kitchen table Robin and her mother shared a cup of coffee.

"How is he doing this morning?" Neena asked her daughter.

Robin shook her head. "Not much different from before, I'm afraid."

She explained to her mother her success in apparently finding Clay's phone number.

"That's great. Did you call it?" Her mother asked with obvious excitement.

"No, not yet." She admitted. "I still am not sure it would be the best thing to do right now. Jamie has enough to deal with."

"I agree, but he doesn't have to know about the attempted contact, does he?"

"Probably not." Robin hung her head, moving her coffee cup in a small circle. "I can't imagine the shock to Jamie if he discovers that all his life I've lied to him about his father."

Neena reached across the table to touch her daughter's hand. "I understand, but we have to decide what's best under the circumstances."

Robin nodded in agreement. "Tomorrow we visit the doctor again to check on the progress of this thing. We've talked before about the risk of kidney damage if this infection can't be contained soon. If that ever happens, we may not have a choice but to contact Clay. I hate to think about it, but Jamie could need a transplant."

Silence settled over the kitchen table as mother and grandmother considered the consequences of Jamie needing a kidney transplant. Suddenly, Robin rose and pushed back her chair. "I do need to get to work. Are you okay with the day here? I've written a brief note on the counter which explains what to do."

"I think I know. Don't worry. I can handle it here. You get to work and I'll talk to you later."

Robin made a last check on her son, who had fallen asleep. She gave her mother a hug before heading for the garage and the short drive to work. A hint of resolve emerged as she drove, thinking she would make a decision about calling Clay Pennell after tomorrow's appointment with the doctor. Certainly for the sake of her son but also for her sake she needed someone to share her deep concern about Jamie's future. Yes, her parents offered some comfort. However, a father needs to know the condition of his son and needs to share with the mother the pain of watching that young son suffer. However, before the father can give comfort and support, he needs to know he has a son.

CHAPTER 37

Clay awoke in the morning convinced of his need to contact, again, the sheriff's office about the white pickup and a person named Miles Hunter. Before leaving for the office, Vicky agreed with Clay's decision. Previous contacts with the sheriff's office included talking with a Stewart Cook. When Clay completed his morning routine, shower, shave, dress for work, and a good breakfast, he sat before the desk in the small office he and Vicky shared. He paged through their personal address book in search of the phone number for the Hennepin County Sheriff's office.

Dialing the number, Clay quickly reviewed exactly his purpose in making the call. He simply had to know about the white pickup, its license number and someone named Miles Hunter.

"Good morning, how may I help you?" The same gentle female voice he heard on previous calls reduced the slight tension Clay felt as he held the phone to his ear.

"Yes, my name is Clay Pennell. I've spoken with officer Cook before regarding a hit and run biking accident I suffered about three years ago. I wonder if he is available."

Yes, he is. May I ask the reason for your call?"

"I have a couple questions I want to ask him about the accident." Clay explained.

"Thank you. I'll transfer your call."

As he waited, Clay moved restlessly with his cell phone pressed against his ear.

"This is officer Cook. How may I help you?"

"Thank you for taking my call. I'm Clay Pennell. I talked to you in the past about a couple hit and run biking accidents."

"Sure, I remember you, Mr. Pennell. I recall you suffered some serious injuries. How are you doing?"

"Thank you for asking. I'm doing fine, even back on my bike weather permitting."

"That's great. How can I help you this morning?" Office Cook inquired.

"I think the last time we talked I asked about a more recent hit and run which involved, I think, a white pickup. Maybe you recall a white pickup was involved in my accident."

"Yes, I recall the discussion."

Clay asked, "Has anything happened with that investigation?"

Silence filled the phone connection. Then Officer Cook admitted, "Unfortunately, no. We've had no other leads except the partial license number mentioned by an assumed eye witness. These cases are difficult to deal with."

"I understand," Clay admitted. "Recently I've met up with a guy who makes me suspicious."

Clay briefly described his encounters with a man named Miles Hunter, who drives a white Cadillac Esclade pickup not unlike the vehicle he briefly glimpsed following his accident. He also explained the guy's strange reaction to learning just how Clay lost a foot. He added the information about the license number which he quoted as LOT 986. Finally, he mentioned his conversation with the eye witness and her recollection of a partial license number.

"I'm sorry to take up so much of your time, Officer, but I'm curious to find out if Miles Hunter really is the driver of a white pickup I see in the fitness center parking lot. Could you determine exactly what kind of vehicle has the plate number LOT 986?"

More silence dominated the phone connection. Then Officer Cook spoke. "You relate a very interesting story. I can appreciate your curiosity about this guy. I do wish to remind you, however, that current privacy laws do limit the kind of information we can disclose. Having said that, give me a minute to do a little search. You said the plate number is LOT 986?"

"Yes," Clay acknowledged, prepared to wait while Officer Cook did his search.

In only a couple minutes which to Clay seemed much longer, Officer Cook apologized for keeping him waiting. "Mr. Pennell, something interesting is going on here. The vehicle with the registration you gave me is not a pickup. It's a sedan. You did say LOT 986?"

"Yes, I did. I don't think I misread it in the parking lot."

"I don't know what happened here. I realize the registration process isn't perfect. Discrepancies like this don't happen very often. Give me a little more time. I think this demands some serious investigation." The officer suggested.

"Thank you. If you don't mind, could you do one more thing right now?"

"What do you have in mind?" the officer asked.

Clay cleared his throat. "Could you search under the name Miles Hunter to see what his registration number is if it is not the one I gave you?"

The officer chuckled. "I guess I can do that since I've already likely violated some part of privacy regulations."

Clay quickly announced, "Look, I don't want to get you into trouble. If you don't think you should do this, please don't."

"No, I think everything will be all right. Just give me another minute."

Clay waited patiently, shuffling from one foot to the other, for the moment again grateful he possessed two feet to shuffle.

"Thank you for waiting. What I gather about Mr. Hunter is a plate with the number LOT 926, close but not the same number you gave me. He is listed as the owner of a white, Cadillac pickup." Mr. Cook paused then continued. "Look, I'm bothered by this discrepancy. Why don't you let me pursue this, and I'll get back to you later?"

"Great. I thank you for your time and your cooperation. Maybe someday we can resolve this whole mystery."

"I hope so. But I'll get back to you as soon as I have something different to report. Anything else I can help you with?"

"No. Thank you so much for what you have done already. I'll expect to hear from you later."

"You're welcome. Glad I could help." Officer Cook wished Clay a good day and hung up.

Clay clicked off his cell phone. Stood for a moment contemplating the conversation he just had with the Officer Cook. It renewed his commitment to finding out someday who was responsible for his artificial foot.

With the conversation completed, Clay relaxed on his way out the door and his drive to work. Though the conversation answered few questions, it did reclaim the assistance of the Hennepin County Sheriff's office. That surely could help in solving the mystery of the whole thing.

Driving to work, Clay revisited the time he spent with the officer. What could have happened to create the license confusion?

Never before did he hear of the state or county making mistakes with vehicle registration. Did Miles Hunter switch plates with someone? Obviously, the plate on his pickup is not the one he should have. Clay grinned. Would attention to the accident ever lose its power to invade his thoughts? Looking down at his prosthetic foot gave him the answer.

His normal route to the bike shop took him through the small suburb of Long Lake. This morning along that route Clay saw a white pickup parked next to a small apartment complex. Though he drove by this complex nearly every morning on his way to and from work, he never previously noticed a large white pickup parked in the lot. Making a quick turn on the street next to the parking lot, Clay wanted to check out the license plate on the pickup. It read LOT 986, the same as the vehicle in the fitness parking lot.

Most of the day found Clay preoccupied with the Miles' pickup, license plate mystery. In the early afternoon, Officer Cook called to confirm for Clay the registration number for a Miles Hunter was LOT 926. The officer assured Clay the situation required further research. He had no further information to convey about either one of the hit and run bicycle accidents. Clay thanked him again and said he would wait for more information as it became available.

After work, Clay drove the short distance to the fitness center where in the parking lot sat the mysterious white pickup. Inside,

Clay engaged in his workout routine, with a furtive eye on Miles Hunter, who devoted most of his time to the weights. Walking to the drinking fountain in the far corner of the workout room, Clay met Miles returning to his weight machines.

Miles stared at Clay. He then held out his hand to stop him. Looking first into his face then down to Clay's artificial foot, Miles asked, "How did you say you lost your foot?"

With surprise at his bringing up the subject again, Clay turned to face Miles. "A biking accident about three years ago, a hit and run biking accident." Clay emphasized the hit and run part.

Miles said nothing. His eyes narrowed to a squint, they ran the entire length of Clay's body. He assumed a dismissive attitude toward Clay and returned to his weight machines. This behavior only added more mystery to an already mysterious situation. However, it also hinted something about who might have caused Clay's crash into the foliage lining the road that autumn morning.

Apparently agitated, Miles stormed out of the workout room without another glance at Clay. Less than a half hour later, Clay completed his workout, eager to return home to his wife and future mother of their baby. Enough time already for one day he devoted to Miles Hunter and the saga of the white pickup. His route home duplicated his route to work. This time, however, a large white pickup followed not far behind.

CHAPTER 38

"Mrs. Foster, I think its much too early to think about that. Right now he rests comfortably in the examination room. Yes, he has lost weight and carries the pallid look of someone fighting an infection. But he's a tough young man who is holding up pretty well." Dr. Luke Gardner sat behind his office desk responding to Robin's hint at the possibility of kidney failure for Jamie.

Robin moved restlessly in her chair stationed in front of the doctor's desk. She crossed her legs and folded her hands in her lap. "I know, but Jamie's not improved much in nearly three weeks. He still suffers nausea and eats very little. I've tried to keep him hydrated. He sometimes even resists that."

"You're doing all the right things. This infection can take time to combat." The doctor turned to a folder on his desk, opened it and scanned the document inside. "Blood tests today showed only a slight increase in blood stain waste. That's to be expected under the circumstances. We will monitor carefully the extent of blood waste which is an indication that the kidney isn't functioning as well as it should." He paused, closed the folder, and looked directly at Robin. "Of course, you know about these things as a nurse. Still that doesn't make dealing with the situation any easier. I understand your concern."

"What's the next step? Should I consider other strategies?" Robin pleaded with her hands.

"Right now, we should continue as we have. I'll want to see Jamie again next week to check his blood. If the blood test reveals no increase in waste, we will continue as we are for another week. If and when we discover an increase in waste, we will have to consider other treatments."

Robin sat up straight in her chair. "I guess that's what I want to know. What other treatments are there?"

Dr. Gardner placed his hands on top his desk. "Of course, we would engage in more thorough hydration and there is dialysis."

The mention of dialysis sounded an immediate alarm for Robin. She stiffened in her chair, emitting a slightly audible sigh.

"Don't let that alarm you. You know its purpose. It doesn't mean anything permanent, just helping the body get rid of waste the kidney can't handle. I think we need to consider that seriously. Jamie's kidneys, at present, aren't doing the job."

Robin understood dialysis. "Can that be done here?"

With a nod of his head, the doctor confirmed it could.

Robin sat silent absorbing what the doctor recommended while thinking about something only remotely related to Jamie's infection. Should she discuss the truth about Jamie's father? Should the doctor know the situation if Jamie did need a transplant?

Robin moved to the edge of her chair. She hesitated, searching for the best way to introduce the subject of Jamie's dad. "Doctor, you know Jamie's dad does not live with us."

"Yes, I believe I read that in one of Jamie's charts."

"I don't think it's necessary to go through specific details. Jamie's conception occurred under rather unusual circumstances which I don't chose to go into right now." Robin swallowed then continued. "The reason I bring up the subject is to ask your advice. Do you think I should contact Jamie's dad?"

Dr. Gardner leaned back in his chair and lightly scratched his left ear. "Of course, that's up to you. However, I think you need as much support as you can get. Tending to a young man fighting this infection can place enormous demands on his mother. Oh, I know your parents are close here in town. But a dad can mean a lot to give support and to hasten recovery."

"I guess I should explain a bit the situation with Jamie's dad." Here Robin breathed deeply about to discuss a subject she had avoided for years. "Jamie doesn't know his dad. He has never seen him. He thinks that his dad died years ago in a bicycle accident. Now what would happen if suddenly he discovers that isn't true?"

Dr. Gardner eyes narrowed as the impact of Robin's explanation induced careful thought. The doctor closed his eyes momentarily then he spoke. "Yes, that does present a dilemma. When is the last time you saw or talked to Jamie's father?

"Not since the night Jamie was conceived. Clay, Jamie's father, stopped in town one night. He was completing the RAGBRAI, you know the ride across Iowa."

"Yes, I know about that ride. I've treated a few who have over extended themselves," the doctor nodded his head and smiled."

Robin returned the smile, folded her hands in her lap, blushed faintly then quietly continued. "Things happened that never should have. He doesn't even know he has a son." Robin slumped in her chair, reaching for a tissue in her purse.

"That is a story. At this time, does Jamie have to know the truth about his father even if you do contact him about his son and his son's illness?"

Robin thought about the doctor's suggestion. "Wouldn't that be dishonest to Jamie?"

The doctor leaned forward in his chair, his eyes set on Robin. "Maybe. I do think, also, a revelation like that could adversely affect Jamie's fight against the infection. However, I think, despite the strange circumstances, Jamie's father deserves to know he is a father and his son suffers from an e-coli infection. At this point, I don't believe Jamie has to know that you have made this contact."

Robin stared at the doctor deeply moved by the advice he gave her. "I suppose you're right. It's been over twelve years since we even spoke to each other."

The doctor stood up from his chair, moved around to face Robin. He placed his hand on her shoulder. "Give it a try, just between you and me. Let me know what you discover. I think it's important."

Robin now stood up. "Thank you doctor. You have made the decision much easier."

"You're welcome. Now, let's check on Jamie so you can get him back home. Also, we need to look carefully at starting periodic dialysis."

Walking carefully with her son by her side leaning heavily on his mother's shoulder, Robin felt some relief knowing now she would make the call she had avoided for months, even years.

CHAPTER 39

"Mom, am I getting any better?" Jamie rested in the car, riding home from the doctor's office.

"What do you think? Are you?" Robin reached across the front seat of the car to squeeze her son's arm.

"I don't know. What did the doctor say?"

Robin considered briefly the importance of telling her son the truth. "He said you are holding your own. He wants to see you again next week to check on your progress. Do you feel better?"

"I think so. It's been so long I can't remember what it's like to feel good any more."

"I know, sweetheart. You've put up a great fight. You just have to keep doing it."

At home Jamie drank more water and nibbled on a piece of toast. The time at the doctor's office allowed him to relax there. Nonetheless, it didn't offer him a comfortable place to lie down and possibly drift off to sleep. In his own room he found the comfort and the quiet he needed to rest his body. Robin made sure she met all his immediate needs, kissed him on the forehead, and quietly left the room closing the door as she did.

In the corner of the living room she sat down in front of her computer. Clay's phone number lay before her, printed clearly on a pad of paper. The hours of doubt that preceded this moment faded when she picked up the phone and dialed Clay's number.

Clay rested in the bike shop office he shared with his boss. Another busy day found him tired, even his prosthetic foot caused a dull pain in his lower leg. The sheriff's office had not called back with any additional information about Miles Hunter and the mysterious license number. In his mind, he felt certain that Miles was the culprit who ran him off the road and compelled him to face over two years of pain and agony over the infected leg and eventual amputation. He longed to bury the past in the past. Until this issue with Miles Hunter reached some resolution, though, that would not happen.

A much happier thought burst into Clay's mind. Today, Vickie met with Dr. Jennifer Price, her obstetrician. The pregnancy, now its second month progressed, so far, without complication. Only this morning Vickie showed the bump in her abdomen, their first child's secure home for the next seven months. Clay smiled as he recalled running his hand over the bulge. Though they had no idea yet of gender, it didn't matter so long as both mother and fetus stayed healthy.

The ringing of his cell phone pulled him back to reality. Typically he received few calls on the cell phone, usually only from Vickie. He fumbled to rescue the phone from its case attached to his belt. He flipped open the cover to study the phone number of the caller. It definitely was not his wife.

"Hello, this is Clay." He met only silence. He repeated, "Hello, this is Clay."

A tiny, female voice asked, "Is this Clay Pennell?"

"Yes, it is." Clay confirmed with growing curiosity.

"This is Robin Foster."

Clay stared into the empty space above the door to the office. He failed to make a connection with the name. "Robin Foster," he whispered to himself. Suddenly, the significance of the name tumbled down upon him. "My God, the Robin Foster from Packwood, Iowa?"

"Yes, that's the one." Robin affirmed in a voice much more confident.

Clay's voice cracked as he caught his breath. "How many years has it been?"

"More than twelve. How have you been? Do you still bike?"

Bridging a span of twelve years produced a cluster of questions which flashed into his mind. Where to begin? With a brief hesitation, Clay answered, wishing to avoid a plunge into the saga of his accident. "Yes, not as often but I still hit the trails when weather permits. How about you?"

Duane A. Eide

"I'm fine. Still stuck in Packwood where I work in the local hospital as a LPN. Do you still work with bikes?"

Clay crossed his legs and leaned back in his chair, listening to the most curious phone call in memory. "Yes, I haven't moved very far either in the last twelve years. I'm still a manager of a bike shop in suburban Minneapolis."

Robin announced, "I don't want to interfere in your day. I just would like the chance to talk with you about an important matter."

Clay thought what could she possibly want after all these years? "Can you tell me about the important matter?"

"Yes, I . . . I can, but I'd rather not discuss it over the phone. Is it possible we could meet sometime soon?"

Clay scratched his head in confusion. What possible matter with Robin could involve him? Is she out to extract money from him? Is she sick with some illness that affects her brain? "I'm sorry. I don't know what this is all about. It's hard to agree to a meeting when I don't have any idea about the subject."

"I'm sorry to bother you, but I'm not doing it for myself. I would prefer to discuss this face to face. For twelve years I've wrestled with this moment." Robin's voice tapered off.

For Clay the mystery engulfed him. "What have you wrestled with for twelve years?"

In a voice again strong and firm, Robin announced, "We have a son."

260

Clay jumped up from his chair. The impact of the announcement nearly took his breath away. Calming his breathing, he whispered, "What did you say?"

Robin paused before answering. "I'm so sorry to alarm you. I couldn't think of any better way of telling you." She paused again before continuing. "Remember the night in Friendship Park. I got pregnant. Our son is now twelve years old and suffers from an E-coli infection that could endanger his kidney function. I felt obligated to tell you." She breathed deeply. "I should have told you about Jamie years ago."

Clay stood staring at the wall, struggling with what he heard from the voice on the phone. He cringed, thinking he has a son. He's had a son for years. He battled his emotions to channel his strength to speak in a clear voice. "I'm . . . Ah, sorry if I sound confused. I am a bit confused right now." Gaining more control, he stated, "I understand your reason for wanting to discuss this face to face." He sat down hard into his chair, running his hands through his hair. He really didn't need anymore distractions in his life. This, however, qualified as much more than a distraction. His son? A father for the last twelve years? It was all nearly incomprehensible.

"I'm sorry, but are you sure I'm the father?" Clay felt compelled to ask.

Robin coughed. Another pause. In a voice firm and confident, Robin stated, "I suppose, you have a right to ask, but I find that slightly insulting. Except for one time, and you know when that was, I've not engaged in careless sex with anyone."

"I'm sorry," Clay responded. "It's more than a mild shock to learn I'm a father."

"I understand that, and I should have contacted you when I learned of my pregnancy. I didn't, and now we have decisions to make about our son. As to your part in Jamie's conception, unless you wish to submit to tests, you'll have to take my word.

Clay closed his eyes. With his hand he wiped away drops of perspiration on his forehead. He said nothing.

Robin waited for his response. When none came, she asked, "Do you suppose we could meet to talk about Jamie's condition? I would really appreciate that chance."

With a calming drifting through his body, Clay proposed, "Look, why don't you give me a couple days to arrange a brief trip to Packwood where we could meet someplace. I need to clear things with my wife and with my boss at the bike shop." He paused before going on. "Look, after the shock of this discovery wears off a bit, I can approach a meeting more rationally. I have your phone number recorded in my phone. Why don't you let me call you back in a couple days when we can discuss specific details of a meeting there in your small town."

"That's fine. I'll wait to hear from you. Thank you."

Clay snapped his phone shut and leaned heavily on the desk. The silence now allowed the remarkable news to penetrate

Clay's thoughts. Should he look into paternity testing? Never did he ever consider such a thing could happen. Certainly, he could not deny that evening in Friendship Park. It happened, and any present doubts failed to alter the fact he enjoyed sex with Robin. It was just a moment of carelessness that overwhelmed both of them that fateful evening. Nonetheless, that moment apparently created a son. Clay would have to accept that. He also would have to accept his responsibility for telling Vicky? Should he explain the whole thing now or wait until after he'd met with Robin? It all happened before he even met Vicky. Still, eventually, he determined, he would explain to her the secret part of his life.

Now even more weary than before the call, Clay moved slowly out of the office returning his cell phone its place on his belt. He helped Ross lock up for the night then slowly walked to his car and the drive home to his pregnant wife to discover what the doctor said about their baby, no longer the first one in Clay's life.

CHAPTER 40

Suspicions about this guy in the fitness center with the artificial foot swirled around Miles' head. The timing of the guy's accident and Miles' run in with the first biker carried a significance beyond mere coincidence. Miles stomped toward his pickup, muttering to himself what a pain in the ass this whole biking incident turned out. Instead of satisfaction at scraping off the road a biker who should stick to the trails, it caused him periods of concern over discovery. He didn't deal well with periods of concern. He expected no interruptions in what he chose to do each day. Nobody would stand between him and his independence. Even his parents found that out. In his mind, he could do whatever he felt like doing. He paid little attention to consequences until now with these damned bikers.

Miles drove away from the fitness facility intending to return to his apartment. Before he left the parking lot, a plan suddenly occurred to Miles. Maybe, he speculated, knowing where this Clay lived would offer some advantage in the future. Each day he met Clay in the fitness center gave him a bit more assurance he finally met the biker he hit months ago. The biker gradually reaching the same conclusion could prove critically serious for Miles. Knowing where Clay lived, Miles convinced himself, could come in handy, maybe.

With a new purpose in mind, Miles circled the fitness area, finally parking in an inconspicuous spot that still gave him visual access to the center's exit. Watching carefully, hoping not to miss the subject of his surveillance, Miles sat gripping the steering wheel of his pickup. In only a few minutes Clay stepped out of the exit door, heading for his car, Miles soon learned was a small Mazda.

When Clay drove out of the parking lot and onto the main highway nearby, Miles waited until he could safely follow without detection. For several minutes he trailed Clay whose route Miles found familiar. A part of it went right by his apartment complex. Much of it followed roads around the Lake Minnetonka Miles traveled almost daily. Soon the route took him beyond I-394 and south to a wooded area not far from the Ridgedale Shopping Center. Following Clay increased in difficulty as the streets narrowed while winding through a neighborhood of modest but attractive homes. A block ahead of Miles, Clay turned into one of those modest homes with an attached two car garage and small entrance porch.

Miles noted the street, slowed to allow Clay to park his car in the garage, then drove directly by the house, noting the house number. With that information Miles experienced a feeling of satisfaction. At least, he didn't feel helpless, knowing now where the person lived who could cause a disruption in his life. With his purpose accomplished, Miles circled back to the freeway with the belief the knowledge where Clay lived gave him some kind of protection.

To celebrate his accomplishment he stepped down on the accelerator igniting his Cadillac's powerful engine. Sixty, Seventy, Seventy-five, the digital speedometer registered the mounting speed. On the inside of the three freeway lanes, Miles whizzed passed other traffic. He loved the feeling of speed, of power, and of dominance on the roadway. Gripping the steering wheel with both hands, he and his pickup formed a well coordinated unit.

Suddenly from behind came the scream of sirens. In his rear view mirrors, Miles could see bright red and blue, strobe lights of a fast approaching police car. He checked his speed. Quickly, he released his foot from the accelerator, considerate enough to yield space to the emergency vehicle. Little did he realize the emergency vehicle pursued him. In seconds, a Hennepin County sheriff's patrol car pulled up next to Miles, signaling him to pull over onto the shoulder. Fleeing the situation flashed through his mind only to fall victim to some remnant of good judgment lingering there.

The patrolman sat in his car for minutes before approaching Miles, who tried to contain a growing anger with this guy Clay who, Miles concluded, was responsible for his predicament. The patrolman cautiously stepped up to the driver's window.

"May I see your license?" He asked politely.

His inflated anger threatened a response with some sarcastic remark. Instead, he reached for his wallet and removed his driver's license.

"Mr. Hunter, you were traveling seventy-eight miles per hour in a sixty-five mile per hour zone. Do you have an explanation for your speed?

Miles glared at the officer, realized the futility of any argument, shrugged his shoulders and mumbled, "No."

"I'm afraid I will have to ticket you for that violation. Also, Mr. Hunter, there seems to be some discrepancy in your license plates."

Miles shifted positions in his bucket seat. With, now, childhood innocence, he looked at the officer. "What do you mean? What's the matter?"

"According to official records, the number on your plates is not the number on your registration records."

Miles shook his head in disbelief. "I can't imagine how that happened. I've owned this pickup for over three years. I haven't changed a thing except the tabs."

The officer stepped back from the pickup, walked to the back and then to the front to inspect again the plates. Returning to Miles' window, he confirmed the discrepancy. "I don't know what happened, but it is a vehicle registration violation. I will have to issue a ticket for that as well. That one requires you to appear before a judge in traffic court."

Miles pounded his hands on the steering wheel. "This is bull shit. I do what is right every year paying big bucks for the tabs and now this chicken shit stuff I know nothing about."

"As I said before, you need to take this up with the judge. I can only issue the citation for a violation. Watch your speed on this freeway." The officer turned and walked back to his vehicle.

Miles struggled to control his anger. He pulled out into traffic heading back to his apartment convinced that he would have to do something about this asshole guy, Clay, or whatever he called himself. He more than anyone else was responsible for these added problems in Miles' life. He would get even.

CHAPTER 41

Clay gripped the wheel, his eyes focused on only the space in front of his car. The revelation coming from the quiet voice on the phone overwhelmed him. He shook his head and banged his fists against the sheering wheel. What to do with the shocking information clouded his thinking. How serious was the infection Robin spoke of. Clay had heard about E-coli but never in any detail.

Driving home, Clay struggled with this new world the phone call exposed him to. Even after the short time since he first heard the news, he started to relax, thinking more rationally about the situation with Robin and their son, Jamie. What should he tell Vicky? Surely, someday he would review with her that part of his life she knew nothing about. Right now he didn't think telling her took on any urgency. Besides he wished to avoid alarming her during her pregnancy. Still, he did feel the obligation to meet with Robin. He also accepted some responsibility for the son he never knew. What that responsibility would entail he did not know. Could Robin use this occasion to seek financial help in raising their son?

Pulling into his driveway, Clay decided he needed to relax, not to arouse concern from Vicky. Knowing the body doesn't respond easily to commands to relax, he, nevertheless, took deep breaths, vowing to concentrate on his wife and on their baby. Upon entering the house, he greeted Vicky with a tender hug, always aware of her expanding stomach.

"How was your appointment?" he asked.

"Great. Everything is normal for now. The baby is positioned just right with no signs of anything unusual." Vicky kissed Clay on the cheek.

"How about you? Are you doing okay?" Clay placed his hands on her shoulders, leaning down to kiss her on the lips.

"Of course, I am." Vicky did a quick turn around with arms spread. "Don't I look okay?" She laughed.

"Honey, you look great. You always look great. Sometimes it's what's inside that counts more than what's outside."

Vicky pinched him on the cheek. "Oh, don't be so serious. Women carry babies all the time. It's part of their role. Now, what do you want for dinner? I do have to return to the office to catch up on a few things I missed because of the doctor's appointment."

"I don't know. I'm not very hungry. Maybe I'll have a sandwich or something light. What about you?"

"That's good enough for me, too." Vicky moved to the kitchen where she assumed control of the sandwich detail.

Clay stepped in behind her, rubbing his hands over her shoulders and neck. "Remember, sweetheart. You are eating for two."

Vicky turned with a big smile to face her husband. "Oh, really. I didn't know that," she chuckled. "Don't worry. I can take care of both of us."

Over a dinner of sandwiches and skim milk, Clay and Vickie discussed her impending advancement to the position of president of Wagner Electronics. Vickie reported that her boss, Madison Wagner, recently confirmed the retirement of Brain Tarlton, the current president. Vickie admitted no regret in seeing Mr. Tarlton leave the company. The brief episode with him in an Orlando hotel room still lingered in a corner of her mind. Clay, too, retained images of Vickie's earlier, painful description of defending herself against the advances of an arrogant, perverted man. Shortly after the new year Vickie would assume her new duties. Her return to the office now, however, had nothing to do with her new position, only a chance to make up for time spent at the doctor's office.

Sitting alone watching the evening news and scanning the morning newspaper at the same time, Clay set the paper aside. He debated calling Robin to establish a time for them to meet.

Setting the time with her then clearing it with both his boss and with Vickie made the most sense.

Clay reached for his cell phone and directed his phone to redial the number from earlier in the day. A few rings brought the familiar voice, familiar since that afternoon, to the phone. Under conditions far less emotional than the earlier call, Robin explained in detail the source of Jamie's infection. She further explained the remote possibility of his needing a kidney transplant. She obviously took no chances with her son's life.

"Have you looked into possible donors?" Clay asked.

"No, not really. You are the first person I've mentioned it to." Waiting for Clay to respond, Robin paused. He said nothing. "You know, you could be one of those asked since you likely could quality as a match for Jamie."

For the moment, the consequence of donating a kidney held no reality for Clay. Accepting the truth of having fathered a son twelve years ago proved almost more than he could assimilate. Agreeing to a kidney donation demanded much more information than Clay currently possessed. With skepticism weakening his voice, Clay answered. "If what you say is true, I would have to consider that."

In a near breathless whisper, Robin said, "Thank you."

Their conversation covered briefly their lives over the past twelve years. She explained her job as a LPN and her pride in their well adjusted, happy son. She emphasized the turmoil of the last few weeks as Jamie battled the infection.

Clay told of his life working in the bike shop, his marriage to Vickie and the accident which resulted in the invasion of an infection causing the loss of his foot. With dismay, Robin listened to Clay's explanation of what happened and what probably still had to happen in the case of the hit and run.

To end their conversation, they agreed to meet on the next Saturday at a family type restaurant in down town Packwood. In preparation for the four hour drive to Iowa, Clay would explain to Vickie his trip related to promoting the traditional bicycle ride across Iowa termed the RAGBRAI for "register's annual great bicycle ride across Iowa." He would also suggest to Ross at the bike shop the value in promoting the near historic event. With promises to meet about noon on the next Saturday, they ended the call, one of the most consequential in Clay's memory. Beyond that, he shivered with the apparent reality of the remarkable truth of his fatherhood.

CHAPTER 42

For several days Miles considered what he would do about the tickets and the order to appear in traffic court. He debated contacting his dad, an attorney. His pride made difficult asking his dad for anything except money. His concentration on the tickets and his confrontation with the law only enhanced his resentment of the one he dubbed as responsible for his misfortune, Clay, the guy with the artificial foot. With little to do and no place in particular to go, the days passed slowly for Miles, who often sat in his apartment watching TV or, at least, sitting in front of the TV paying only casual attention to what appeared on the screen.

The last few years produced profound changes in Miles' life and it all began with the cyclist he ran off the County Road 19 so many months ago. In his foggy interpretation of fairness, he couldn't imagine how a moment of revenge on a God damned biker could screw up his life the way it did. Of course, he never for an instant assumed any of the blame for his miserable life. Without a job, with occasional help from his parents whom he rarely spoke to except when he needed spending money or rent money for his apartment, and no desire to search seriously for a job, Miles drifted deeper each day into a growling bitterness that accentuated his lifelong defiance. He hated his life and the people he identified as responsible for what it had become.

Soon he would have to achieve some release from the hostility that threatened to explode at any time, especially during the idle afternoons when he sat, useless, resisting the urge to put his fist through walls closing in on him. For several days he avoided the fitness center. Too many things invaded his mind to think about lifting weights or about his physical condition. Besides, there, he might run into that Clay fellow. Right now he didn't need that reminder of who caused most of his problems.

Trying to determine what he would do to improve his life, Miles sipped on a can of beer. Since he quit his job working for his father, Miles faced daily shortages of money. Still he only reluctantly considered seeking a job. His dad offered him to return to the law office to resume his duties there. Miles rejected the offer, expressing his disdain for what he called slave work. Nonetheless, he felt no compunction about asking his dad for money.

The ring of his cell brought Miles back to the reality of his shabby living room. He glanced at the tiny screen to read his dad's name. At first Miles refused to answer only to realize the stupidity of alienating his father any more than he already had. "Hello," he grumbled into the cell phone.

"How you doing, son? We haven't heard from you for a while." Mr. Hunter spoke softly, all to familiar with the explosive tendencies of his son.

"All right, I guess." For only an instant Miles considered telling his father about the traffic tickets. He dismissed it.

"Have you found another job yet?" Mr. Hunter believed he knew the answer but asked to keep the conversation alive.

Miles tossed his head in a gesture of disgust. "No, I haven't. Nothing out there worth looking at."

"You have been looking, then?" His father took some satisfaction in that.

"A little," Miles mumbled.

"You know you can come back to the office. There's always room for one more." Only one of several times Mr. Hunter made this offer.

"Yeah, and spend my time emptying waste baskets and sweeping floors."

"There's much more to do around the office than that. You have to want to do it."

"And, I suppose, I don't," Miles sneered into his phone.

Mr. Hunter made no response simply because what Miles said reflected the truth. "Have you heard any more about the hit and run bike accidents?"

"Look, Dad," Miles raised his voice to a near shout. "I resent your snooping into my life. I've told you enough I know nothing

276

about any damned bike accidents, and I don't like when you bring it up all the time.

"I'm sorry. I'm not snooping. I'm just curious if you've heard anything more about them."

"Why should I? It's ancient history."

Silence filled the phone waves. "Is there something you need?" Mr. Hunter asked.

"Not right now."

"If there is, be sure to let us know." Mr. Hunter knew the futility of trying to persuade his son to do anything including asking for help in any form. "Your mother greets you. Take care."

The connection ended, Miles deposited his beer can in the kitchen sink and reached into the fridge for another. The short conversation with his dad cooled his temper by distracting attention away from the complications crowding his life. With a sudden resolve derived from the brief conversation with his dad, Miles reached for the phone book. He returned to his sofa, sat down, and opened the thick Minneapolis phone book. He would make a call to this Clay. Each day he saw him at the fitness center increased his belief that biker he ran off the road three years ago was Clay. Clay's making the same connection could prove disastrous for Miles. He needed to use his powers of intimidation to persuade Clay to keep his damned, big mouth shut.

Miles plopped the phone book on his lap. What the hell was Clay's last name. Shit, Miles thought, how could he find a phone number if he didn't know his last name? Stupid, he muttered to himself, tossing the phone book across the floor. Miles slapped his knees, stood up, committed to some kind of action. He could no longer hold his resentment within. If he couldn't threaten over the phone, he would do it at Clay's front door. After all, Miles did know his address.

A grin replaced the frowns of frustration. Miles grabbed three more cans of beer to accompany him on his drive to see his buddy, Clay whatever.

CHAPTER 43

Clay headed south on Interstate 35 toward the Iowa border and his noon meeting with Robin Foster, whom he hadn't seen in twelve years and who allegedly shared with him a son. With a touch of guilt he explained to Vicky the reason for his quick trip to Packwood, Iowa, one of the small towns on the across Iowa bike tour. She understood without question the explanation of his intention to establish a closer connection between the bike shop and this traditional bike ride. Ross, at the bike shop, greeted with enthusiasm Clay's idea of promoting the tour.

The last time Clay made this drive occurred in late summer twelve years ago. Now in the early winter, he drove cautiously on roads recently dusted with snow. The sun shined brilliantly off the sun covered fields and interstate median. Clay mapped out his route well in advance, a route that would take him south to Mason City and then southeast to the small town of Packwood.

Passing through the eastern part of Iowa, Clay noted the near desolation of harvested corn fields now showing only occasional clumps of partial corn stocks that survived the harvest and the subsequent cultivation. Driving through the flat farm land, he noted the small clusters of farm buildings and storage elevators that dotted the area as far as he could see.

The first sign noting Packwood eighteen miles ahead reinforced the reason Clay made the trip. Leading up to his morning departure from home, he suffered moments of anxiety regarding the trip and about Robin's assertion that he was the father of her son. However, gradually he accepted the visit with Robin as vital for confirmation of her claim. That acceptance helped to calm his nerves. Now, though, approaching his destination, his stomach quivered and his mouth turned dry as he passed the sign welcoming him to Packwood.

Robin awoke early on Saturday morning to prepare herself for the meeting with Clay and to ensure Jamie's comfort while they waited the arrival of his grandmother who would look after him in his mother's absence. Still plagued with vomiting and diarrhea, he did show some small improvement from two weeks ago. However, the burden of his confinement made him restless and moody.

Earlier, Robin explained to her parents her contact with Clay. They supported her completely in her decision to contact him. Later in the morning, Robin's mother would arrive, as she did nearly everyday, to look after Jamie. As time neared for her departure, her nerves tingled and her stomach contracted though the importance of the meeting helped mask her anxiety as it had Clay's.

At 11:30 the hostess guided Robin to a quiet corner in the restaurant for the planned noon meeting with Clay.

"Could I get you something to drink?" The hostess asked.

Seated, Robin thought for only a moment. "Maybe an ice tea. Thank you." Shortly, a waitress placed a glass of ice tea on the table in front of her. "Would you like to order?" The waitress inquired.

Robin explained she awaited the arrival of a friend. Then they would order. Sipping her ice tea, she sat by a table set for two giving her a direct view of the entrance to the restaurant. Nervous about the meeting with Clay, perhaps in only minutes, she stiffened when her cell phone interrupted her quiet contemplation. Clay called to inform her of his approach to Packwood and, maybe, she could give him precise directions to the restaurant where he assumed he would soon arrive. She quickly gave him the directions. Closing the phone, Robin sat back in her chair wondering what Clay looked like after the passage of so many years.

She ran her hands through her hair, adjusting it behind her ears. Previously, concerned only with discussing her son's condition with his father, she completely ignored her own personal appearance. At this moment, though, she thought about how she looked to him after all these years. In her own mind she had changed little over the twelve years. Though she recognized the relative insignificance of appearance, she still entertained some curiosity knowing that in a few minutes the man she had not seen in twelve years and the father of her son would walk through the door on which she focused her eyes.

The thought no sooner occurred to her when through the door walked this dark haired, handsome young man who stood in the doorway surveying the small restaurant dining room. Robin stood up. Her heart literally skipped a beat, and a trickle of tension descended her back. She stood up from her chair and moved toward the man she recognized immediately as Clay Pennell.

Clay froze. He studied the young woman who approached him. His mind whirled back twelve years to the waitress who served him at the church dinner following his day long bike ride. She hadn't change a bit. Like then, she retained an attractive figure, short brownish hair and an engaging smile. With outstretched arms he advanced to embrace Robin carefully and discreetly. "It's good to see you again," Clay whispered in her ear. Seeing Robin with her innocent smile, her sincere greeting, and the courage displayed in her contacting him out of concern for her son chipped away at the misgivings haunting Clay since the initial phone call.

Robin stepped back, "Yes, it's been such a long time. Thank you for coming so quickly."

"Thank you for calling me, letting me know about Jamie." Clay found impossible referring to him as "their son." However, looking into Robin's eyes, he remembered as bright and sparkling now dulled by worry with a hint of pleading, he couldn't image her attempting to deceive him about her son.

Robin reached for Clay's hand. "We have a table right over there. Let's get comfortable. You've had a long day already." She led him to the table where they sat down across from each other. Their eyes met in silence. Robin spoke. "My goodness, you haven't changed a bit in all these years. How have you stayed so young?"

Clay reached across the table to touch Robin's hand. "Probably the same way you have." Smiles spread across the face of each.

Robin took another sip of her ice tea. "How was the drive down here to marvelous Iowa?"

Clay smiled. "Very uneventful. A chance to see the beauty of harvested corn fields with corn stocks peeking through patches of snow."

Robin grinned at the reference to Iowa corn. "Sadly, you missed the glory of the tall corn stocks before harvest. People around here really do see beauty in acres and acres of tall corn stocks."

"Kinda like wheat fields in Minnesota." Clay moved his chair closer to the table.

A waitress stood next to the table to ask about beverages and to hand out menus. Clay ordered an ice tea; Robin a refill. They delayed ordering a lunch. With the return of the waitress and their drinks, Robin and Clay quietly sipped their ice tea.

Setting his glass down and folding his hands before him on the table, Clay asked, "How is Jamie doing?"

Reaching into her purse on the floor beneath her, Robin withdrew a picture of their son. "Not very well, I don't think. He's suffered this infection for several weeks now, missing school and missing out on being a young man." She handed Clay the picture. "This was taken at his twelfth birthday party when he ate the contaminated hamburgers. At least we think it was the hamburgers."

Clay studied the picture. "A handsome young man. Looks like his mother." He smiled, directing his eyes again to the picture to notice something very familiar about Jamie's smile which removed for Clay virtually all doubt about the identity of his father.

Silence returned to the table. The waitress arrived to take their order. When she left, Robin straightened in her chair and slowly shook her head. "God, where does one begin after twelve years?"

Clay touched a twitch on his nose and looked deeply into Robin's eyes. "At the end, I think. What happened before makes little difference. What happens now makes all the difference, particularly for Jamie." He paused. In thought, his eyes narrowed, his brow furrowed. "What does happen now?"

Robin breathed deeply. "First, I think, we need to remove any doubt about your role in Jamie's birth." She gazed with intensity at Clay. "You sounded skeptical on the phone, and I can understand why. Learning suddenly that you're a father is quite a revelation." She smiled.

Clay moved restlessly in his chair. "Yes, it was a revelation." He reached across the table to grasp Robin's hand. "I believe you. I don't think you are the kind of person to make up something about a son." He paused. "I repeat. I believe you. And ask again. What does happen now?"

Robin lowered her gaze, with a tissue, dabbing at the corners of her eyes. She exhaled deeply. "Thank you. What happens now is we meet with the doctor again next week to check on kidney function and try to control the diarrhea and the dehydration. Depending on the results from that appointment, we may have to seek advice from the doctors at the Mayo Clinic in Rochester." Robin reached into her purse for a tissue she used to dab tiny tears.

Clay reached across the table again to squeeze Robin's hand. "I'm so sorry you've had to face all this alone. Fate has a fickle hand sometimes. Is there anything you need from me or want me to do?"

"Of course, I would love to tell Jamie about his father. I would love to think we were a normal family. Clay, we are not, and that's the way it is. I do have my parents here to assist me, and they have been wonderful down through the years."

With their lunch served, silence returned to the table. "What have you told Jamie about his father?" Clay asked.

"Only that he was killed in a bicycle accident when Jamie was a mere baby." Robin hung her head, reluctant to look directly at Clay. Looking up, she continued. "I don't know if that was the right thing to do. I didn't think telling him the truth was a good foundation for a mother-son relationship."

"I would have to agree with that. Do you think he should ever know the truth?"

Robin shrugged her shoulders. "I . . . I really don't know. I don't know what he would think about my lies to him all these years if suddenly he discovers his father lives. I guess that decision will have to wait until after this present crisis has ended."

"I definitely would agree with you there, too. We will simply have to wait and see what happens."

Deep seriousness claimed Robin's face. "One thing I should tell you about what you can do. If Jamie's condition does not improve, if his kidneys continue to lose function, he might need a kidney transplant. You, Clay, could very likely prove a match for Jamie." She hastened to add, "Now, remember, the situation has not gotten there yet. In a couple weeks it could." She paused to reach for the strength to ask Clay the critical question, "Would you be willing to give Jamie one of your kidneys if needed, and you are a good match?"

Clay moved his plate off to the side. He glanced down at the table before lifting his eyes to look at Robin. The ambivalence of previous days faded the longer he sat with her even though he understood little about what a kidney donation entailed. "I would do that. You don't really need to ask."

Robin leaned forward, covering her face with her hands. Tears seeped through her fingers as she tried to control her emotions. She reached for more tissues. "I'm sorry I'm such a baby, but you have just made me so happy to know that if needed I could count on you."

Each order a light dessert. For almost an hour, they discussed the last twelve years. Clay talked about his job in the bike shop, his wife and her pregnancy, and his accident leaving him with a prosthetic foot. Robin talked about the shock of her pregnancy, the marvelous support from her parents in this very conservative, small town, her growing up with their son, and her work as a LPN.

Standing outside the restaurant with a brittle early winter sun slowly making its journey in the western sky, Robin and Clay embraced in an expression of good bye. She promised to keep in touch about Jamie's health. Clay promised to help in any way he could.

Driving northwest out of Packwood, Clay squinted from the sun's glare. In his mind he thought about all Robin and he discussed during their extended lunch. Uncertainty clouded so much of the future of their son. However, Clay felt sure about one thing, his return to Packwood, Iowa.

CHAPTER 44

Miles stormed out of this apartment, headed to his cherished pickup. The cool December air failed to cool the growing rage that settled over him as he considered his status in life and the possibility that Clay could make his life even worse with his potential for connecting Miles to his biking accident and the artificial foot.

Committed in his goal to teach this Clay a lesson, he roared away from his apartment building toward I-394 and Clay's home south of Ridgedale. The one previous visit to the area left Miles with only a vague memory of where Clay lived. Nonetheless, in fading light of late afternoon, Miles circled several blocks before driving passed the house he now recognized with its covered front entrance and a bike figure attached to the mail box. He drove by the home, proceeded to the end of the block, turned around, and headed back to the house he was certain belonged to Clay.

Lights filtered through the curtain covering the large front window. With the sun still inching toward the horizon, the outside lights on both the garage and the front entrance were dark. Miles pulled into the driveway, rammed the shift into park, but left his pickup running. He stepped out onto the driveway, his determination increasing as he advanced closer to the front door. He climbed the four steps, looked around for evidence of any neighbors watching, and searched for the doorbell. One press produced a ring inside he could hear. Immediately following the sound of the door bell, a young woman peeked through the curtain covering the circular window in the door. She opened the door only far enough to peer out to ask, "May I help you?"

Miles stood tall and menacing outside the storm door. He tried the handle. The door was locked. He stepped back to ask in a loud, intimidating voice, "Is Clay here?"

The woman guarded the door carefully. "No, he is not. What do you want?" Vicky stood tense and ready to slam the door if this huge, threatening person tried anything.

Through the glass of the storm door, Miles screamed, "Tell that chicken shit husband of yours he'd better forget about his bike accident if he knows what's good for him!"

Vicky tensed, still holding the door firmly. She saw the rage in Miles' eyes. She took no chances and slammed the door in his face.

He yelled, "God damn you bitch. Nobody slams the door in my face." He stepped back, raised his leg and pushed it through the glass storm door. The window shattered; glass fragments scattered around the front entrance. Miles stood shaking with anger, staring at the closed front door. He heard sirens. Did that bitch call the cops? Not wanting to face them again, he kicked pieces of glass out of his way and hurried to his pickup. Tires squealed as he backed into the street. The sirens faded, likely not headed in his direction. Police would not pull him over ever again.

Unable to intimidate Clay with his threats only sustained the anger that shadowed Miles almost daily. He sought the release he always derived from his pickup. The feeling of power the roaring engine gave him lured him back to the freeway and north away from the congestion of the Twin Cities. Traffic thinned. Early evening found light traffic on I-94. Miles gripped the steering wheel, glancing at the speedometer which registered eighty-five miles per hour.

Miles grinned his delight as traffic headed to the Twin Cities whizzed by on the other side of the median. He concentrated on the road ahead, falling victim to increased speed, now over ninety miles per hour. He claimed the left lane as his, rushing by anything in the right lane. Though the state highway department took good care of particularly the interstate system, it couldn't eliminate the ravages of winter's ice and snow. In sheltered parts of the freeway, not even the road salt could completely remove patches of ice or compacted snow.

Miles held his speed steady at ninety miles per hour. With the setting of the sun, darkness rushed in. It now surrounded him.

He stared straight ahead at the stream of his head lights, a jumble of thoughts tumbling through his mind. Most of those thoughts fashioned a miserable life filled with nothing but disappointment and people who took advantage of him. Not even his parents understood him. Now this bastard biker threatened to make his life even worse, whining around about this accident shit. Miles pounded the steering wheel with the heel of his hand. No one took advantage of him.

The drift back into his self-pity took his attention away from the road ahead as well as the reckless speed he maintained. Approaching a curve through a sheltered area, Miles ignored the dangers some times lurking there with patches of ice spreading over portions of the road bed. Suddenly, turning the wheel produced nothing from the pickup. The front wheels did not response to the turn. Instead they slide on the ice. Miles panicked applying pressure on the brakes which only threw the pickup into a skid sideways down the roadway.

First one way than another, the pickup fish tailed across the freeway. Widely trying to gain control, Miles turned the wheel one way and then back. Nothing helped. In the beam of his headlights, he saw the guard rail directly in front of him. In seconds his pickup crashed through it, sailed over a steep embankment, and rolled several times, coming to a stop in a tangle of trees, dirt, and metal.

Darkness covered the area, the only sound a beep that survived the violence warning of the need to secure seat belts. Miles lay crunched between the air bag and the roof of his cherished pickup, unconscious and temporarily free from the anger and resentment of a tortured life.

CHAPTER 45

The northern sky glowed with reflected light as Clay approached the outer suburban limits of the Twin Cities. His drive from Packwood took a little longer than he anticipated, his concern for early winter road conditions slowing his progress. In minutes he would drive into his driveway, his mind teeming with thoughts of his conversation with Robin and what he would tell his wife about this day. His quiet drive through northern Iowa and southern Minnesota gave him time to reach one important decision. He would tell all to Vicky, the ride twelve years ago, his meeting Robin, her pregnancy, Jamie, his illness, everything. His pursuit of Miles all but buried under issues far more important.

Outside lights welcomed Clay home. A glance at the front door introduced him to the broken window. A tiny shock shot through his stomach concerned about the possible cause of the broken window. With little hesitation he parked his car and rushed into the house without even lowering the garage door. Vicky met him as he entered. She rushed to take him in her arms, tears trailing down her cheeks.

"What's the matter, sweetheart? What happened?" Clay asked desperate for an exclamation.

Vicky sobbed then gained control, stepping back to look into her husband's eyes. She swallowed. "This big, burly guy came to the door. He asked if you were home. I said no. He tried to open the storm door. I slammed the front door and locked it. He screamed some vulgarity then he must have kicked the window in the storm door."

Clay stood facing his wife, his anger festering. "It was that damned Miles something, the guy I suspect was responsible for my accident. He's the one I've seen so often at the fitness place." He moved to take his wife into his arms. "Honey, I'm so sorry you had to face that brute. This whole mess has gotten to a point where the police need to do something. This guy is dangerous."

Clay placed his arm around Vicky's waist and guided her to the living room where they sat together on the sofa. He wiped away a tear that settled on her cheek. "The important thing is he didn't do anything more than break the storm door window. We can't go on concerned about if he will return or what he will do next. The guy's crazy."

Clay leaned back into the sofa. Vicky turned to face him. "How was your day in Iowa?"

Clay looked down at the floor then rested his head against the back of the sofa. The resolve he reached driving home from Packwood gave him the courage to address the topic he had avoided for twelve years. He reached to grasp Vicky's hand. "Sweetheart, I've something to tell you."

Vicky removed her hand from Clay's grasp, a look of alarm crossing her face. "Okay. I'm listening."

To relieve a bit the anxiety skipping through his body, Clay stood up and moved away from the sofa. Finding a place for his hands in his pockets, he turned to face his wife. "Honey, this all happened before I ever met you. Over twelve years ago I did what I wanted to do for years, ride across Iowa on my bike, a ride that has a big history behind it."

Vicky raised her hand to halt his explanation. "Look, Clay, if this doesn't relate to me or to us, you don't have to tell me. It probably is none of my business."

Clay exhaled deeply. "Vicky, no it doesn't relate directly to us, but it does relate to me and that makes it relevant to us."

"That's fine."

Clay seated himself across from Vicky in the sofa chair. He fixed his gaze on her. "At the conclusion of that ride I met a young girl. In a rare, unguided moment for both of us, we made love. The next day I completed the ride and returned home to the Twin Cities. I didn't hear another word from this girl until a few days ago. She called to inform me . . . ah she told me I have a son."

Vicky's head shot back and her mouth dropped open. She stared at Clay. No words could express her surprise. She spoke none.

Clay shook his head. "Believe me, I had no idea. The reason she made the effort to contact me was to tell me that her son, our son, has an infection that threatens to damage his kidneys. She felt compelled to tell me this as his father and also as a potential donor in the event that he might need a transplant."

Clay rose again and sat next to his wife. He put his arm around her shoulders; she leaned close against him. They sat shrouded in silence.

Finally, Clay took another deep breath. "Sweetheart, I love you. You know that. This has nothing to do with our love for each other or for our baby. I don't want anything to intrude on our relationship. I do think I have some responsibility to this young man who is a product of a careless moment."

"Clay, I'm sure this story is not unique to you, and I admire you for telling me about it. Also if you don't question the truth of your role in this boy's conception, I certainly will not." Vicky paused to wipe a tear from the corner of her eye. 'You are so right. That young man does need your help in whatever form you can give it." She reached for Clay's hand and squeezed it. "I love you too, Clay. You are so right about something else. This really doesn't have anything to do with our love."

"Thank you for understanding." Clay reached over to kiss his wife on the cheek.

"I have one question I feel I have to ask. You probably asked it, too, at least to yourself. Does your son's mother have any desire to seek money from you? I know that's a harsh question under the circumstances, but I needed to ask it."

"Absolutely, a critical question," Clay acknowledged. "The subject never came up though I considered asking it. The young boy's mother, Robin, as far as I can tell, is worried about one thing, her son's infection that hasn't improved much apparently in several weeks. Besides, she does have a good job and very supportive parents."

"That's good." Vicky reached again for Clay's hand. "What about the kidney donation? What do you think about that?"

"Vicky, that's a decision we will have to make. I guess that does relate to both of us. Right now, as I said before, I feel an obligation to this young boy who I have never seen. His mother will keep me informed of his status. If that time comes, we will have to decide."

"I know we will do the right thing." Vicky leaned against her husband ready to accept the kiss he placed upon her lips. She chuckled as their lips parted.

"What's so funny?" Clay asked through a broad grin.

"Your trip really didn't have anything to do with the bike ride across Iowa, did it?

"You're very shrewd to figure that out," Clay joked before admitting. "It didn't today, but it sure did twelve years ago."

Both stood up, for an instant consumed with the importance of the issues they just discussed. Breaking the silence, Clay announced, "You know, sweetheart, I'm hungry. I haven't eaten since lunch."

"How about a pizza?" Vicky offered, as they walked together toward the kitchen.

"Sounds great. If you would call for the pizza, I will call the sheriff's office to report the visitor who disrupted your life this afternoon."

"Fine, a deal." Vicky turned to reach for the land line phone. "By the way, I almost forgot. My mom called earlier to day to ask about plans for Christmas. She hinted about getting together with us here along with your parents."

"Good idea. We'll have to consider that." Clay moved back into the living room. He reached for his cell phone to call again about a time and a person in his life he would rather forget.

CHAPTER 46

Clay's call to the sheriff's office informed him that law enforcement officials were investigating the actions of Miles Hunter. The spokesperson at the sheriff's office thanked Clay for his call but could not disclose any other details about the case because of privacy laws and laws restricting release of information during an ongoing investigation. The call confirmed for Clay Miles' last name.

His late afternoon visit to Clay and Vicky's home created concern for both of them. The ringing of a phone or the sound of the doorbell ignited a tenseness in their house that never before existed. They talked about the threat Miles posed, but dismissed as unlikely any serious personal or property damage he would do. Still, this guy apparently imposed few limits on his own behavior. The little contact Clay had with the guy convinced him he was responsible for the accident that cost him his foot. To Clay, he likely was also responsible for the more recent hit and run that put another cyclist in the hospital. From what Clay knew, the other cyclist also survived. That did not reduce the severity of hit and run accidents involving a vehicle and a bike.

For three days, Clay and Vicky felt on edge in their own home. However, they pursued their individual daily routines. The discussion of Clay's other life before meeting Vicky, his son, and his son's fight against kidney failure assumed a vital place in their lives without disrupting the harmony of their relationship. Vicky took pride in her husband's courage and confidence to share with her the details of this long ago moment of passion. She also found satisfaction in knowing that her husband trusted the strength of her love, while believing in her unequivocal acceptance of his explanation.

Vicky and Clay relaxed, she in the kitchen preparing a light dinner and he in the living room resting his tired leg. The evening news failed to attract his attention. Typically, following a long day at work, they found little time to watch TV at all, not even the news. However, maybe the uncertainty of the situation with Miles Hunter, induced Clay, at least, to pay a little more attention to the media expecting he might hear or read something to allay their concerns. On this evening he did.

A report about an accident on I-94 northwest of the Twin Cities caught Clay's attention.

At the same time Vicky, from the kitchen, asked, "Would you like a snack before dinner?"

The question divided Clay's attention. "Honey, just a minute. Something interesting on the news. Come here, quick."

Vicky rushed into the living room. "What is it?"

Clay sat up straight in his sofa chair staring at the TV off to this left. "I'm not sure. Something about an accident on the interstate. Let's listen."

Vicky sat down on the sofa prepared to give her undivided attention to the TV.

The local TV news reported a passing motorist noticed a damaged guard rail west of the Twin Cities on I-94. The motorist stopped to search the area when he discovered the badly damaged white pickup at the bottom of a ravine. Apparently, the driver lost control on patches of ice covering the road way at that spot, plowed through the guard rail and into the ravine. Suddenly, the picture of a pickup filled the TV screen. Severely damaged, tangled in brush, and partially submerged in shallow wetlands failed to conceal its identity as a white pickup.

Seeing the picture brought Clay to his feet to move in closer to the TV screen. "Do you think what I'm thinking?" He turned to face his wife.

"Yeah, if you're thinking that pickup belongs to this Miles . . . ah, what's his name, Hunter, then I am thinking the same thing."

The reporter continued to explain that the victim, a young man in his thirties, lay trapped in the wreckage for more than ten hours. Still the motorist found him alive. Officials air lifted the victim to Hennepin County Medical Center in Minneapolis. There, according to the TV, doctors reported the man, whose name officials declined to release, suffered multiple injuries including a broken back and severed spinal cord. However, hospital officials expect the man to survive.

Clay and Vicky sat mystified by the news. They looked at each other across the living room. The report included compelling evidence, the white pickup, to connect Miles to the accident. Still, skepticism prevented a rush to any immediate conclusion.

Nonetheless, they both flirted with the same thought. Could this really be the guy who ran Clay off the road or were they victims themselves of wishful thinking?

That the victim of the accident suffered life altering injuries neither Clay nor his wife considered without compassion. Nonetheless, a young man they hardly knew caused months and months of pain for both of them. In Clay's mind, this same young man recently threatened Vicky. The authorities' eventual identification of this young man as the one who disrupted their lives would definitely temper their compassion.

With the conclusion of the news story, Clay returned to his sofa chair and rested his leg on the stool he often used for that purpose. Neither he nor Vicky spoke a word, both considering the implications of what they heard and witnessed on the TV.

Finally, Vicky interrupted the silence. "I'm not sure about that story, but dinner is almost ready. Do you want to eat here?"

Clay looked up as his wife as if just awakened from a light sleep. "No, no, I'll eat in the kitchen." Standing up, he stepped closer to his wife placing his arm around her waist. "Sweetheart, wouldn't that be something if our suspicions prove right?"

Vicky smiled, punctuated by a distinct nod of her head.

The next day a local newspaper confirmed the identity of the accident victim. It was Miles Hunter, the son of a prominent Twin Cities attorney. Clay knew nothing about the Miles he met at the fitness center. Still, he was convinced this definitely was the Miles he knew. The newspaper article included a brief review of Miles and his troubled life. It also reported the conclusion of doctors at HCMC that his spinal cord injury would ensure his spending the rest of his life in a wheelchair. The article also included information about possible charges pending against Miles. They included hit and run and tampering with vehicle license plates. The article contained little detail about the potential charges except to note that the Hennepin County Sheriff's office, for quite some time, considered him a person of suspicion in two hit and run accidents involving cyclists.

Clay felt confident in the identification of the accident victim as the same person who ran him off the road and who recently intimidated his wife. For confirmation or simply for his own satisfaction, he called the sheriff's office, asking to speak with Mr. Cook with whom he spoke several times before. Reluctant to reveal much detail about the case, Office Cook did confirm to Clay that the vehicle involved in the accident was the notorious white pickup with the altered license plates. Now, no question remained as to the identity of the victim.

Clay greeted with relief the news of Miles' fate, the conclusion to an issue that shadowed him for months. He couldn't dismiss the irony of the gleaming white pickup, which for months commanded his attention, almost serving as a casket for Miles. In the future, he expected the media would have more to say about Miles Hunter. Now, though, he could concentrate on an even more important matter influencing his life, the health of a son whom he had yet to meet.

CHAPTER 47

"Mom, do I have to go to the dialysis place again? I was there only a few days ago." Jamie ate breakfast with his mother, who took the day off work to accompany her son to the hospital for the treatment.

The last few weeks brought a significant improvement in Jamie's condition. Careful attention to hydration to flush his system finally had rid his body of the E-coli infection. With that victory came the return of Jamie's appetite, his energy, and his desire to go back to school. However, the infection left his kidneys unable to perform their cleansing function. Dr. Gardner recommended temporary dialysis to allow Jamie's body to gain the strength lost during the long siege of infection.

"Yes, you do have to have another session." Robin spoke with little patience. The many weeks of worry about her son's condition limited her tolerance for explanations that her son frequently requested. "It may be something you would rather not do, but look how much you have improved."

"I know. When will I get to go back to school? It's been so long I don't even remember where it is." Jamie laughed at his search for humor.

"I guess, when Dr. Gardner says you can." Robin softened the tone of her voice. She sipped from her cup of coffee. "Your tutor has helped, hasn't she?"

Jamie nodded his head in agreement. "Yeah, I suppose she has. But it's not the same."

Robin rose and moved her chair back from the table. She approached her son, ruffled his hair allowed to grow below his ears, and squeezed his shoulder. "I know, honey. It's not the same. The last few weeks have been tough on you and on me, too." She placed her hand under Jamie's chin, turning his head to face her. "No, it's not the same, but it's much better than it was. You have put up with this dialysis for now until the doctor decides what to do next."

Jamie looked into his mother's eyes. "What is the next thing?"

Robin dropped her arms to her sides and stepped back to stand behind her chair. She positioned her hands on the back of the chair, in an almost defensive position. "Dr. Gardner has mentioned the possibility of a kidney transplant. Maybe you don't remember, but he mentioned it to us a while ago only as a last resort. You can't go on with kidneys that don't work very well. It's a big decision. We'll talk about it with the doctor. Right now, we need to get going for the appointment at the hospital."

Jamie obediently pushed back from the table to follow his mother to the car and the short drive to the local hospital, a very familiar drive for both of them.

CHAPTER 48

"Good morning, sweetheart." Vicky turned to face her husband snuggled deep in blankets at the edge of their king size bed.

Clay smiled, stretched, and reached out to tap his wife's nose. "Good morning. Merry Christmas," he uttered with a voice emerging from a deep sleep.

"Merry Christmas to you, too." Vicky rolled to a sitting position on her side of the bed. She stood up then turned to face Clay still nearly concealed in bed covers. "What time did we say they were to come for Christmas dinner?"

Clay raised up on one elbow. "I guess about two o'clock. Isn't that what you said?"

Vicky rustled her hands through her thick black hair, trying to restore a little shape denied by the night on the pillow. "I don't know what happens to my mind, sometimes. That time simply slipped away."

Clay chuckled. "It's your age, honey. Forgetfulness is a part of growing old."

Vicky picked up her pillow and playfully tossed it at her husband. "What do you know about memory? As I recall, you didn't even remember our commitment to spend Christmas Eve with your parents last night."

"Oh, I was just kidding. How could I forget spending Christmas Eve with my parents when we've done it for years?"

"Yeah, sure." Vicky made her way to the bathroom. "I have to get at that turkey if we plan to eat early this afternoon."

Rarely did their parents, the Dumonts and Pennells gather for any occasion. Over the years, Vicky and Clay celebrated special occasions and holidays with either her parents or his, rarely both. Harold, Clay's father, and Edwin, Vicky's father, never seemed very compatible. From the very earliest meeting, they had little to talk about. Edwin's life spent as a successful, Wisconsin farmer and Harold's life as a retired salesman failed to blend. In addition, their personalities contrasted: Edwin domineering, opinionated, Harold unassuming and congenial. Still, on those occasions that brought them together they managed to carry on a halting but friendly conversation.

Vicky quickly completed her bathroom routine. Returning to the bedroom, she noticed Clay had already made the bed and disappeared someplace. She changed into work clothes ready to tackle the preparation of a Christmas dinner for six people. Not particularly devoted to cooking, like everything else in Vicky's life, through sheer determination, she succeeded. Today she needed success since both mothers in law took great pride in their culinary talents. Vicky insisted, though, she cook the dinner, all of it.

In the kitchen stirring up stuffing for the turkey, Vicky concentrated on her duties for the moment ignoring the sudden disappearance of her husband. Clay approached Vicky quietly and touched her shoulder. She jumped.

"Sorry. I didn't mean to scare you." Clay stood behind his wife clutching a small gift wrapped box.

She turned to face him, hands sticky from mixing the stuffing. "I didn't hear you come. Where'd you'd go?"

"To collect what Santa brought."

"I thought we did that last night at your dad and mom's" Vicky looked with surprise at the wrapped box. "Is that for me?"

"Of course, it's for you. Do you want to open it?" Clay handed her the box.

"Sure, but not with sticky hands." Vicky turned to the sink, washed her hands, then reached for the gift. "I thought we weren't going to exchange gifts between us."

A feigned look of horror crossed Clay's face. "You mean you never bought me anything from Santa?"

Vicky's shoulders slumped, contrition cross her face. "No. I'm sorry."

Clay stepped forward embracing his wife in a gentle hug, the only type of hug he practiced during her pregnancy. "Honey,

I'm only kidding. Yeah, we did agree to not sharing gifts this Christmas. Thinking about our lives, my God we have so much to celebrate. I had to buy you something. Open it."

Vicky was not one to rip into a gift. Instead, she methodically removed the string then pealed away the tape. At last she reached the box, about four inches by ten inches. Clay stood by watching her meticulous unwrapping of the gift. Removing the cover, she turned back the tissue paper. Inside the box lay a highly polished, wooden desk plaque engraved in large, block letters, **President**.

A smile spread across Vicky's face. She reached for Clay's chin, stepped closer to him to kiss him on the lips. "Honey, this is so special. What a great gift. Thank you."

Clay looked into her deep, dark eyes. "Not everyone gets to be president of the company. I'm so proud of you and your success." He pulled her slightly closer, returned her kiss while she grasped the plaque behind his back.

Only days before the Christmas holidays, Madison Wagner, CEO of Wagner Electronics, summoned Vicky to his office. The time for Christmas bonuses produced a minor parade into his office. For weeks, Vicky entertained the thought of her promotion to president of the company. Madison previously discussed that possibility with her. The current president, Brian Tarlton, faced retirement at the close of the year.

Simply believing Madison would offer her the position didn't make it real. However, on this day she likely would receive the offer or a bonus or both. To her excitement and deep gratitude, Madison offered both. On January 1 she would assume her new duties as president of Wagner Electronics.

The exhilaration of that moment endured through the days leading up to Christmas Eve and Christmas Day. Christmas Eve at Clay's parents included a lengthy discussion of Vicky's new responsibilities as well, of course, of her pregnancy.

Vicky stepped back from Clay and held up the plaque to study its craftsmanship. "It's perfect. I can see it prominently placed on my desk at work. Thank you for your thoughtfulness." She handed the plaque to Clay. "Would you take this? I've got to get back to the turkey."

Vicky and Clay spent nearly every Christmas Eve with his parents and nearly every Christmas Day with hers. Last evening they exchanged gifts with Harold and Agnes Pennell, mostly gifts dealing with the impending arrival of the first grand child. Today, however, would find the Pennells and Dumonts gathered for Christmas Day dinner.

At one forty-five Vicky's parents arrived followed minutes later by the arrival of Clay's parents. Bundled up to combat the cold of this Christmas Day, the two sets of parents eagerly shed their coats to take a place in the warmth of the living room.

Following Merry Christmas greetings all around, Vicky brought in snacks. She and Clay hastened to make their parents comfortable. Inquiries about beverages produced requests for coffee, wine, as well as beer, one of Harold's favorites. As the guests relaxed on the sofa or a chair, quiet settled over the group.

Standing at one end of the living room, Clay asked his in-laws, "How were the roads from Wisconsin?"

Edwin sat up straighter, placing his glass of wine on the table before him. "Clear as can be. A bit of patchy ice on the bridge over the St. Croix that's all."

With that comment, the conversation drifted through a variety of topics, Edwin dominating most of them. Vicky's promotion and her pregnancy received the most attention. Also the condition of Clay's foot entered into the conversation. That introduced the recent accident involving the person Clay believed was responsible for his amputation. More questions framed the conversation dealing with Miles Hunter and the eventual contact between him and Clay. They all agreed what happened to Miles deserved their sympathy. They also agreed if he in fact is found guilty of the charges, justice would be served.

One topic Clay and Vicky avoided talking about to their parents was the reality of Clay's son. Only recently did Clay disclose the truth to Vicky. They discussed the need to tell their parents. They determined telling them would serve no real purpose. Yes, someday they would likely tell them. That day had yet to arrive. However, with the remote possibility of Jamie needing a kidney transplant, Clay could very likely serve as a donor. That could have implications for Clay, Vicky, their baby, and the grandparents, sufficient justification for telling them now.

Seated around the dining room table, the last bites of a fabulous Christmas dinner finding their way into contented mouths, Clay moved his chair back from the table, a serious look on his face. "There's something Vicky and I haven't told you." The comment drew instant attention from those seated around the table. "It's not . . . ah, it's not something of immediate danger or anything like that." Clay fumbled for what he wanted to say. Eyes from around the table focused on Clay. No one said a word. They all waited for Clay to disclose whatever he and Vicky hadn't told them.

Clay moved slightly closer to the table. "A long time ago I rode in this traditional bike ride across Iowa. The ride was the fulfillment of a dream." He paused, looking over at his wife who sat next to him. "Not only was it a dream come true it also made me a father."

Mouths dropped. Eyes looked with astonishment at others around the table. Silence hung heavy over the Christmas Day table. Vicky reached to place her hand over Clay's.

Clay squeezed Vicky's hand, moved aside his dinner plate, and folded his hands on the table in front of him. He looked around the table first at his in-laws then at his parents. "I didn't know about my son until a few weeks ago. I don't need to go into any details, but a few weeks ago the boy's mother contacted me with information about my son's battle with an infection that could affect his kidneys."

Those around the table sat transfixed waiting for Clay to go on. Clay cleared his throat. "Vicky and I decided we should tell you about this situation." He looked down at his hands folded before him. Looking up, he made brief eye contact with their guests. "I could be asked to submit to an evaluation as a donor. I've not heard anything about it in the past few days, but we wanted you to know the truth." Clay stopped, leaned back in his chair, expecting questions.

Harold spoke first. "Son, what a shock. Thank you for sharing this with us." He paused then added, "How old is the young boy?"

"About twelve."

"What about his mother? What does she do?" Harold asked.

"She's an LPN in a local hospital in Packwood, Iowa." Clay clarified.

"Have you seen the boy?" Clay's mother asked.

"Only pictures."

"Do you intend to meet him?" Agnes inquired.

"I don't know. That depends upon his mother. We will have to seriously consider that." Clay paused debating about going on. "She has told him his father died in a bike accident. How would a young boy feel about his mother who lied to him about his dad?"

Edwin spoke next. "I certainly can understand that. A delicate matter. On another point, if you do qualify as a donor, would you agree to donate?"

Clay glanced at Vicky. "We have discussed that too. We both agree I would donate."

"Aren't there serious risks to that?" Edwin remarked.

Clay looked at his father-in-law and took a deep breath. "I suppose any type of surgery has risks. From what we've found out, with today's medical technology those risks are small."

"Can you live normally with just one kidney?" This time his mother broke her silence.

"From what we understand yes, that's not a problem." Clay assured her.

The impact of the revelation tended to dull the flow of questions. Learning that Clay was already a father to a twelve year old son proved more than adequate to occupy those around the table with personal thoughts, not questions needing explanation.

With dinner complete, each person assisted Vicky in clearing the table. From the kitchen the group retired to the living room where the conversation probed more deeply into the existence of Clay's son, kidney transplants and the future of the relationship between Clay and his son.

By the time darkness ushered in the evening, Vicky's parents needed to drive back to Wisconsin, Clay's to their home only minutes away. Along with the good-bye hugs came an unspoken expression of love and compassion for Clay, Vicky and the decisions they would have to make, perhaps, before the arrival of the new year.

CHAPTER 49

From the corner of the small room crammed with equipment needed for dialysis, Robin watched as the technicians prepared Jamie for another two and a half hour session of mechanically cleansing his blood. In her heart she sobbed for her son who for several months battled E-coli infection and now kidney failure.

During the dialysis sessions Robin watched near by as her son submitted to the lengthy procedure instead of playing soccer or even attending school with his friends. Today, her mind drifted back several months to those early signs of problems following Jamie's twelfth birthday party. Abdominal pain, nausea, and diarrhea prompted Robin to take her son to the doctor. The diagnosis shocked her, E-coli poisoning. Weeks of careful attention to his condition followed with critical attention to ensuring he received adequate hydration.

Studying her son, immobile and still frail, attached to the dialysis machine, Robin's feeling for his condition surged. How much he sacrificed over the months: little contact with friends, no soccer which he loved, only day after day of dealing with a body fighting desperately against an insidious infection, threatening his young kidneys. A friend who also contracted the E-coli poisoning, presumably from food eaten at the local fast food restaurant where Jamie celebrated his birthday, luckily fought off the infection before it damaged his kidneys. Robin smiled to herself, grateful for the recovery of Jamie's friend. She looked over at her son, closed her eyes and thought, if only Jamie had been so fortunate.

Jamie's battle prohibited his attending school. To date he had missed over three months of classes. Of course, Robin worried about his falling behind in school. However, her far greater concern was the gradual decline in kidney function. Besides, Jamie enjoyed school, always performing near the top of his class. In recent weeks, a tutor met with him three times a week to assist in bringing him up to date with the rest of his class. A decision allowing him to return to school awaited the counsel of Jamie's doctor.

"Excuse me, Mrs. Foster. Sorry to disturb you." A nurse stood next to Robin.

The nurse's presence rescued Robin from her concentration on Jamie's past few months. She looked up at the nurse. "I'm sorry. I guess I got lost in my own thoughts."

"I understand completely. Your son has shown real courage through it all." The nurse glanced down at her clip board. "Dr.

Gardner asked if you could meet with him now while Jamie finishes his session?"

Robin stood up from her chair. "Of course. Where should I meet him?"

"In his office. If you are ready, just follow me, and I will take you there." The nurse turned to lead Robin out of the dialysis room.

A short walk through the hospital corridor passed the admitting area brought them to a group of offices including that of Dr. Gardner. A gentle tap on the door produced an invitation to enter.

Dr. Gardner moved from behind his desk as Robin followed the nurse into the office.

He approached Robin, placed a hand on her shoulder, and smiled. "Thank you for coming. I didn't wish to interfere with you while the session continued, but I have a rather urgent appointment later. I did want to discuss your son's situation today while both of you are here. Please sit down." He directed Robin to a chair in front of his desk. He then thanked the nurse who turned toward the office door, closing it behind her as she left.

The doctor returned to his place behind his desk. Sitting down, he opened a file placed in front of him on the desk. He studied it for a moment then looked up at Robin. "Mrs. Foster, I wanted to talk with you today because, I think, we need to assess where we are with Jamie's treatment."

Robin met the doctor's gaze, nodding her head.

"According to his records, Jamie has gotten dialysis two times a week for, ah," the doctor studied the record before him, "for five weeks. Previously, you reported no serious problems in between sessions. Is that right?"

Robin shifted in her chair. "Yes, that's right. His appetite has improved; he sleeps well, and doesn't complain about any pain or discomfort." She glanced down for an instant. Looking up at the doctor, she smiled, "He is very disappointed about missing school, though."

"I can understand that. He's gone through some very tough times for anyone but especially for a twelve year old. Is he still getting tutoring help?"

"Yes, he is, about three times a week." Robin confirmed.

The doctor leaned back in his chair and steepled his hands in front of him. "That he is only twelve years old is a major factor in decisions that we have to make soon. Again, according to his records, his kidneys have not regained their function. Blood tests reveal that they perform minimal cleaning. Most of it done by dialysis." The doctor paused, a frown creased his forehead. "I think we need to consider Jamie's future. I don't think we can expect a young boy to continue this dialysis. Life for him offers much more than that."

Robin sat unmoving. She studied the doctor, quite sure where the discussion was leading. She said nothing.

"Some time ago, we discussed in a general way a kidney transplant. I know that sounds drastic and to some extent it is. However, in Jamie's case I think it's time for us to seriously consider that alternative. As I already stated, he has a long life to live. We must make it as enjoyable as possible for him."

The doctor stopped, waiting for a response from Robin. She took a deep breath, looked off into the emptiness of a blank office wall, then directed her attention to the doctor. "I understand what you're saying. Of course, I agree about Jamie's life. He can't spend it sitting tied up to a machine. But, I . . ." Tears gathered in her eyes. She reached for a tissue in her jacket pocket. "I'm sorry. It's such a big thing to decide for Jamie. It will be with him the rest of his life." Robin dabbed her eyes.

"You certainly don't have to be sorry. I understand your feelings. It's not easy to make these decisions that have life long implications. I think we need to begin the evaluations that will determine if Jamie qualifies for a transplant, place him on the transplant waiting list and start a search for a possible match among your family and friends."

Robin slumped in her chair. Dr. Gardner stood up and moved around to the front of desk. He dragged another chair closer to Robin's. He sat down facing her. For the next half hour he explained in detail the entire kidney transplant procedure. He pointed out the nature of the surgery, the length of recovery, the threat of complications, and the potential for a life free of worry

323

over kidney function. He also addressed the obvious advantage of a family or friend, kidney donor. He advised Robin that a donor would face a minimal stay in the hospital following the surgery and would likely face a life without complications. He assured Robin that a donor can function very well with just one kidney.

Throughout the explanation, Robin sat listening intently even though she was familiar with much of it. Over the past few weeks she researched the detail of a kidney transplant both for the donor and the recipient. Nonetheless, when it involved a close family member no amount of research could reduce the apprehension.

When Dr. Gardner stopped, Robin looked down at her hands folded in her lap. Looking up, she said, "Thank you for the explanation. Nothing takes away some of the fear better than an honest discussion. I think I understand what we have to do, but what is the next step?"

The doctor moved back his chair, stood up and returned to his place behind the desk. "I've instructed the staff to bring Jamie here after his session has finished. I think he needs to be part of the decision. At least, he needs to know the plans for his future."

Robin nodded her head. "I definitely agree."

As Robin voiced her concurrence with Dr. Gardner, a tap at the door announced the arrival of Jamie along with a staff person. Robin jumped up from her chair to greet her son who stood mildly bewildered by the seriousness that pervaded the office. Dr.

Gardner also approached Jamie, placing his hand on his shoulder. "How did it go today?" he asked.

Jamie shrugged his shoulders. "All right, I guess. I got all my blood back."

"That's good," the doctor smiled in agreement. "Why don't you sit down next to your mother." He guided Jamie to one of the chairs in front of the desk. The staff member inconspicuously left the office, closing the door as she did.

Robin reached down to give her son a hug before sitting in the chair she occupied during Dr. Gardner's long explanation. The doctor sat behind the desk, closed the folder still placed before him, then looked up at Jamie. "Son, your mother and I have had a long conversation about you."

Jamie smiled and raised his eye brows in acknowledgement of his place at the center of the conversation.

Dr. Gardner's voice assumed a serious tone. "Jamie, what your mother and I talked about while you went through your dialysis involved a possible kidney transplant."

The topic surfaced before with his mom, making it less startling. Still, coming from the doctor implied more than a general discussion with his mother. Jamie said nothing. He looked at his mother and then back at the doctor. "Do I need a transplant?"

The doctor leaned forward, folding his hands on top his desk. "Your mother and I agree that might be the best for you. You don't want to stop by here every few days to sit for nearly three hours while a machine does what you possibly can do better with a transplanted kidney."

"Would I be able to go back to school, play soccer?" Jamie asked.

"Yes, you certainly could." Dr. Gardner confirmed. "You would have to be careful for a while, but, yes, we expect you would return to a life appropriate for a twelve year old."

Jamie turned to look at his mom, his eye brows raised in curiosity. "Would I have no more doctor's appointments?"

"After you healed from the transplant, maybe a visit to see Dr. Gardner twice a year."

Jamie shrugged his shoulders, tilted his head. "Okay, I guess."

"Jamie, that's great." As before, the doctor rose from his desk chair and walked around to stand next to Jamie and his mom. "Look, a lot needs to be done before we talk about dates for surgery, which incidentally would be done at the Mayo Clinic in Rochester, where they have some of the best facilities and surgeons who perform kidney transplants all the time."

"Aren't you going to do it?" Jamie asked.

"No, we don't have the facilities here. I assure you the doctors at the Mayo Clinic will do a great job."

Again, Jamie voiced his agreement, "Okay with me."

Before Robin and Jamie left the hospital, Dr. Gardner scheduled another appointment to evaluate Jamie's qualifications for a transplant. He also advised Robin to explore a possible friend or family donor.

Walking across the hospital parking lot at the conclusion of another long day at the hospital, Jamie asked, "Maybe I'll get a new kidney as a present for Christmas?"

Robin placed her arm around her son's shoulder. "Maybe you will." To herself, she said, maybe your father will deliver it.

CHAPTER 50

Clay closed his eyes in concentration, gripping his cell phone. "I'm so sorry to hear that. What a tough decision."

"Yes, it was." Robin confirmed.

Clay rearranged new winter cycling clothes when his cell phone vibrated in his pocket. He received few calls at work, mostly from Vicky. A moment of tension accompanied the call. Concern for Vicky's pregnancy always occupied a corner of his mind. Checking the caller ID on his cell phone established the caller as Robin, not Vicky. Recently, calls from Robin also commanded his attention since the initial call weeks ago and after his trip to meet her in Packwood, Iowa. Quickly, Clay escaped to his office where he could talk in relative privacy.

"When did you make the decision?"

Suddenly, he heard only silence. Then Robin took a deep breath. "During our last visit to the hospital for Jamie's dialysis." Clay sensed she tried to contain her emotions.

Clay repeated, "I'm sorry for Jamie . . . for you. What's next?"

Robin cleared her throat. "Jamie's doctor reported little return of kidney function. He emphasized Jamie's age and the burden of dialysis for anyone but especially for a preteen."

"What does Jamie think about the decision?" Clay asked.

"Well, he doesn't like the dialysis. He only wants to get back to something normal in his life." She paused again, then continued, "The doctor is convinced that further treatment will do no good. He spoke to Jamie about it. Jamie's ready."

"A brave guy. What's next?" Clay moved behind the desk to sit down.

In a voice much more calm than earlier, Robin explained, "Finding a donor is the most important thing. According to the doctor, a five year waiting list exists for a cadaver kidney."

"God, we can't put Jamie through five more years of what he has faced so far. I've checked online about what's involved in selecting a donor. I learned some general information. What's the truth?"

"Obviously, the donor must have the same blood type as the recipient. Beyond that, I guess, common sense takes over." Robin answered.

"Vicky and I have talked about this possibility. We agreed that if needed, I will be available for testing to see if I qualify."

Clay heard a gasp and then silence. As before Robin struggled to control her emotions. "That's great. I prayed you would say

that, but I understand if you need to talk to your wife about it."
She paused. "Excuse me for a minute."

Clay waited for her to collect her composure

"I'm sorry," announced a frail Robin voice. "Clay, I want you
to know that I'm first in line for finding out about compatibility.
Only if I'm not, will I ask you to get involved. You must
understand that."

"Look, Robin, I understand completely. I also understand
how difficult this has been for you. I want you to know when the
time comes I will do what I need to do."

Again Clay waited for a response. Robin cleared her throat
then in a voice barely above a whisper replied, "Thank you so
much for your willingness to get involved. You don't know how
much I appreciate your cooperation."

"Really, it's a privilege . . . an obligation."

"No, it's more than that. It's . . . it's wonderful." Another
moment of silence preceded her next comments. "A problem
we face in finding a donor is my small family. After me it's my
parents who might be too old. Of course, Jamie has no siblings. A
few relatives are around but nobody very close."

"Yes, I can see that's a problem. Even my parents are probably
too old. By the way is there an age restriction?" Clay asked.

"I don't think so. The doctor didn't say there was. Good
general health is important. I suppose common sense would tell
about selecting an older donor."

"I guess I would agree with not asking our parents to donate, even if they qualify, unless there are absolutely no other alternatives."

"Yes, I think that's the only sensible thing to do." Robin confirmed.

Clay stood up from his chair, to move around to the front of the desk. "Look, Robin, we can't resolve much right now until the tests are given. I feel confident that things will work out. I will discuss this with Vicky and let you know. Is there an urgency for the transplant?" Before Robin could answer, he added, "Oh, I know getting it done is so important, but we have some time, right?"

"Yes, we do. Thank you so much for your help. I will wait to hear from you."

Clay asked briefly what a donor evaluation involved, then reaffirmed his confidence in a successful conclusion to the many weeks of agony Jamie suffered. The phone call ended with a promise to talk soon. Clay closed his cell phone, replaced it in his pocket, and leaned against his desk. He stared blankly at nothing, his mind swirling with questions about the whole process of donor evaluation, preparation, and recovery from kidney transplantation. Intermingled with all those questions were thoughts about the recipient and what he must face, especially when he's only twelve years old.

The rest of the day found Clay preoccupied with the phone conversation with Robin. He faced no reluctance in submitting to the evaluation, but what if his tests proved him incompatible, then what? A wave of emotion still moved through his body whenever he thought about "his son." What of his prolonged infection and his amputation? Would they be critical factors? Would compatibility exist with other family members? In the event that nothing else worked, could he justify asking his parents or Robin's parents to undergo evaluation? At their age, could they deal with major surgery and its possible complications?

Returning to an empty house, Clay slumped in his favorite, living room, sofa chair and clicked on the TV to pass the time until Vicky arrived home from the office. Since advancing to the position of president of Wagner Electronics, her time spent at work hadn't changed much. She still devoted, on some days, twelve, thirteen hours to her job. Clay grew accustomed to her irregular schedule, those times months ago when he questioned her need to spend so much time at the office gradually faded into oblivion. He now took pride in his wife's success.

"Honey, Robin called this afternoon." Clay announced to his wife after she joined him in the living room upon her return from the office.

"Did she have news about the condition of Jamie?" Vicky harbored no resentment after learning the truth about portions of Clay's life before she met him. She supported him in his concern

332

for his son's health. She rejoiced in the prospect of having a child of their own.

"Yes, she did. Apparently Jamie needs a kidney transplant. His kidneys just aren't functioning like they should."

Clay's revelation produced a halt in Vicky's breathing. She did know about Jamie's health problems. Still hearing the reality of the transplant shocked her. "That's too bad. What a shame a young boy has to put up with something like this. How long has he faced this kidney problem?" Vicky asked.

"Well, the kidney problem only the last few weeks, I guess. Before that he battled this infection, and we know about battling an infection."

"That's for sure. What happens now?" She asked.

"We need to discuss my offering to undergo the evaluation to see if I qualify as a donor." He stopped and folded his hands on his knees. "Maybe I should back up a little." Clay affirmed. "Before we go any farther I need to say that, of course, Robin will be the first tested. If she qualifies, then there's no need for me to get involved that way."

Vicky smiled. "Oh, I assumed that. Still you have to be prepared to do what you need to do. You know, we've discussed this before. Have you changed your mind at all?" Vicky moved closer to the edge of the sofa.

"No, I haven't. I just need to know if you approve."

Vicky slid across the sofa to sit at the end closest to Clay's sofa chair. She reached out to grasp his hand. "Sweetheart, you know I support you in this. If you feel you need to do this, and I think you do, then, of course, do it."

Clay slipped out of his chair to kneel in front of his wife. He grasped both of her hands and locked his eyes onto hers. "Vicky, I love you. I love your compassion. I love your understanding. I am so proud of you as my wife, as a corporate president, and soon as the mother of our child." He leaned back on his haunches. "Yes, I do need to do this if circumstances demand it and the sooner the better to give Jamie back his life."

Their light dinner afforded them the chance to discuss as much as they knew about the details of the qualification testing, of preparation for the surgery, the surgery, and the recovery. Clay relayed what Robin told him over the phone: blood, urine, and radiology tests formed the basis for determining compatibility. As an LPN, Robin possessed a familiarity with kidney transplants most others lacked. Still she spoke with Clay in general terms. She touched on the surgery itself and following surgery the three to four day hospital stay for the donor. She reassured Clay that a person can lead a very normal life with just one kidney. Hearing that assurance, Vicky smiled and quipped, "I can believe that. We lead a perfectly normal life with just one heart."

Their dinner completed, Clay and Vicky got up from the table, reached for each other to conclude their discussion with a long, tender embrace, Clay always wary of pressuring Vicky's bulging stomach where each passing day their child grew bigger.

CHAPTER 51

In the days since Robin informed Clay of the necessity of a kidney transplant for their son, Clay waited expectantly to hear from her regarding the testing to determine her qualification for a kidney donation. Clay moved restlessly around the house, trying to find something to occupy his time. Vicky's day stretched well beyond his, at least it did on this day.

Since the phone call from Robin with the revelation about Jamie, Clay devoted the time during those private moments to asking himself about his fatherhood. Before Robin's phone call, he, of course, categorically, had no reason to think about his role as a father except as related to Vicky's pregnancy. However, learning about Jamie prompted a list of what-if's in Clay's mind. What if Robin had informed him of her pregnancy when she discovered it? Would he have encouraged her to carry the baby full term? Would an abortion have been an option? Would he have married Robin if he had known about her pregnancy?

Besides these thoughts, Clay frequently thought about fatherhood. Though without resentment, he still considered all he had missed as his son advanced from one year to the next. He wondered about all those times he played with his dad. Would he have done the same with Jamie? Would Jamie like biking? How proud Jamie likely would have made Clay's parents.

Clay stopped by the kitchen sink to have a glass of water. He took a long drink, set the glass on the counter, then stretched back with both hands grasping the counter. For an instant he stared blankly at the window above the kitchen sink. With some resistance he coaxed his memory back to reality. What happened, happened. Nothing he could do about the last twelve years except to make himself available if needed to intercede in his son's life. With a shake of his head, he stepped away from the kitchen counter, reached for his cell phone, and dialed Vicky's private number.

Robin, too, fought to control her restlessness and anxiety waiting for the results of her tests to determine suitability for giving one of her kidneys to her son. The day before she had traveled to Rochester for the necessary, initial tests. Now she simply waited for the results.

Her days, recently, found her spending most of her time away from work discussing with her son the details of what he faced with transplant surgery. Dr. Gardner, on the latest office visits, tried to allay Jamie's fears about the procedure, assuring him that despite the seriousness of the transplant, he would emerge healthy and ready to resume his life as a young teenager.

Still, watching his mother's restlessness, Jamie asked, "When will you find out about the tests?"

Robin sat down next to her son, who rested on the living room sofa. "I should find out any time now. The tests tell the story very quickly."

Jamie studied his mother. "Why did you have to go to Rochester for the tests?"

With a deep sigh, Robin answered, "Jamie, a kidney transplant is pretty common nowadays." She exhaled again, cautious to avoid scaring her son about the seriousness of the procedure but still wishing to avoid deluding him with a dishonest assessment of the potential dangers involved. "It also is serious. Not every hospital is equipped to do all kinds of surgeries. We are just lucky that one of the best hospitals in the country is so close to us."

With a tip of his head and flick of his eyes up and to the right, Jamie looked at his mother but said nothing. Suddenly, small furrows creased his forehead; a thoughtful look crossed his face. "What happens if you don't pass the tests?"

"Then we search for someone else who might share some compatibility with your system."

"You're my mother; why wouldn't you work?" Jamie asked in mild confusion.

"Well, son, the body is a very complex thing. A mother doesn't necessarily have the same blood type, for example, as her child. Without that she wouldn't qualify."

A puzzled look persisted. "Why wouldn't your blood type be like mine?"

Robin resisted introducing the subject of Jamie's father. Right now, though, she had little choice. "Remember, your father had something to do with things like a blood type. That's true with other parts of your system."

Jamie sat silent, now more thoughtful than confused. He looked up at his mother again. "I guess we can't ask him to take the test."

Robin worked to hold back the tears that mobilized in her eyes. "No, we can't, but we will find someone."

"What about grandpa?" Jamie offered.

"Maybe, that's a possibility." Robin stood up to ask Jamie if he wanted a sandwich, his appetite much improved over only a few weeks ago. While they ate their sandwiches, Jamie asked additional questions about his mother's work schedule while he recovered in the hospital and about school, if he would ever catch up to the other kids in his grade. Robin did the best she could to explain to him that all would work out since she already had arranged for time off from work and for a tutor to help him keep up. She reminded him not to worry about those details. He needed to gather his strength to ensure when the time came for the transplant he would be ready.

Jamie listened intently to his mother then responded with a smile, "Kinda like getting ready for a big soccer game, maybe."

Robin returned the smile, "Yeah, maybe."

The next morning the Mayo Clinic informed Robin she did not reach a level of compatibility that would allow her to donate her kidney. When she recovered from the shock of that information, she knew she must contact Clay immediately, realizing the search for a suitable donor grew more urgent with her rejection.

The call came as Clay ate his lunch in the bike shop office. Nearly breathless, Robin explained the results of her tests. The reality of her rejection sent a shiver through his spine. All the previous conversation with Robin and with Vicky failed to prepare him for this crucial time which would take him once more to the Mayo Clinic where he might be asked to save a life, his son's.

CHAPTER 52

Smoke from roof top chimneys curled upward in the brittle morning air; ice crystals formed delicate patterns on foggy windows. Early February in Packwood, Iowa, traditionally included snow, ice, and below zero temperatures. This morning as Jamie, his mother and grandparents prepared to make the drive to Rochester's Mayo Clinic and Hospital the temperature hovered just above zero, but to make their three hour drive less tense the roads stood clear of any snow or ice.

For the past several days frequent communication with the hospital in Rochester finally confirmed a date for Jamie's kidney transplant. The disappointment of discovering Robin's incompatibility quickly turned to excitement upon their learning that Clay's tests proved him compatible. With that news, Robin worked quickly to coordinate with the hospital and with Clay to set the date for the surgery. Now, tomorrow that day would arrive.

"Mom, how long will I be there?" Jamie sat on a kitchen chair observing his mother's meticulous assembling of luggage and coats and shoes.

Robin stopped to face her son. Her voice hinted of impatience. "Honey, we have discussed that several times already. You probably will be in the hospital for several days. It all depends on how the surgery goes and how quickly your body accepts the new kidney.

Jamie closed his eyes as if thinking of another question. He said simply, "Okay."

As Grandpa warmed the car outside, Grandma and Robin carried out the few essentials needed for the hospital stay. That stay would include Robin for a few days while hospital staff monitored Jamie's early recovery from the surgery. With the last piece of luggage stored in the car, Robin approached Jamie still sitting in the kitchen.

"It's time big guy. Here, let me help you with your jacket. You go out to the car. I'll lock up and be there in a minute." Robin guided her son toward the door.

"Mom, I can walk by myself." Jamie announced.

"I know. I'm sorry." She reached out to brush her hand through his hair, dulled by his long confinement.

A somber silence pervaded the car as Robin's father headed out of Packwood toward Rochester, Minnesota, a nearly two hundred mile drive. In the back seat, Jamie stared out the side window where he saw only barren fields of harvested corn, a familiar sight across Iowa. Next to him, Robin, for the moment, sat engrossed in her own thoughts about the impending surgery and the chance for a normal life for her son. How many times during the past few months did she pray for a return of a normal life for him? Now, she grasped for confidence that it would happen.

She reached across the rear seat to touch her son's arm. "You okay?"

Jamie looked at his mom. A faint smile spread his lips. "Yeah, I guess so." His eyes narrowed in a squint. "What did you say was the name of the guy who is going to give me one of his kidneys?"

"Clay Pennell." Saying the name in front of her son never failed to produce a twinge in her stomach.

"Why is he doing this? He doesn't even know who I am?"

Robin took a deep breath. "Jamie, we've talked about this before."

"I know, but why would he?"

Robin turned to face Jamie. "Look, some people have big hearts. They are willing to help others in need. Mr. Pennell put his name on a donor list for kidneys because he is a wonderful man who is willing to share a kidney to help people like you to lead a normal life."

"Will I ever meet him?"

"If you want to, I'm sure you can." Robin smiled at her son. "That probably wouldn't happen until after the surgery when you are all healed up."

For the next several minutes silence returned to the car. Grandpa concentrated on the road, thankfully clear of snow or ice. Grandma had listened to the conversation in the back seat but didn't join in. Mother and son now studied the winter landscape that stretched beyond the highway.

Jamie broke the silence. "Are Grandma and Grandpa going to stay at the hospital too?"

"No, they will stay at a motel for a couple nights until the surgery is over. Then they will go home to check on things there. They'll be back though."

That thoughtful look returned to Jamie's face. "What about your work? How are you going to do that?"

"Honey, don't worry about those things. I'm taking off work for a few days. What's important now is you."

By early afternoon they arrived at the Mayo Clinic and Hospital where the staff greeted them and began the process of registration and preparation for the surgery scheduled for the next day. In less than half an hour, they sat in a typical, hospital room with a large adjustable bed, two basic chairs, a wall mounted TV set, a closet, a bathroom, and a window overlooking, of course, a parking lot.

Grandpa put his arm around Jamie's shoulder. "Well, son, this will be home for a few days. What do you think?"

Jamie shrugged his shoulders, "It's okay, I guess."

A light tap at the door ushered in a middle aged man about six feet tall with black hair sprinkled with gray. Good afternoon, I'm Dr. Walker. I will be doing the surgery on your kidney. And you are, I bet, Jamie Foster."

Jamie nodded his head, offering his hand to that of Dr. Walker.

Dr. Walker introduced himself to the others before devoting a short time to discussing the time schedule for Jamie's procedure. He asked for any questions. Robin and her parents likely harbored many but refused to ask them at this time. Only Jamie asked, "Will I feel anything?"

The doctor emitted a chuckle. "No, you won't feel a thing and before you know it, you will be walking out of here with a new kidney and a whole different life than you've had the last few months." The doctor looked quickly around the crowded room then at Robin. "Please excuse me. I won't interfere with your getting settled. I'll see you early tomorrow morning." He moved toward the door. Turning, he gave Jamie a vigorous thumbs up.

Three hundred fifty miles north of Packwood, Clay and Vicky prepared for the drive to Rochester, the surgery, and the anticipated two to three day stay in the hospital for Clay. Only days before,

Clay made another drive to the Mayo Clinic for confirmation of his compatibility as a donor for Jamie. The tenacious infection he fought following his accident offered a concern for his acceptance as a kidney donor for anyone. Nonetheless, the tests revealed no lingering effects of the infection. His prosthetic foot also made no difference to his compatibility.

On this cold, early February morning, Vicky and Clay carried to the car the few items he would need during his short hospital stay. They departed the Twin Cities, thankful for good winter driving conditions on the way south to Rochester. As with Robin and her family, Clay and Vicky drove in silence, each facing moments of anxiety about the impending surgery. The time they spent in days past discussing the possibility of Clay's donating a kidney to his son precluded any more discussion of that decision.

Entering the reception area of the hospital brought back vivid memories of the time over two years ago when they arrived for the surgery that amputated Clay's foot. Like the last time, this time he would also lose a part of his body. However, this time it would give back a normal life to a young twelve year old boy.

"Good morning. How can I help you?" A pretty young receptionist greeted Clay and Vicky standing before the reception desk.

"Yes, good morning. I'm Clay Pennell. Tomorrow, I think I'm scheduled to donate a kidney to Jamie Foster."

The receptionist checked her schedule to confirm quickly the scheduled surgery. "Yes, Dr. Walker will meet with you as soon as you are settled in your room. Also, then, you may complete necessary paper work. Please have a seat and a hospital staff will direct you to that room. Thank you."

In a few minutes, a male staff member joined them in the reception area. Holding hands, Clay and Vicky followed the young man, nervous, yes, but more important, confident in the outcome of the transplant and proud of their role in it.

347

CHAPTER 53

"But what if he doesn't come?" Jamie sat with his mother in a family counseling room on the first floor of the Mayo Clinic and Hospital.

Robin looked up from the magazine she paged through. With a smile she reassured her son, "Yes, he will be here. It's only a little after ten o'clock. The meeting was scheduled for ten thirty."

Jamie squirmed in one of the several chairs spaced around the counseling room. Unlike many doctor and dentist waiting rooms, this one gave patients and family members an attractive, comfortable place to consider important questions typically having to do with health. With chairs and sofas strategically placed around the room, families could find in the room privacy along with an escape from, perhaps, traumatic moments requiring painful decisions about loved ones.

Today, though, would prove a happy gathering in the room. For several days, Robin coordinated with Dr. Walker the first meeting of Clay and Jamie. The day of the surgery, now over two months ago, offered little time for the drama of a first meeting. Far more important were the preparations for the surgery to remove one of Clay's kidneys as a replacement for one of Jamie's.

Both surgeries had included no complications. Dr. Walker and his team worked diligently and efficiently to complete the surgeries in less than two hours. Jamie's body responded quickly to reject the foreign kidney. However, the anti-rejection medication, likely required for the rest of his life, performed its function well. In just days his body with the help of the medication allowed the new kidney to resume its critical function. The whole procedure confined Jamie to the hospital for fourteen days while the hospital staff monitored his body's reaction to the new kidney, the function of the kidney, and the condition of the relatively small incision needed for the transplant.

Within hours of the surgery, Jamie walked the halls of the hospital, exercising his young body to avoid muscle atrophy. During his hospital stay, Robin committed herself to her son, the hospital providing her with a small sleeping room only doors away from her son's room. Each day saw the return of Jamie's strength as well as his vitality.

Each day, too, saw in Jamie a growing restlessness, an eagerness to return home to resume the normal life of a preteen which had evaded him for so many months.

Despite the restlessness, Jamie complied with whatever the hospital staff requested. Nurses talked about this young kid in Room 206 who entertained them with his sense of humor and with his unending need for explanations of why the staff did what it did during his recovery. The monitoring devices for his vital signs intrigued Jamie, who asked each day the meaning of all the numbers.

The day before his discharge from the hospital, Dr. Walker reviewed with Robin and Jamie what to expect in the weeks to come. Gathered in his office, Jamie and his mother relaxed on a small sofa while Dr. Walker sat on a chair in front of them. Dr. Walker spoke first. "Everything looks okay for your going home tomorrow. You've done well."

A broad grin revealed the delight Jamie felt in hearing that. "Can I play soccer in the spring?"

Robin laughed as did the doctor. She reminded Jamie, "You know there are things maybe more important than soccer."

"Well," Dr. Walker expressed, "to Jamie that may not be true. I will say, though," the doctor focused his attention directly on Jamie, "and Jamie please remember this; for the immediate future you need to avoid too much physical exertion. You need to let your body become familiar with that new organ you received. To help it do that, you need to remember to take your anti-rejection medication."

Jamie nodded in understanding.

"As far as soccer is concerned, we have to wait and see over the next few weeks how everything works out."

Robin moved forward on the sofa, turned and smiled at her son sitting next to her. "Though he might not admit it, he is eager to return to school. You know, he has missed so much."

Jamie raised his eyebrows as if to say, "Oh, Mother."

"I understand about school," the doctor added. "I don't see any reason why he can't return after his two week check up which we will do here. By the way, I realize the distance you have to travel to get here. Depending on Jamie's progress, maybe in the future you can have check ups with Dr. Gardner back home."

"Thank you, doctor," Robin responded.

"Of course, when you leave the hospital tomorrow, you will receive a complete set of instructions about what to do and not do. Please remember, though, that Jamie's transplant did not make him into some invalid. With common sense, he should soon return to the life of a twelve year old boy." The doctor paused, studying both Robin and Jamie. "Are there any pressing questions?"

Jamie's eyes brightened. He half raised his hand to speak. "Will I get to meet the guy who gave me a kidney?"

Robin jumped into answer the question she heard so many times already. "Honey, we've discussed that. You know that you will when the time comes."

"Mom, when is that?"

"Jamie," the doctor cautioned, "you must understand that sometimes organ donors are reluctant for whatever reason, to meet the recipients of their donation. I don't think that's true with yours, and I'm certain that the time will come when you can meet him.

In the over two months since Jamie's discharge from the hospital, he made impressive progress, regaining lost weight, regaining his quiet but engaging personality while making strides to catch up with his classmates in school. Now the time had arrived for the fulfillment of his desire to meet the person who gave him a kidney.

Clay and Vicky made the familiar drive to Rochester. In the two and one half months since the crucial surgery, Clay's recovery required only days. In a week after the surgery he returned to work at least for half days, reminding him of those weeks and weeks of dealing with infection and a prosthetic foot. In frequent contact with Robin, he learned of the impressive recovery of their son. A recent contact asked Clay about meeting Jamie. Of course, he experienced an increased desire to meet his son. He also experienced increased anxiety about that meeting. Still, it was what he wanted, at this time, more than anything else.

A hospital staff directed Clay and Vicky to the office of Dr. Walker, who, along with Robin, arranged the long awaited meeting between Clay and Jamie. Only Dr. Walker of the Mayo Hospital staff knew of their father-son relationship. Under the circumstances, Dr. Walker supported Robin and Clay's decision to shield Jamie from the truth about his father.

Dr. Walker greeted Clay and Vicky at his office door. "How are you doing? Clay, you look great as do you Mrs. Pennell."

"Thank you. We're fine. Excited to be here." Clay spoke for both of them.

"Yes, this is an exciting time for you and certainly for Jamie, who has been persistent in meeting that guy who gave him a kidney."

Clay smiled and grasped Vicky's hand as the doctor directed them to follow him to the family counseling room. As they walked through the corridor, the doctor turned to announce that Robin and Jamie arrived very early for the ten thirty meeting. He then smiled to say, "Apparently, what I've been told is that Jamie displays less patience than does his mother."

The doctor, Clay and Vicky stood before the door of the family counseling room. Clay's stomach tingled with nerves; perspiration gathered at the base of his neck. The doctor tapped on the door. Robin's voice invited them to enter. Opening the door, Dr. Walker raised his left arm in an invitation for Vicky and Clay to enter. Inside the room Vicky and Clay stood side by side. In front of them sat Jamie and his mother.

Dr. Walker stepped up beside Clay. "Jamie, I want you to meet Mr. Pennell, who made possible your kidney transplant." The doctor then placed his hand on Clay's shoulder. "Mr. Pennell, this is Jamie Foster."

Clay stepped forward as Jamie rose from his chair. They stood facing each other, frozen in time. Emotion surged through Clay's body as he stood before his son, seeing him for the first time. In that instant he noticed something familiar about Jamie's eyes and the shape of his mouth. Tears threatened to cloud his vision, but Clay suppressed them, moving toward his son with hand outstretched. Jamie grasped his father's hand, stood straight and tall, already taller than his mother, and said, "Thank you very much, Mr. Pennell."

Clay cupped his hands around Jamie's. "You are so very welcome. I hope everything has gone well since the surgery." Some of the tension gradually began to drain from Clay's system. For an instant, regret over his son not knowing his father joined the other emotions he felt. Nonetheless, he supported Robin's decision.

Jamie nodded his head. "I'm even back in school full time now."

"That's great."

During this dramatic moment, Vicky stood silently watching the meeting between father and son. Of course, she had never met Jamie nor had she met Robin. With the introduction of father and son, Clay turned to his wife. "Vicky, I want you to meet Jamie, who now must carry a part of me around with him even when he plays soccer."

Vicky smiled and extended her hand which Jamie took in his. "It's so good to meet you, Jamie. I've heard so much about you and how brave you have been through all your troubles."

Clay stepped closer to Jamie, placing his arm around his shoulder. "Jamie, I want you to meet my wife Vicky."

"Hi, Mrs. Pennell." Their hands met a second time. "Thank you for sharing your husband with me." Laughter further reduced the tension in the room.

Through the months of contact between Clay and Robin, Vicky had yet to meet Robin. The introductions so far found Robin observing from her chair near Jamie's. Clay guided his wife closer to Robin, who as they approached, stood up. Clay stood between two very important women in his life. "Vicky, I want you to meet Robin, Jamie's mother who has been so brave and courageous through all this." Next he turned his attention to Robin. "Robin, I want you to meet my wife, Vicky."

They both stepped forward to an emotional embrace. First Vicky voiced, "I'm so happy to finally meet you."

"Thank you," Robin, for a moment choked with emotion, whispered to Vicky. Dabbing her eyes with a tissue, Robin took a deep breath before saying, "Thank you for your husband's wonderful gift." She slowly shook her head. "Really, we can never thank you enough."

With introductions complete, Dr. Walker invited all of them to stay as long as they wished in the counseling room. If they needed refreshments, they could simply call the number listed on the phone. They didn't need refreshments. They needed time to relax, time to corral galloping emotions, and to acknowledge the marvel of compassion. With several hours to drive home, Robin explained they better get started in an attempt to beat the sunset. All four stopped to thank Dr. Walker then walked outside to the warm April sunshine with a promise to stay in touch and a hint at celebrating Jamie's thirteenth birthday by joining for a day the Register's Annual Great Bicycle Ride Across Iowa.

CHAPTER 54

Six months later

"What are you writing?" Clay hesitated on his way into the garage carrying a bassinet filled with baby blankets.

Vicky sat next to the kitchen table, checking items off a list. "I'm only making sure we're taking what we need for the trip to Iowa."

"Is not as easy as it used to be, I guess. Keisha has added a few details to most of what we do." Clay squeezed through the service door with his load to add to the luggage already stored in the trunk.

On a hot night in mid July, the lives of Clay and Vicky changed dramatically with the arrival of a seven pound, ten ounce baby girl. Combined with Clay donating his kidney to Jamie Foster, Vicky's pregnancy added more excitement and concern to their lives. With only minor complications including a few days in the eighth month that required Vicky to stay off her feet for several days, her pregnancy progressed normally.

Named Keisha Louise Pennell, the healthy baby girl enlivened the Pennell household with her demands for nourishment, dry diapers, and motherly affection. Clay adapted well to his role helping Vicky with the baby. However, the thrill of fatherhood refused to fade. During those private moments holding this tiny miracle, Clay experienced an overwhelming pride. Moments like these also reawakened his regret at not having shared the same thing with his son. However, what he missed with his son could never be recovered. His daughter, though, gave him another chance to experience the extraordinary thrill of becoming a father.

Maternity leave for Vicky gave her the opportunity to relax during those final crucial weeks and to face the often hectic periods of a new baby's demands. Thankful for Clay's willingness to share in responding to those demands, Vicky now prepared to resume her job as president of Wagner Electronics. First, the Pennells would travel to Iowa to join in the celebration of Jamie Foster's thirteenth birthday. This trip marked the first to include Keisha, consequently, Vicky's diligence in making a list of what they needed for the baby while on the road.

Clay returned from the garage. "I think we've got it all. The bike is on the trunk rack so I hope we don't have to open the trunk again for a while." He stopped in the kitchen entrance. "We should really get going. It's a long drive."

"Yes, I just need to check on Keisha's diaper and make sure we have extra formula. That's it."

The weeks since the transplant and the thrill of Keisha's arrival brought routine back to Clay and Vicky. Clay, of course, worked long hours at the bike shop and did what he could to help Vicky with the baby. He even found a few hours to spend biking, many days back and forth to work. Occasionally, he did take an extended ride on the weekend. Invariably those rides would evoke memories of rides in the past, particularly one ride that nearly ended riding all together.

The name of Miles Hunter would forever rest in the depths of Clay's memory. Nonetheless, rarely did this name surface. When it did, Clay typically was near the scene of his accident on that fateful autumn morning. Clay heard little about Miles following the accident that placed Miles in a wheelchair for the rest of his life. Some weeks after the accident, Clay heard from his friend, Stewart Cook, from the Hennepin County Sheriff's Office, that Miles confessed to the two hit and run accidents involving cyclists. His confinement to a wheel chair influenced his sentencing. A compassionate judge refused to assign any jail time. Instead, he sentenced Miles to several hours of community service that required him to talk with groups of young people about responsible driving. According to Mr. Cook, the experience produced a remarkable change in the formerly belligerent bully who despised cyclists.

Clay faced no problems with his prosthetic foot or with his recovery from the surgery to remove his kidney. Most often he never really gave the foot any thought. Sometimes after a long day at the bike shop, he would seek relief at home by removing the foot and elevating his leg while relaxing in his favorite chair. Of course, on some of those extended days, both legs needed special favors. After his short hospital stay following his kidney donation, Clay rested at home a few days before returning to work. At first, frequent check ups with his local doctor found no complications. Ultimately, the same good conditioning that enabled him to adapt to the prosthetic foot enabled Clay to suspend any more check ups unless a need arose. One never did.

"Boy this is a small town." Vicky commented as their long day driving through the Iowa corn fields came to a close.

"Yes, it is, like a lot of others around here." Clay consulted his directions Robin sent to guide them to her house. In his previous visit to Packwood several months ago, Clay did not visit Robin and Jamie's home.

With little difficulty, the Pennells located the Foster home. A modest, two story house on a block of modest, two story houses, it reflected the good care afforded it over the years. As they pulled into the driveway, Jamie burst through the front door, followed less energetically by his mother. Jamie waved his arms then approached the car, waiting for it to stop. When it did, Clay quickly opened his door and stepped out onto the driveway. Vicky checked on the sleeping Keisha then opened her door to get out of the car. She moved around to the other side of the car to stand next to Clay.

"You made it." Jamie proclaimed.

"We sure did." Clay reached for Jamie placing both hands on his shoulders. "How you doing?"

"I'm fine. I played soccer for the first time yesterday." Jamie boasted.

Vicky reached for Jamie's hand. "Good to see you again. Wow, you're back to soccer."

Robin moved to give Vicky a brief hug. "Thank you for coming. I can hardly wait to see that new baby."

"Yes, she's growing fast, already nearly three months old."

Clay gave Robin a soft hug, a self imposed caution considering their relationship of thirteen years ago. "How have you been?" Though the two spoke regularly after the surgery and in planning the trip to celebrate Jamie's birthday, their contact proved sporadic.

Robin smiled. "Everything goes well. How's the baby?"

"Sound asleep in the back seat."

Robin moved closer to the car while Vicky retrieved their daughter from the special infant seat.

"Oh, my, she's beautiful. Look at all that black hair, just like her mother." Robin stretched her hand to touch Keisha's tiny head. She announced to her guests, "Let's go into the house. I'm sure you're tired and hungry from the long drive. Jamie, why don't you help Mr. Pennell with their things."

In the house Robin helped Vicky and the baby get settled in the living room while Clay and Jamie carried in the luggage and special bags filled with baby supplies. With that accomplished, they sat in the living room reestablishing a relationship that started for all of them only months ago. Of course, the conversation focused on two topics, the new baby and the function of Jamie's kidney. All reports from his doctors confirmed that Jamie's kidney worked efficiently and would continue to do so provided he took the anti rejection medication. Also from all reports, except for a few sleepless nights for Clay and Vicky, the baby did extremely well.

"So tomorrow is your birthday." Vicky commented to Jamie.

Jamie nodded his head. "I hope it doesn't end up like my last one." He could hardly forget the infection presumably caused by the contaminated hamburger he ate at his last birthday party.

"Say, Jamie," Clay interrupted. "You ready for a short bike ride tomorrow?"

"Yeah, I am."

Robin quickly reminded them that the Across Iowa bike tour would very likely make the route crowded. Besides they would not have official registration allowing them to participate. "I suppose that doesn't matter all that much. Who's going to know?" She commented.

"No, I don't think it will make any difference." Clay agreed. Sitting listening to talk of the bike tour, he couldn't help but remember thirteen years ago when this time of year he road into Packwood only to leave as a future father.

All evening the conversation dwelled on the significant events of the past year. Later Robin's parents arrived to meet the Pennells for the first time. They did not have a previous opportunity to do so. In preparation for the birthday festivities of the next day, the conversation ended early allowing all to get some rest, especially Clay and Vicky, who faced a potentially fussy baby thrust into a strange environment.

"Are you ready, birthday boy?" Clay asked while he removed his bike from the bike rack.

"Yep." Jamie answered.

"About how far is it to the tour road?"

Jamie thought briefly, "Oh, about maybe a mile."

"Okay, let's go." Clay announced.

Standing in the front lawn, Vicky and Robin waved good bye as Clay and Jamie rode off.

Clay's mind swirled with memories of the last time he rode the across-Iowa tour. What a difference thirteen years make. Only months ago he didn't even know Jamie existed. Now Jamie carried with him one of Clay's kidneys and was about to join the man he knew only as the one who donated a kidney, not his dad, on a short ride along the current, across Iowa route.

Approaching the highway serving as the current route, Clay cautioned Jamie about the crowds they might meet. "Just remember, follow at a safe distance behind me. That way we can avoid any problems."

Turning left onto the two lane highway that served as the tour route, Clay and Jamie blended in with a cluster of riders. Comfortable with the speed, Clay glanced back at Jamie, who rode a few feet behind him. "We're going to get around most of this group so follow me."

Clay carefully pulled out and around the bikers in front of him. He announced, "On your left." Then he glanced back at Jamie, who smiled. Clay glanced a second time to capture that smile so remarkable and so much like one, he envisioned, of a three year old kid taking off on his first bike ride without training wheels.

Jamie pedaled harder to keep up with Clay. As he passed the line of bikers, he smiled, sat up straight, and announced "On your left."